"If you think we aren't already involved, you might as well think again,"

Oren said, holding out his hand. His gaze was steady.

Lorena tried to hold to her good sense, but it was crumbling. She put her hand in his. "Haven't you ever heard of passing through the friendship phase first?"

He drawled, his voice full of sex, "Oh, lady, we passed the friendship phase that first night in your kitchen." He tugged her to him gently, offering her the chance to say no.

But she didn't.

Lorena went into his arms, her heart pounding. Her blood warmed rapidly, deliciously. She wrapped her arms around his neck and met his kiss, opened her lips and her soul for him. She forgot everything and became simply a woman enamored of this man.

Dear Reader,

Happy New Year! May this year bring you happiness, good health and all that you wish for. And at Silhouette Special Edition, we're hoping to provide you with a year full of books that are chock-full of happiness!

In January, don't miss stories by some of your favorite authors: Curtiss Ann Matlock, Myrna Temte, Phyllis Halldorson and Patricia McLinn. This month also brings you *Far To Go,* by Gina Ferris—a heartwarming addition to her FAMILY FOUND series.

The January selection of our THAT SPECIAL WOMAN! promotion is *Hardhearted* by Bay Matthews. This is the tender tale of a woman strong enough to turn a gruff, lonely, hardhearted cop into a true family man. Don't miss this moving story of love. Our THAT SPECIAL WOMAN! series is a celebration of our heroines—and the wonderful men they fall in love with. THAT SPECIAL WOMAN! is friend, wife, lover—she's each one of us!

In Silhouette Special Edition, we're dedicated to publishing the types of romances that you dream about— stories that delight as well as bring a tear to the eye. That's what Silhouette Special Edition is all about— special books by special authors for special readers.

I hope that you enjoy this book and all the stories to come.

Sincerely,

Tara Gavin
Senior Editor

Please address questions and book requests to:
Reader Service
U.S.: P.O. Box 1325, Buffalo, NY 14269
Canadian: P.O. Box 1050, Niagara Falls, Ont. L2E 7G7

CURTISS ANN MATLOCK

SUMMERTIME

Silhouette®

SPECIAL EDITION®

Published by Silhouette Books
America's Publisher of Contemporary Romance

Dedicated to my dear friends who are with me now in our
ripe summertime: Karen, Dixie, Genell, Miss Susan and
fellow Mucketts.

"Its name is Public Opinion.
It is held in reverence.
It settles everything.
Some think it is the voice of God."

—Mark Twain

 SILHOUETTE BOOKS

ISBN 0-373-09860-X

SUMMERTIME

Copyright © 1994 by Curtiss Ann Matlock

This edition published by arrangement with Harlequin Enterprises B. V.

® and TM are trademarks of Harlequin Enterprises B. V., used under
license. Trademarks indicated with ® are registered in the United States
Patent and Trademark Office, the Canadian Trade Marks Office and in
other countries.

Printed in U.S.A.

Books by Curtiss Ann Matlock

Silhouette Special Edition

A Time and a Season #275
Lindsey's Rainbow #333
A Time To Keep #384
Last Chance Cafe #426
Wellspring #454
Intimate Circle #589
Love Finds
Yancey Cordell #601
Heaven in Texas #668
*Annie in the Morning #695
*Last of the Good Guys #757
*True Blue Hearts #805
*Summertime #860

*The Breen Men

Silhouette Romance

Crosswinds #422
For Each Tomorrow #482
Good Vibrations #605

Silhouette Books

Silhouette Christmas Stories 1988
"Miracle on I-40"
To Mother with Love '92
"More Than a Mother"

CURTISS ANN MATLOCK,

a self-avowed bibliophile, says, "I was probably born with a book in my hand." When not reading or writing—which she does almost constantly—she enjoys gardening, canning, crocheting, and motorcycling with her husband and son. Married to her high school sweetheart, the author is a Navy wife and has lived in eight different states within a sixteen-year period. The nomadic Matlocks finally settled in Oklahoma, where Curtiss Ann is busy juggling two full-time careers—as a homemaker and writer.

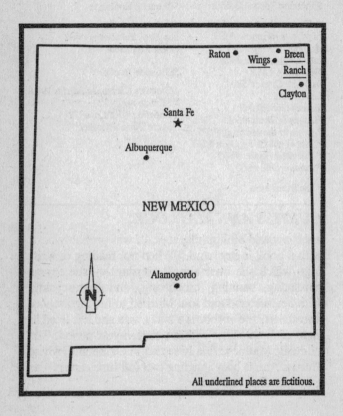

Raton • Wings • Breen
          Ranch
          Clayton •

Santa Fe
★

Albuquerque
•

NEW MEXICO

Alamogordo
•

N

All underlined places are fictitious.

Chapter One

Lorena Venable was single, had two grown sons and a responsible job with the Community Savings Bank. She went to church on Sundays and belonged to a quilting club, all of which equaled a slow and peaceful life and was exactly how Lorena intended. That was why it came as something of a shock to find herself being accosted by an intense, belligerent, half-drunk cowboy. It certainly wasn't a situation she had much experience in handling.

She'd come to the rodeo with Prima Gonzales and Mary Jean Owen. That in itself was unusual; Lorena didn't go out much, with girl or guy friends. She hadn't had a date in eight months, and she hadn't been to a rodeo in years. She was having a good time, though. It all reminded her of summer nights back in her teen years. She'd reached an age when recalling those was sweet.

She'd been on her way to the rest rooms—slipping away while the grand entry was going on and the rest rooms would be mostly empty. Three men—Saturday-night cowboy types with their perfect summer straw hats, big silver belt buckles and shiny snakeskin boots—were coming away from the men's room. Chuckling and walking a little unsteadily, they appeared to have had a number of beers. The next moment one of the men broke away from the other two and stepped in front of her.

"Hey, baby, remember me?"

Baby wasn't a term she cared for, but in the scheme of life Lorena had come to consider this of small consequence. As for remembering, the light was too dim for her to recognize, much less remember.

He tilted back his hat, allowing light from the pole lamp to shine on his face. "George Silva. I didn't imagine you'd forget me."

Yes . . . George Silva, in his late twenties, part-time mechanic, part-time stock dealer. She'd turned down his application for a personal loan last month because he was also most-time unemployed. "Hello, Mr. Silva." No matter that he made her skin crawl, politeness was part of her world.

"*Mr.?* That ain't friendly. Why don't you call me George, and I'll just call you Lorena?"

He leaned close, and both the scent of alcohol and his gaze swept her. Lorena was well aware of being normally attractive, and she received her share of manly attention. Her looks weren't why she didn't date; there simply weren't any eligible men of her age around who interested her. She didn't find George Silva's attention much of a compliment, however. He was the sort to be proving himself with any female, regardless of her attributes.

"I'm not interested, *Mr.* Silva," she said in her most proper tone, which could be very proper, and tried to step around him.

But he shoved in front of her, brushed her arm. She drew back, and when her gaze caught his, something inside began to be frightened. Her proper tone had simply been fuel to his fire, she thought quite suddenly. There was no one else around; all attention was focused on the grand entry going on in the arena. All except George Silva's buddies, who stood some distance away, watching and grinning. Lorena's temper flared, and she tried to keep it in control. She didn't want to make a scene. And she was a rational, adult woman. She could deal with this.

He said, "Now, I'm just bein' friendly, Lorena. Can't blame a fella for enjoyin' talkin' to a pretty gal like you. I heard you're divorced. Bet that gets lonely, huh?"

"Please get out of my way." She gave him a look designed to wilt the most hearty soul.

But the light was dim, and the look went over his head. He said, "There's no call to get uppity, Miz Banker Lady. You know, I ain't never kissed a banker lady. I sure bet I could make you a little less lonely."

Before she knew it, he'd grabbed her arm. He was strong, like a big sack of concrete anchoring himself to her. She pulled, and her heart jumped into her throat. She was about to kick the fire out of him when a voice sounded behind her.

"Is this man botherin' you, ma'am?"

Over her shoulder Lorena saw a long, lanky man. Another cowboy—the real variety, wearing a rather bent straw hat, a crisp shirt, creased blue jeans and holding a worn bronc saddle.

Before Lorena could say anything George Silva said, "I don't recall anyone askin' for your help, *cow*boy."

The lanky man shifted and said in a low, amicable voice, "We all came here to have a good time, so let's not cause a ruckus. The lady isn't interested, so the polite thing to do is to let her go about her business."

George Silva let go of her then, turning his total attention on the lanky cowboy. Lorena stepped backward. Looking at both men squaring off, she thought that George Silva had to outweigh her rescuer by at least fifty pounds.

Uh-oh was the thought that came to Oren Breen's mind. "There's no reason to get physical about this," he said. He didn't need to defend his pride; that never did take a dent, anyway.

"You should have thought about that before you stepped into my business, boy." And the heftier man shoved Oren, sending him stepping back to catch his balance.

Oren had the sinking feeling he was about to be beaten to a pulp. He wasn't a hand at fighting, a fact everyone knew. He mostly tried to stay away from anything that resembled an altercation. Though, if pressed, he never backed down, and he always strove to give back. It was just that generally he never gave back as much as he got, and if one of his older brothers wasn't there to step in, he usually got the stuffing beaten out of him.

To his profound amazement, however, this time was different.

To start with, he saw the first punch coming and managed to take only a glancing blow. He held his own in the scuffling, too; his opponent being at least half-drunk was a definite plus. And then Oren was smart enough to toss the bronc saddle at the man's feet, so the guy tripped all over it. Next Oren got off a good clean punch into his opponent's belly that sent the ole boy tumbling backward—right into one of the few remaining mud puddles around. The guy plopped down, sending mud squishing and water spraying.

That made that ole boy madder than a hornet. His face turned red, and fire shot out of his eyes. There he was—a hulk of a hornet sitting in mud. Oren couldn't do anything but laugh. He was still laughing when the guy came up out of the mud and ran at him like a raging bull. Oren felt so exuberant that he hit him again and sent him reeling right back into the mud.

Then a couple of deputies arrived, so the fight was officially ended, and Oren was left standing. The winner! He felt as much relief and amazement as pride. His entire life, he'd always been the one on the ground.

A small crowd had gathered, and now faded away. As they left, several people he knew told him, "Way to go, O.T." It was a nickname he'd had since school, his middle name being Till. Two of the Hunsicker sisters came over with his hat, which had been knocked away. Corinne Hunsicker, with a highly worried look, sashayed over to inquire whether or not he was hurt. He assured her that he wasn't and tested his nose, a bit surprised to find it wasn't bleeding. But then, he hadn't gotten very angry at the fella, and as far as fights went, this one could really only be classified as a good scuffle.

As he dusted off his hat he saw the woman he'd helped looking at him. She walked toward him as he settled his hat on his head. She smiled tentatively, and he smiled broadly. Any man would smile inside and out at her. She was pretty, with brown hair piled loosely atop her head, satiny skin, long lashes and striking dark eyes. Brown, he thought, though the light wasn't good.

"Thank you for steppin' in, though I'm awfully sorry you had to get into a fight because of me." Her speech was soft, almost cultured.

"No problem. Wasn't much of a fight, anyway." He thought then that her eyes were definitely brown, and that her face was like cream, and that she was a full, womanly woman, not a girl. And doggone, if she didn't look familiar to him.

"Still, I do thank you...." She was about to say more, but a dark-haired woman hollered to her from the stands, telling her to come on, that the bareback bronc riding was starting. She started away. "Thanks again." Her smile flashed.

Oren was left standing there, watching her disappear. She looked back at him once; he didn't miss that. And he noticed her particular way of walking, which was sexy and regal at once, like a sensual queen in brown Wranglers and an ivory lacy blouse, with fancy silver earrings swaying with every step.

They hadn't gotten to exchanging handles, and he regretted that, he thought, as he lifted his bronc saddle and headed for the chute area. But he thought her friend had called her Lora—though he hadn't clearly heard.

The familiarity swept over him again. He wondered where he knew her from. Maybe he'd taken her picture some other place. She hadn't acted as if she knew him, though.

As he hefted his bronc saddle he put it all down to the familiarity a person has when recognizing something they like in another person. He hadn't missed the certain warmth in her brown eyes. No, sir, he hadn't missed that, though it was true that a lot of women looked at him with warmth. And he wasn't bragging, because it wasn't to his credit that he appealed to women—that had been passed through his blood and came from God. Women liked Oren Breen, and Oren Breen liked women. He was his father's son.

As he neared the chutes Jada came hurrying toward him, wobbling on her tiny, high-heeled boots, weighted down with his camera equipment, which he'd dumped on her for safekeeping. Her face was drawn with concern.

Jada Cobb was in her late forties but didn't admit to anything past thirty-nine, had fiery red hair that curled to the middle of her back, a shape to stop traffic on an interstate and a heart as big as Texas. On and off, for the past couple of years, she and Oren had called on each other when they had somewhere to go and needed a date or simply wanted company. They were friends. Jada's presence kept women from hitting on Oren, and his kept men from hitting on her. Also, the past year Jada had taken up photography, and he'd been teaching her all he knew.

Her worried gaze searched him. "Monte just said you were in a fight."

"Yep. A bit of one," he said as he dropped his saddle to the ground and touched the sore spot at the corner of his eye where the guy's first punch had grazed him. It had begun to throb.

Jada looked it over, then said, "You mean to say you were in a fight, and that's all you got?" She looked suspicious. "Your nose isn't even bleeding."

"Well, I guess I never got very mad," Oren said, then added, "And I won."

Jada looked skeptical. "Oh, come on. You've never won a fight in your life."

"Well, I have now." He thought maybe it should seem more important, but somehow fighting had never been important to him. It seemed a silly thing for grown men to do, and yet plenty of them did it.

Jada said she had to get a picture of him on this historic night. She put his camera to her eye and backed up, carefully, in those tiny black boots. Oren put on a proud smile for her, and then his gaze went beyond her to the spectator stands, scanning for the brown-haired woman. He saw her sitting at the nearest end of the stands, third row up. Picked her out as if he had some invisible connection with her. She seemed to stand out, like a queen. She sat between two women, so apparently she wasn't here with a man.

He almost asked Jada if she knew who the brown-haired woman was. Jada knew at least half the people in the world. But a sudden strange shyness stopped him. What he was feeling suddenly seemed too private.

Minutes later he was preparing to enter the saddle bronc event and wondering what the brown-haired woman would think of him out there, riding high and wild, all of which just went to show that there were parts of him that would never grow up. But he sure enjoyed life.

"What in the world possessed you to enter the bronc ridin'?" Jada asked. "You haven't been on a bronc in five years." There, in the artificial brightness of the tall pole light, she tried to keep her voluptuous body balanced as she

slung his camera over one shoulder and his bag over the
other.

He'd done it to experience the feeling, so he could better
capture it in his photographs. That had been the logical
reason. A second reason had gone deeper. Bending to fas-
ten his colorfully fringed leather chaps around his legs, he
said, "Oh, I imagine for the same reason you wear those
fancy boots."

With a puzzled frown she looked down. "These boots
make me feel sexy and feminine."

"That's right," Oren said, and Jada chuckled.

A couple of young women he knew only by sight walked
by and said, "Good luck, O.T. We'll be rootin' for you."
Their eyes were bold in conveying a couple of other, more
intimate messages, too. Jada told him to keep his mind on
what he was about to do, because she didn't want him to get
killed, leaving her to have to find another ride home.

"Here's your macho gear." She helped him gather his
saddle, halter and bronc rein, lastly plopping his camera
back on him.

He kissed her cheek for luck and headed off to the bucking chutes, feeling like a cocky son of a gun. His eyes
scanned the stands, drawn by the brown-haired queen.

"Well, good golly," Rudy Crow said as he got to the
chutes. "I figured you'd get properly scared and back out."

"Oh, I suppose I'm properly scared...but my Caddie
needs waxin'." Rudy Crow had bet him that he wouldn't
make a full ride, the wager being a wash and wax of the
loser's vehicle.

"You're pretty confident for an out-of-practice rider."

"I learned by the time I was five how to stay on a bronc,"
Oren said.

Rudy cut his eyes at him. "Okay. You can stay on any old
way, so let's make it that whichever of us wins has to come
out with a score above sixty-five."

"You gettin' nervous about losin', Rudy?" Oren teased while he paused to snap a shot of two fellas working the chutes.

"I'm just tryin' to make certain things are fair."

Oren had Rudy pose quickly before getting up on his bronc. Rudy laughed and said he would expect payment if the picture sold, then added with pleasurable wickedness, "I'll come visit you in the hospital. You drew Hellion."

Oren climbed up on the rails. The guys there were grinning at him. He looked the horse over. The animal was a rather squatty sorrel with a lot of white showing around his small eyes. His chest and legs were powerful enough to send Oren over the moon. A man would never get on one of these animals if he thought along those lines, though, so Oren didn't dwell on it. He would get the job done, that was all. His gaze strayed across the chutes to the brown-haired woman.

He gave the care of his camera over to a fella as a couple of others helped him to saddle Hellion and then to settle himself atop the bronc. The horse was hot, damp and quivering between his thighs. The animal was a seasoned pro and knew how to play the game. He was itching to get out there to the challenge of getting this man off his back. Oren's blood raced with the challenge, too.

He took the camera back long enough to capture a close-up of Rudy in the adjoining chute. He tried for several as Rudy went flying out, but Hellion started jumping around beneath him.

The buzzer sounded the end of Rudy's go. Rudy had made it a full ride, and the pickup men rode in to get him off. He hopped to the ground and held his hands up to a cheering crowd. A score of seventy was called.

It was Oren's turn. Adrenaline raced, and his heart beat like a rapid tom-tom. He readjusted himself atop the bronc and remeasured the plaited rein, which was all the handhold he would have. Then quickly, instinctively, his gaze scanned the stands, again finding the brown-haired woman. Like everyone else, she was looking this way. He wondered again what she would think of him.

Lorena heard the announcer say, "Our next rider is Oren Breen." Surprise blocked out the rest of the announcer's words.

She scanned the rodeo program. There it was in black and white.

Oren Breen. No wonder he'd looked so familiar, and her mind traveled back to a summer day nearly twelve years ago. He was then and was now the spitting image of his daddy.

She stared at him atop his horse in the chute. Yes, it had been twelve years ago that she'd last seen him, because her Jaime had been eight. Oren had been eighteen, all full of himself. Of course, she'd heard some about him these past weeks, because Nicky had gone to work out at the Breen ranch. Other than growing into a man's thickness—and not much of that—Oren hadn't changed much. He still had that way about him—boyish, relaxed as a wet noodle and with a grin to charm the birds from the trees.

The chute opened, and the horse bearing Oren Breen came shooting out, ducking and bucking, spinning and whirling. Lorena wiggled her bottom on the hard bleacher seat, then froze. Her breath stopped in her throat as the horse neared the rail. *Oh, my Lord, don't let it . . .*

Oren rode with a graceful rhythm, one hand tight on the braided rein and the other flying high. It seemed an impossible feat for him to stay on the bucking horse's back. Watching, Lorena had her hands in fists, her muscles tight, every part of her trying to help him. The buzzer sounded, and the cheer went up as the pickup riders moved in. Lorena stayed tight, knowing the danger wasn't over. But when Oren slipped smoothly over to the pickup horse, she clapped, then put her fingers in her mouth and gave out a shrill whistle.

"Good grief." Prima stared at her. "I didn't know you could do that."

Lorena blushed. "A talent left over from childhood."

Her gaze shifted back to the arena and Oren walking back to the bucking chutes. He waved an arm. And then it seemed he was looking right at her. He smiled, and she smiled in return. For that split second her spirit flew with high feeling.

Then Mary Jean said, "Mmm-hmm. He can park his boots underneath my bed any time."

Lorena and Prima both laughed, and Prima teased, "Is that what you do between husbands?"

Lorena silently echoed Mary Jean's sentiment, though she would never say so. And she averted her gaze from the young man. As the mother of grown sons, she didn't need to be indulging in carnal thoughts about the son of a family friend, who was also her son's employer and somewhere around ten years younger than herself.

During the remaining events Lorena very discreetly watched Oren moving here and there, taking pictures. When he came down in front of the stands and aimed his camera up at her, she very carefully kept her face turned to the arena.

Mary Jean elbowing her and pointing at him didn't help one bit. Mary Jean said he was scouting Lorena out, and Lorena told her that maybe it was Mary Jean he was scouting. Mary Jean liked that idea. She made eyes at him, and he grinned at her.

Lorena felt a stab of disappointment. Then she very firmly told herself that it was silly to think he was paying her any attention. She was imagining it. He was a handsome man who, according to rumor, had all the feminine attention he could want. And there was a very flashy red-haired woman with him tonight. Mary Jean was the one to spot her and point her out; Mary Jean didn't miss a thing like that.

Still, Lorena couldn't seem to keep her eyes from returning to him—and it did seem that he often looked her way.

The last Oren saw of the brown-haired queen was her
getting into a car with her two companions—a slender, dark-
haired woman and a shapely, poofy-haired blonde. His own
vehicle was parked several cars away and out of the light. He
and Jada were stowing his gear in the trunk.

"Do you know who that woman is?" he asked Jada on
impulse.

"Who?" She followed his gaze.

He pointed. "That one gettin' into that red Crown Victoria over there. Underneath the light pole, gettin' in the
back." Since she was getting into the rear seat he didn't
think the car belonged to her.

Jada shook her head. "Can't say I've ever met her." She
shot him a speculative smile. "Why?"

He shrugged, not letting his disappointment show. "She
just looked familiar, and I can't place her." He wished he
hadn't said anything.

He slammed the trunk and took Jada around to the passenger side. He caught sight of the Crown Victoria pulling
out into the stream of traffic leaving the rodeo grounds.

Oren's car was a classic Cadillac convertible. The top was
down now, the way it was for most of the summer. Oren
figured a person might as well not have a convertible if he
didn't use it. He didn't worry much about people stealing
anything, either, because his basset hound, Harvey, went
most places with him and had sense enough, and was lazy
enough, to spend most of that time in the car. As quiet and
mellow as he looked, Harvey would show a stranger a different side if he put his hand into the car. He was lying in the
front seat now, and Oren had to move him to the back. He
buckled the seat belt around him, too.

As he entered the stream of traffic Oren kept trying to see
ahead and locate the Crown Victoria, see which direction it

took, but he never found it. Not that seeing the car and which direction it went would tell him anything more about his brown-haired queen.

They drove home through the balmy Southwestern night, listening to an oldies radio station coming out of Amarillo. That was Jada's favorite music. Oren liked all kinds. He let Jada off at her apartment above the old brick drugstore she owned in Wings, New Mexico, and continued on a few miles north to his home at his family's ranch. It was nearing midnight. The house was quiet and dark, except for the light his sister-in-law, Annie, always left burning for him above the kitchen sink. Oren had been born in this house, had lived here all his life. He lived here now with his eldest brother, Matt, and Matt's wife, Annie. Lately, for a number of reasons, he'd been thinking it was time to move out. Only there was nowhere else he wanted to live.

He went directly to his darkroom to develop the shots he'd taken that night. He'd gotten some good ones, including two of bronc riders that pleased him immensely.

Oren was a sometime photographer. That was how he thought of it. He would go for months taking pictures all over the place, and then he would tire of it and set his camera aside for months. He made some money with his photographs, sold to magazines and newspapers if the spirit moved him, and sometimes he sold prints to individuals. Occasionally, he even worked on commission. He'd been doing that tonight, shooting pictures of the rural rodeo for a horseman's magazine back East. He didn't make much money at any of this, however, though he had won a couple of awards for his pictures and was becoming known for them. He didn't need the money, and money didn't mean a lot to him, either. Simply living to the fullest was his main goal in life.

The two shots that really interested him were of the brown-haired queen. Like all those he'd shot that night, these two were in black and white. He liked working with black-and-white film best. With his telephoto lens he'd managed to get a very clear close-up of her. He held up the glossy, still-wet print and gazed at it for long minutes.

Where did he know her from?

He did know her, of that he was certain. The memory was way back in the ragged edges of his mind. Yet he couldn't place her.

The next day he asked his brothers Rory and Matt who she was, but they didn't know. They weren't certain about her looking familiar to them. Rory said yes, Matt said no. Oren thought to ask his dad, but at first Big Jesse was away in Denver, and when he returned, the occasion to show him the photo didn't come up. By then Oren felt too self-conscious and didn't want others to think he'd gone around the bend for this woman. Funny, but in this one case he didn't want people to know how he felt. This feeling, this face on the glossy paper was his to treasure, and treasures had a way of fading when exposed to the light of others' views.

Just as in his entire life he'd never, until that night, won a fight, Oren Breen had also never been in love. He was known throughout the county as a fun-loving country boy, a charmer, a man who drew women the way clover drew bees, and who knew how to enjoy them, too. People said he was too busy flirting around to settle for just one woman.

However, the truth was that he'd never met a woman who could equal Annie, his brother's wife. He could have loved Annie, if he would have allowed himself. And that was a treasure he kept to himself, too.

Over the following weeks he kept a lookout for the brown-haired woman wherever he went, though the chances of seeing her seemed awfully slim. He even found excuses to go down to Dalhart looking for her, for the car she'd been in. Once he spied a woman going into a bookstore in Dalhart, and he ran up to her, but when she turned around he discovered he'd made a complete fool of himself. The woman wasn't his brown-haired queen.

He kept the photographs of her in his darkroom, and over the following weeks he would take them out, gaze at them and wonder who she was and if he would ever see her again. She became his fantasy woman, and he halfway didn't want to learn anything about her, because this way he could make up stories about her in his mind.

He never would have predicted that he would meet her again by going right to her house. It happened two weeks later, on the night of his thirtieth birthday party, when her son got a little crazy and dented the door of Oren's Cadillac.

Chapter Two

His family gave him a party for his thirtieth birthday, and when the Breens held a party, it was a blowout. This one had begun at four that afternoon, with over sixty guests gathering for a barbecue in the shade of the big trees down near the pond.

They had all feasted on ribs prepared by Kelly, of Kelly's Tavern and Lemonade Parlor, and chili that Oren's dad, Big Jesse, had cooked up. There had been horseshoe contests and games of checkers and chess, horse racing and just plain visiting. Now, at past eleven, forty-some celebrants were still going strong in the tractor barn that was decked out with colorful Chinese lanterns, sawdust scattered on the floor, and a live band on a makeshift stage. The adults were laughing and talking, dancing and romancing, while the younger ones entertained themselves by climbing all over the giant Massey Ferguson tractor that had been moved into the rear doorway and sat there as if plugging a hole.

Oren claimed Annie for a dance. She was standing beside Matt, with Matt's arm around her shoulder. Oren took her hand, shot his brother a teasing grin and swung Annie out onto the floor—very carefully. They were all careful with Annie these days, because she was four months pregnant with a baby she'd been praying to have. Since the doctors had been skeptical about their chances of having another baby, Matt and Annie had been taken almost by surprise. Annie's first pregnancy had been difficult, and they were all holding their breaths about this one. So far, Annie was in perfect health, and this night she glowed, as beautiful as a desert rose.

The dance was a slow one. Oren held Annie loosely and waltzed her around. She smiled broadly at him. Next to them, Oren's dad, Big Jesse, danced with his wife, Marnie. Married two years now and parents of a toddler, they still acted like newlyweds. Aunt Ina, all straight and tall, danced with her latest boyfriend, a skinny little man whose nose came right to her breasts. Jada, in a crimson, off-the-shoulder dress, was waltzing with Kelly, who amazed them all with his fancy footwork. Rory was dancing with his wife, Zoe, and their twin little girls, all at once, and Miss Loretta, the postmaster of Wings, her white hair teased high on her head, had corralled wizened Turley and was making him dance, though it looked more as if he was just lifting his feet in place. The fiddler made his fiddle weep, and the singer sang a mournful tune.

The next minute a very disheveled Corinne Hunsicker came running in, hollering for Jesse. "He crashed! He's killed hisself!"

Big Jesse sprinted after Corinne, and everyone else followed, running out into the graveled yard and over to where Oren's Cadillac was parked at the edge of the grass. There, crashed nose first into the driver's side door of the Caddie, was one of the green garden tractors. Seeing it, Oren stared in disbelief at the tractor, then at the demolished door. Oren's hound, Harvey, had his front paws up on the door and was gazing over at Nick Venable, who was lying on the ground.

Nick sat up with a grunt. He wasn't dead. He was, however, drunk as a skunk. A few seconds later it came out that the accident was a result of a race between two young ranch hands—Nick on this garden tractor and Bobby Tafoya on the yellow one—both of them under the influence of way too many beers and lust, which had started them showing off for the older and very lovely and sexy Corinne Hunsicker.

Bobby was swaying, and Nick was stumbling, and Oren was aiming to kill them both.

Spitting fire and a few choice oaths, he went at Nick first, lifting him off his feet and throwing him against the fender of the Cadillac. "You wrecked my Caddie!" Oren let go and looked at the car door, then went at Nick again.

"Oren . . ." It was Annie. She laid a hand on his arm. He turned to look into her grass green eyes. "It was an *accident.*"

Still gripping the young man, Oren breathed deeply and ground his teeth. He looked from Annie back to Nick, debating. Big Jesse stepped in and asked Nick if he was hurt. Oren released him and turned away. His gaze passed over the tractor and the dented door of his precious car, and his stomach sank low enough to drag the ground.

His beautiful car. A classic '58 Cadillac, with the rear fender fins, mint condition, original engine and upholstery. New flamingo-pink paint job. Oren was as proud of it as a man was his child.

Annie squeezed his hand, and Jada came over and gave him a tissue. His nose had begun bleeding. He jammed the tissue beneath his nose and pressed the nerve above his top lip, stemming the flow.

It didn't help any that Matt said in his irritating bigbrother tone, "It can be fixed, Oren."

"Yeah, it can be fixed," Oren mumbled into the tissue.

"What's wrong?" Matt said to Annie. "I was just pointin' out that it isn't the end of the world."

And Oren said, "Matt, sometimes you jack my jaws. Just don't say anything. Okay? Jada, do you have another one of these?" Jada passed him another tissue, and he pressed it to his nose, thinking that he could ride a bucking bronc without a scratch, and here he stood with a bloody nose from temper.

That sort of broke up the party. As if abandoning Noah's ark, people started leaving two by two, everyone wishing Oren a happy birthday, along with offering their condolences about the Caddie. Nick Venable didn't have a scratch and had sobered up enough to see what he'd done, and had become all apologetic, too. Oren wished he would quit saying how sorry he was, because every time the kid opened his mouth Oren wanted to put his fist in it.

Rory and Sandy, their foreman, helped Bobby Tafoya over to the bunkhouse. Matt and Big Jesse started to take Nick Venable there, too, but Nick kept insisting he had to go home.

"I promised...my mom. I told her I'd get home, so's I can be there in the mornin'. If I'm not, she's gonna be mad as a wet hen." He actually tried to find his keys, but he couldn't get his hand into his pants pocket.

"I'll take him," Oren said. His nose had stopped bleeding as quickly as it had started. He was simply mournful now.

Nick looked at him and shook his head. "No, sir. I'm okay.... I can drive myself." He still couldn't get his hand into his front pants pocket.

Oren said, "You could drive, but gettin' anywhere without killin' someone may be a problem."

Nick looked sick, as if he thought for sure Oren was going to drive away and kill him on the sly. He finally got his hand into his pocket, but he couldn't get his keys out.

Big Jesse voiced the opinion that maybe Nick should have to see his mother tonight, and Rory said he thought that was cruel. Zoe volunteered to bring the boy some coffee, but Big Jesse said he thought it would take a gallon, and he wasn't hanging around half the night to see the boy get sober. "Let the boy get the full effect of all this," was his opinion.

"You sure you want to drive him?" Matt said, when just he and Rory and Oren were left standing there on the gravel driveway. Nick tried to stand straight but resorted to leaning back on the Cadillac.

Oren cast him a crooked grin. "I'm not gonna take him out and beat him up, big brother."

"I didn't say you were. I just thought you might not feel so generous as to take him down to Clayton. Me or Rory could take him."

"Naw... you guys have Annie and Zoe and the kids. Besides, I need to go for a drive, so I might as well head on down to Clayton."

Nick had started away toward his own truck, so they had to go get him. Harvey was moved to the back seat, and then Nick had to be helped into the passenger seat. Oren climbed over the smashed door.

"You feel sick, kid, you make sure you hang over the side," he told Nick. He sure didn't want his white leather seats puked on.

"Oh, I'm okay.... I'm feelin' a lot better now." As they pulled out onto the blacktopped county road he said, "I can pay for havin' your car door fixed. I really will. You don't need to be tellin' my mom."

"I imagine you'll be payin'. As for tellin' your mom, that depends. We'll see how I feel when we get there, so I'd advise you not to throw up on my seats."

The night air blowing in was downright sharp, but it was the best thing for a kid who'd had too much to drink, and Oren enjoyed it, too. He stopped once, though, and put on the denim jacket he had in the back seat. Nick had to make do with shivering. Five minutes later the kid mumbled, "I'm gonna throw up."

Oren pulled over quickly. Nick, clumsy as a newborn calf, got the door open but couldn't seem to get out. Oren gave him a shove that sent him sprawling. Listening to the kid retching, he almost felt sorry for treating him so roughly, but by heaven, it would be a darn sight easier for the kid to recover than to clean the interior of his car. And the kid should learn the hazards of drinking.

Finally the retching stopped. Oren leaned over and saw the kid lying flat out on the ground. He told himself to remember being eighteen as he grabbed some napkins from the glove box and went around to lift Nick up and wipe his face. The boy had slobbered on his shirt, too. The smell made Oren queasy and doubly glad the Caddie's top was down. He reflected that his birthday had been anything but dull.

Nick lived with his mom, Lorena. She'd been Lorena Sandoval before she'd married, and the Sandovals were old friends of the Breens. Lorena's dad, Max Sandoval, had coffee with Big Jesse at least once a week and had for about twenty years. Oren often wondered how two such opposite men could be friends; Max was as stern as he was sour, and Jesse was as fun loving as he was mellow.

Oren wasn't certain where Nick and his mother lived and shook Nick awake to give directions. In his fuzzy state of mind Nick wasn't certain, either. They went down three wrong streets before Oren thought to ask the kid his address. Most anyone would automatically recite their address, no matter how far gone he was.

Oren found the house and pulled to a stop in front. There wasn't a curb; there weren't many curbs in Clayton, and there weren't neighborhoods of houses that all looked the same, either. Each had a look and personality of its own. This house was two story, built in the twenties or thirties,

American traditional remodeled to have a hint of the Southwest. The porch light was on.

Nick got out of the car all right, but appeared none too steady with his first steps, so, with a sigh, Oren got out to help him. Their footsteps echoed loudly on the wooden porch flooring.

There was a light showing inside. Nick couldn't find a house key. Just as Oren was about to use the fancy brass knocker in the middle of the smoky-blue door, the door opened and a woman stood there. Familiarity flickered inside Oren for a split second, and then recognition dawned like the bright sun after a week of storms.

It was his brown-haired queen.

Her eyes widened with surprise. Oren, for his part, was awfully surprised, too. This was where he knew her from. She was Lorena Venable.

Nick said, "Hi, Mom."

"Oh, my God, what's happened? Nicky?" Getting a good whiff, she made a face and drew back. "Good Lord, you've been drinkin'!"

"Aw, Mom...I'm sorry." The boy seemed struck almost sober, and straightened up. "I had a little too much to drink, but I'm fine."

Oren let go of his arm, which turned out to be the wrong thing to do. Nick took a step, stumbled over the doorsill and pitched forward to the floor, taking his mother with him.

Lorena Venable jerked herself from beneath the boy in a way that said she found this all a shock to her sensibilities. Oren wanted to laugh but, being a prudent man, he stopped himself. He kept staring at her, thinking how this was a miracle. He'd found his brown-haired queen, and she was an old friend of the family. He had to be the luckiest man on earth.

Nick was up on his hands and knees, apologizing his head off and sounding sick as a dog. Oren stepped in to give him a hand up. In the process he got a good look at Lorena Venable's legs clad in black tights.

"I'll get him up to bed," Lorena said tightly.

Both her look and her words were a hint for Oren to leave, but he didn't take it. "I'll help. He's a pretty good weight." He wasn't about to leave now.

Keeping a firm hold on Nick, he helped the boy up the stairs. Lorena tried to help, too, but she didn't do much more than get in the way. She realized this and dropped behind, just where she would be sent tumbling if Nick missed a step.

Nick kept saying he was sorry, that he'd just wanted to see what it was like and that he hadn't thought a person could get drunk on beer. All the standard excuses of an eighteen-year old boy. Lorena said she hoped he was finding it all worthwhile, and her voice was mother-sharp.

Upstairs two bedrooms opened off the landing, with a bath in between. Nick headed toward the bedroom on the right. His mother reached in and switched on the light. It was a teenage boy's room, only a whole lot neater than Oren's had been, or was even now. In fact, it was what Oren would term excessively neat.

He let Nick sink onto the bed, where the kid automatically rolled onto his stomach. Lorena slipped in front of Oren, practically pushing him aside, then bent to turn Nick over and unbutton his shirt.

With Lorena's head bent close to Nick's, Oren noted the resemblance between the two. Both had chestnut brown hair and brown eyes. He could see her as a mother then, too, one fussing over her son, as mothers were supposed to do.

He left them and went downstairs. He thought that Lorena Venable didn't realize her son was a man grown. She treated Nick about the way Matt tried to treat Oren. Though he guessed a mother had more right. And he supposed anyone who would drink enough to make himself wish he was dead had to be pretty much of a child, no matter whether he was eighteen or eighty-three. He guessed humans were an odd species.

His natural curiosity led him to look around the living room. *So this was where his brown-haired queen lived.* The sofa and chairs were the round-backed and stuffed-arm kind that invited a person to stay for a while. A quilt was folded on the corner of the couch, as if waiting for someone to take a nap. The wood pieces were all thick, warm oak. Nothing matched, except the colors, which were shades of blue, tan and brown. It was an inviting room. Friendly and warm. It all matched what he'd imagined about his brown-haired queen.

As far back as he could recall, he'd known Lorena Venable. Known *of* her was a more accurate description. Oren knew old Max Sandoval best, because old Max had been a district judge, and Oren had been up before him a couple of times for disturbing the peace. There had been that time he'd tied firecrackers to a remote control car and sent it out among the horses in the Fourth of July parade. And then he'd had some traffic violations that had definitely qualified as disturbing the peace. Remembering these incidents, he suddenly had more empathy for Nick Venable. No, he wouldn't tell Lorena about Nick's escapade tonight.

Not counting the rodeo, the last time Oren could recall seeing Lorena had been the day she'd come to the ranch with old Max to buy a horse for her sons. She'd ridden the horse herself, and she'd been a good rider, had barrel raced back in high school. And, come to think of it, she'd been really pretty that day, with the sun shining like gold on her brown hair. Figuring quickly, Oren realized that had to have been about twelve years ago, because he'd had a broken arm from a car wreck, and he'd done that when he was eighteen. Max Sandoval had made certain he paid a hefty fine for that incident, too, because Oren had wrecked two parked cars in the process of wrecking his own. Empathy for Nick grew by leaps and bounds with these memories.

From what he'd heard somewhere along the way, Lorena was divorced, had been since her sons were small. She'd moved up to Denver and lived there until a couple of years ago, when she'd come back here to her hometown and gone to work at the Community Savings Bank. Her oldest son, Jaime, was in college in Denver, and Nick was eighteen, had graduated high school the past year and was looking toward college, too.

There were a couple of photographs on the mantel— posed portraits, one of Nick, his senior high picture, and another of a young man at about the same age, most likely Jaime. It was when Oren walked over to see them that his interest was drawn to the adjoining room.

Bright light came through the curtained French doors, which were standing open, almost as if inviting him to come and see. He stepped into the doorway.

It was a study, with a desk and shelves filled with books and files and papers. He had to smile at the clutter, and thought *Hurrah!* Here was life.

There was a cleared space around a computer on the desk, but books and things were stacked on top of the monitor. There were some *Money* magazines and *The Wall Street Journal,* and the titles of the books all sounded financial. Not a novel in the bunch. Tucked here and there on the shelves were trophies and ribbons from the boys' ventures in basketball and high school rodeo. There was one dusty and tarnished trophy for barrel racing bearing the name Lorena Sandoval, and Oren figured a couple of the ribbons stuffed at the back were hers.

On the other side of the room was a big flowered chair, the kind his aunt Ina would love. There was a quilt hanging on the wall, the kind that won prizes at state fairs. Intricately made, it depicted a ranch scene, like a primitive painting, complete with animals, even little chickens, children playing, a cowboy working cattle.

There was a small oval quilt ring on a stand beside the flowered chair and a quilt in it, obviously in progress. A woman of intellect and artistic ability, Oren thought. And she still liked horses, because they were on the quilt, appliquéd on pillows, pictured around the room.

He tucked his hands into his pockets and strolled over quickly, getting a closer look at the quilt on the wall and the one in progress, and the fine teacup and saucer on the table beside the chair, and the stack of mystery novels tucked on the other side of the chair. What he was doing could be construed as snooping, so he headed back to the living room. He wasn't averse to snooping, though he did have a certain code about it. He never touched anything, never opened drawers or closets or even so much as lifted a magazine to see what was underneath. And he never got caught. He expected everyone else to treat him with the same politeness.

He stood there in the living room, waiting for Lorena Venable, his brown-haired queen.

Chapter Three

Lorena wanted to smack Nicky and cuddle him to her breast, both at once. And it frustrated her no end that she could do neither. He was past feeling her smack and far past the age of being cuddled by his mother.

She worked out her energy by tugging off his shirt, boots and jeans, and she wasn't any too gentle. Nicky grunted and told her to leave him alone, then chuckled and called her Corinne. Lorena rolled the shirt inside the jeans to carry downstairs and put right in the washer.

He was lying there, on his back now, snoring, and she got worried about him throwing up and choking himself. That had happened to Juanita Jennings's husband. Gil Jennings had come home drunk, and Juanita had been so tired of it she'd let him lie out in the yard. Sometime in the night Gil had gotten sick but hadn't roused enough to sit up, so it had just run back down his throat and suffocated him.

Tugging and pulling, Lorena got Nicky turned on his side near the edge of the bed. It raised her spirits when he roused and again told her to leave him alone. Apparently he wasn't at the dead-drunk stage. She got towels from the bathroom and spread them on the floor, just in case. All of this didn't seem like something a person who'd gotten a college degree and become a banking executive was supposed to have to do. Though it *was* what a mother did, and she was a mother and would be for the rest of her life, even when her boys were grown and gone.

After she'd opened his window she came back and stood gazing down at him, at his glossy brown hair and tawny skin. Tears welled in her eyes.

She hardly ever cried; she'd learned long ago that tears didn't seem to wash away her ache but only made her feel worse. Sniffing them back, she reached down and caressed Nicky's brow. He looked so young... but he just barely resembled the little boy she'd brought into the world and who used to hold tight to her fingers. He used to like to hold her last two fingers best, because they fit into his small hand.

Slowly she lowered herself to the edge of the bed, her mind flying back through the years. She'd raised two boys by herself. After the divorce, and pretty much before the divorce, too, Tony's fathering had consisted of sending support checks and Christmas presents and calling on birthdays. She'd helped them take their first steps, helped them learn to ride their first bicycles, helped them learn to drive their first cars.

How could they be eighteen and twenty? It seemed like yesterday that she'd been sitting at the table with them and making double-decker peanut butter and jelly sandwiches. Now Jaime was gone, a young man riding high on his agenda, as he called it, and she was losing Nicky to adulthood, too. They'd been her life. But all mothers' boys grew up and went away. It was a fact of life, and she wouldn't want them to stay little forever. She even remembered the day when she'd realized she was herself again, Lorena Venable, a woman, more than Jaime and Nicky's mother. That had been a joyful day.

Then she started thinking about how one day her sons would marry and have children, who would call her grandma, and she would sit in the place of honor at the end of the table, and suddenly it seemed as if her life was just whizzing by.

The tears came back then. Stupid, silly tears. Crying couldn't hold back the years.

She brushed them aside and rose. She would read Nicky the riot act tomorrow about this drinking business. He wasn't so old she couldn't do that. Though, of course, she had to be thankful, because her boys had always been so good, hardly giving her a bit of trouble. But plenty of worry. Mothers certainly had enough of that, she thought as she switched out the light and headed downstairs. And mothers always got the dirty clothes, she added to herself, gingerly carrying the soiled shirt and jeans.

She wondered where Oren Breen had gotten to. He'd probably left. For an instant all that she'd felt when she'd seen him weeks ago at the rodeo swept over her. She paused on the stairway. Then she thought, no…none of that. What she had to say to him would all be about Nicky, anyway.

It was with a bit of surprise that she saw him standing in the doorway of the den. And he grinned at her. "Hi. We meet again. I'm Oren Breen, in case you're wonderin'."

"I put two and two together. You look just like your daddy and brothers."

He raised an eyebrow, looked at her a moment and then said, "How's Nick?"

"Drunk." Lorena clung to her ire, which was safe. "Do you make it a habit to take teenage boys out drinkin'? He is only eighteen, and since he works for you, I'm presuming you knew that."

"Lorena, I didn't take him drinkin'. He got drunk all on his own, and it was out at the ranch, on beer. He wasn't out bar hoppin', drinking rotgut whiskey and chasin' fast women.''

She wanted to slap that faint grin off his face. "Beer is alcohol and has the same effect as whiskey—it just takes more of it. And it doesn't matter where it's served to him. He's still a minor, and he still got drunk.''

"Yes, ma'am, I guess that's true. But it wasn't like anyone served him—it was come-and-get-it style. We had a barbecue today, with a big metal cooler full of beer, just like always. Someone always stops the little ones, but Nick hardly qualifies as one of those. Nick does a man's job, working for us, and it does seem to me that at eighteen, when a person's old enough to kill for his country, he's old enough to decide about drinkin' beer or not.''

He spoke very quietly, reasonably, just as he had that night to George Silva. And he made such sense. It irritated Lorena no end.

"Well, I thank you for bringing him home" was the most she could bring herself to say. She stepped toward the front door.

"Does it entitle me to a cup of coffee?''

That stopped her, brought her head swinging around. He stood there in the middle of the room, as easy and friendly as an eight-month-old hound dog. Cocky as all get-out, just as he had been the other evening at the rodeo. As she recalled, he'd always been like that, and so good-natured there was no arguing with him. Her daddy called him a cloudhead.

Oren said, "I thought I smelled some already made.''

She nodded and raised an eyebrow at him. "It's the hard stuff—caffeine loaded.''

"Just my style.''

"Mine, too," she said, stepping toward the kitchen. "It never affects me. I can drink several cups and go right off to sleep.''

"Me, too.''

He followed her into the kitchen. She felt his eyes on her back and thought how she didn't have a stitch of makeup on, and no bra, either. She didn't need makeup, she thought, because she didn't need to impress Oren Breen. Good golly, he was hardly more than a boy, at least considering *her* age. She did feel funny about the bra part, though. But her shirt was of a thick enough fabric, and full, too. She didn't think he could tell.

She put Nick's soiled clothes in the laundry room, then stepped back into the kitchen. Oren was looking at the For Rent sign she'd just finished painting.

"This is probably the fanciest For Rent sign I've ever seen," he said. "What are you renting?"

She turned on the water to wash her hands and said, "The house next door." The sign was much more than required—black calligraphy letters against a smoky-blue background, paint left over from doing the front door, with filigree designs in tan and pink along the edges. She liked to do things like that.

Oren held the towel toward her—the blue checked one.

She took it without touching his hand, but felt as if she had. "Thank you." It sure seemed odd to have a man in her kitchen, handing her a towel, in the middle of the night.

She'd brewed the coffee just before he and Nicky had arrived, and the pot steamed. She poured two cups full, handed him his. "Do you take sugar or milk?"

"Black, thanks." He sipped the coffee and appeared to savor it.

She spooned sugar into her coffee, a fourth of a teaspoon, which was all she ever allowed herself. "I thank you again for steppin' in when you did the other night. I wasn't handlin' any of it very well." She hadn't wanted to speak of it, but it was there, and it would have been impolite not to mention it. She hoped he didn't think she'd enticed George Silva, which was silly of her.... All she was feeling was silly. She drank her coffee and kept her gaze on it.

"I imagine you were doin' all you could with a guy like that. Some guys just can't take no for an answer."

"It wasn't what it seemed—not totally. I think Mr. Silva was really tryin' to get back at me for turning down his loan application at the bank. I've had some people get bitter with me, but never like that. I'm just sorry you had to get into a fight because of it."

"No harm done. Actually, it was quite a good experience for me. I'd never won a fight before."

"You've never won a fight," she repeated.

"Nope. Not even back in high school. 'Course, I might have, if I'd been on my own more, but it seems Rory or Matt has always been around when I managed to get into a scrape, and they always stepped in to protect me." There was a certain knowledge and sparkle in his eyes. "Neither of them happened to be there the other night."

"I'm glad it worked out so well for you."

He grinned and leaned back on the counter. "I thought you looked familiar when I saw you, but I couldn't place you."

"I didn't place you, either," she said. "Not until the announcer said your name. You made a good ride."

He looked shy. "Aw, I gave up ridin' broncs years ago. I just rode that night because of a bet...and to get the feel of it again for my pictures."

"Is that what you're doin' these days—professional photography? From what Nicky said, I thought you worked out at the ranch."

"I do, mostly. Guess I'm a jack of a lot of trades but a master of none. That night I was doin' shots for *American Horseman* magazine," he said with shyness, as if uncomfortable talking about his accomplishments. "They're runnin' a series of articles on grass-roots rodeo. Mostly I take pictures for myself. And how about you?" he said, adeptly shifting the conversation to her. "Looks like you make pictures with quilts. And that you still like horses. I saw the ones in your dining room. And I did peek into your study.''

He didn't say that he hoped she didn't mind him looking around. She liked that, for some odd reason.

She said, ''I do that for myself, too.'' They exchanged understanding looks.

They each fell silent for a long minute, drinking their coffee. Before Lorena even realized, she was noting how lean and lanky Oren was. How hard. She looked back into her coffee cup.

Oren said, ''You were invited to the barbecue today. All the families of the hands were. Didn't Nick tell you?''

''Yes.'' She moved to sit on the tall stool. ''But I had shopping . . . and Saturday afternoons are my afternoons to be lazy.'' She couldn't say that she hadn't gone because she'd been afraid of seeing him again. That was just ludicrous. She hadn't been afraid. . . . She'd simply chosen not to see him again. Yet here she was, oh, so glad to see him now. And that was a feeling she set aside quickly. ''So how was it? As I recall, the Breen barbecues of the past were generally bang-up affairs.''

Oren agreed with a wry smile that the barbecue had been as bang-up an affair as it always was.

''It was for your birthday, wasn't it?'' she asked, and then she just had to say, ''So, how old are you now, Oren?''

''Thirty, and lucky to be here. Many's the time I thought I wouldn't make it.'' He grinned at her above the cup, and his blue eyes seemed as vibrant as sparkling stars. For an instant she simply stared at him. She'd never seen eyes quite so blue, like a cloudless sky at noon on a midwinter day. And they were looking at her as if . . . as if he were quite interested in her.

Flustered, she averted her gaze and asked, ''How's Nicky doin' out at the ranch?''

''Matt seems highly pleased, and when a person can please Matt, they've gone some. It's Matt and Rory he works for, really. 'Bout all I do at the ranch these days is keep the books.''

"And what does Jesse do?''

Oren grinned. "Oh, he's around, and we all work for him.''

"Well, I appreciate you all givin' Nicky the job. I'll be paying for college expenses in the fall, but he'll have to earn his own spending money. And it's good for him to have to learn what hard, physical work is like. Then he can see the value in a college education.''

"We're glad to have him. Good hands aren't easy to come by.'' He drank deeply of his coffee, then looked thoughtful. "You know, though, a lot of fellas get college educated and come back to the ranch.''

"Not as a ranch hand.''

He inclined his head in agreement. "That's so. And I guess being a ranch hand won't earn anyone a fortune, or in some cases a lot of respect, but it is honorable work done by a vanishing breed. And a ranch hand doesn't have to worry about stock prices or the weather. He just does his job and enjoys the out-of-doors, relaxing when the day is done. And if he's good, he'll always have food and a roof over his head, without having to worry about a mortgage,'' he finished, adding emphasis with a poke of his cup.

"True,'' Lorena agreed slowly, "but he'll have to risk frostbite in the winter and sunstroke in the summer.''

"There's a down side to any job.''

"A person with a college education has a much wider choice of down sides,'' she said with wisdom born of her years.

"You have me there.''

"I had you all along.''

He chuckled at that, a deep sound that compelled Lorena to smile inside and out. He said, "You make me think about goin' back to college. I had two years and decided it wasn't doing anything for me, so I came home. Until this minute, I never regretted it."

"You had more of a choice than Nick does. Leaving college, you still came home to a job and a future waiting for you," Lorena said. "And you weren't a ranch hand."

"I was for Matt—still am, sometimes," he said, and there was a cutting edge to his humor.

Making himself at home, he reached over to pour another cup of coffee, then refreshed hers, too. His hands were tanned and rough. He had a relaxed and fluid way of moving, a sensual way that held her eye and brought a pleasurable warmth stirring in her belly.

His hair was deep brown and wavy, his face handsome enough to earn him a living as a model, but with just enough rough imperfection to cut the pretty-boy image and give him real character. He looked like any other well-groomed cowboy on a Saturday night, wearing one of the starched rainbow-colored shirts that were so popular at the moment, a tooled leather belt with a silver buckle earned for bronc riding, denims creased so sharply they could cut, and brown snakeskin boots. It was obvious he enjoyed dressing. Idle scraps of sensual thoughts flitted through her mind, like what his bare shoulders might look like, or his bare chest, or his bare . . .

She brought her thoughts back in line. A trick of the night—that was all her feelings were. It most certainly did seem strange to be there, talking with him, alone, in the middle of the night. Not something she would normally have occasion to do, or would even consider doing. It verged on the improper, according to the rules she lived by. Maybe that was why it was so much fun.

And maybe, just a little bit, she was flattered by his attention. Flattered and enjoying the way his blue eyes crinkled and sparkled, the way her breasts and blood warmed and tingled. But tomorrow, in the light of day, it would all be gone, and that bore keeping in mind.

They went on talking about everyday things such as the weather and changes in the county, and about their respective rodeo experiences in years past. No, she said, she didn't go to many rodeos these days, since her sons had finished with it. He didn't, either. Yes, she exhibited her quilts on occasion, though she'd never sold any; that made quilting like work. Same for his photography, though he had sold several of his, mostly to fellas he thought were smart asses who would pay through the nose to have a flattering picture of themselves. She laughed at that—such a cocky son of a gun, like his father, and she told him so. He took it as a compliment and then said she wasn't at all like her father. As he had reason to recall, her father was tough as nails. She wasn't offended but amused, and she told him how her father called him cloud-head. He laughed at that.

Of course, all good times come to an end, and this one did, too. Lorena was surprised at the hour, and at feeling disappointment because he was leaving. But that was foolish, so she set it aside and properly walked him to the front door.

As she opened the door she told him it had been nice visiting. He agreed, and then he asked her to dinner.

Lorena first stared at him and then averted her face. *Good Lord, he'd asked her for a date!* Had she in some way revealed her silly little fantasies?

At last she said, "Thank you for askin', Oren, but I don't think so," and she looked at his chin. There was never a good way to decline a date; a woman just had to do the best she could. Most times she felt so foolish, and she certainly did this time. This time she wanted to go, which was the most foolish thing ever. And she hoped to God he couldn't tell any of that.

He said, "If it's because you already have plans, maybe you could go Wednesday?"

She looked up. He was gazing at her with his blue eyes, patient as Job and warm as the sun.

She shook her head and smoothed back her already smooth hair. "No, but you certainly flatter me."

"Are you involved with someone?"

"No...not that it is any of your business."

He stepped forward, took hold of the edge of the door and gazed down at her, his face only scant inches from hers. She could feel the air vibrating between them. She kept her gaze on his shirt.

He said in a very low tone, "I'd really like to take you to dinner, Lorena. Or a movie. Or we could go to the races...anything. I'd just like to enjoy your company. That's all. I'm not tryin' to get in your bed or anything like that."

Good grief! He was frank, she had to give him that. She forced herself to look him in the eye. "Oren, when you were barely in elementary school, I was graduating."

A wry grin tugged at his lips and his eyes. "What does that have to do with now? Are you wantin' my school records before you'll go out with me?"

She shook her head and didn't know what to say. She pulled the door wider. "I've enjoyed visiting with you, Oren."

"Me, too. That's why I asked you to dinner."

"Oren, if you're lookin' for a fun fling with an older woman, go look somewhere else. I'm not up to it."

Teasing mischief slipped across his face. "I asked you to dinner, and you have us in a fling. I don't know now if I want to go out with you, Lorena—you're too fast for me."

And so she was embarrassed, though she refused to show it. "Good night, Oren," she said primly. "Thank you for bringing Nicky home and for the conversation."

He most gallantly inclined his head. "Thank *you*, Lorena. It has been a pleasure." He went through the doorway. Then, to her surprise, he paused and turned back, looking down at her with a long, deliberate look. "You might not admit to what was goin' on between us tonight, but it was there just the same."

She shut the door in his face.

She stood there, holding her breath, her hand still on the knob. She listened to his footsteps as he left the porch.

Then, very carefully, she moved the edge of the sidelight curtain with a finger and peeped out, watching him head away down the walk toward the car parked in front. Good golly, the car was a classic Cadillac—a pink one, no less! She'd seen it around on a number of occasions. She'd noticed the driver, too, though she hadn't placed him as being Oren. She hadn't looked at the driver hard enough to recognize him. It had been the car that had drawn her eye; she'd always had a penchant for hot cars and hot horses. Not hot young men, she thought, as she watched him walk around to the driver's side. He had a long-legged stride.

He paused and looked at the house. Lorena jerked back from the window and pressed herself against the door. She surely didn't want him to see her there. And she couldn't imagine why she'd been watching him in the first place.

The clock beside her bed read two o'clock by the time Lorena had gotten undressed. In her pink silk robe she sat in front of her dressing-table mirror, running a brush almost absently through her hair. She paused, dropped the hand holding the brush to her lap and peered more closely at the mirror.

The light was good, but fixed to flatter. Her hair was brushed back and fell prettily around her face. Thanks to family heritage, her hair was a shining brown, with only a stray gray hair here and there that she would pull out whenever she found it. Devoid of makeup, she was colorless, as she'd been when Oren had seen her. As far as the mirror was concerned, she could be any age from twenty-five to fifty-five.

What had Oren seen that had attracted him?

She had great cheekbones. Her mother always said that, though Lorena wasn't certain exactly what made good cheekbones. She had fine lines around her eyes and looked upon these with mixed feelings. A part of her wished never to age, but another part was glad to be past the confusions of her youth and took the lines as badges of a good life well lived. She had, however, gone so far as to begin a list of good plastic surgeons.

She touched her lips. They had always been thin, and they would never again be the lips of a twenty year old. Cosmetics offered all sorts of remedies, but Lorena didn't find that they helped her any.

No, the fact was that she wasn't a fresh young thing anymore, and she really didn't want to be. Yet she wasn't old, either. She was, she thought, a woman in her prime.

Her work and her life in general were fulfilling. Some people had to drag themselves to work, but Lorena was one of the fortunate few who loved what she did.

She loved working with figures. Columns of figures made her pulse race, and, as a loan officer, she got to give away money. Not her own money, but other people's, and she got a great charge out of that. What could be better? She helped people. Her boss, Paul Martinez, was sometimes skeptical of some of the people she qualified for loans, but no one she'd qualified had ever failed to repay, contributing to the perfect circle. And now she was in charge of a new bank service—customer investments. She got to counsel customers on how to invest their money through the bank. It was a challenge that enabled her to work more with figures and make everyone more money.

Outside of work she had her quilting, which in its way was a working of figures, too, and she had her home, her family, her friends, her love of the country and community. She had everything she could want, almost. There was one thing lacking—sex.

If Lorena had had to put her hand on the Bible and tell the truth of it, the truth would be that she was forty years old, in the best of health and startlingly good shape and the prime of her sexuality. She was a woman comfortable with her own sensual nature. She acknowledged it, even enjoyed the earthiness within herself as being a vibrant part of her being. Years sucked the life from a person, but Lorena had learned that those years could never take away her awareness of herself. She savored this, triumphed in it. Unlike the earthly body, this inner awareness never aged but remained forever young.

There was one drawback to all this, though, and that was her current situation: namely, living a celibate life, which she had been doing for more years than she liked to think about. Except for one brief, crazy fling, she had been all alone since her divorce from Tony nearly sixteen years ago. And both her marriage and crazy fling had left her with absolutely no desire to get involved with another man.

She cried sometimes when alone, and sometimes she took cold showers, but usually half an hour on her weight bench worked best. She might have desire, but not for involvement. It had been said that a woman came into her own in her forties, and Lorena was certainly finding that to be true. She had come to know exactly who and what she was, and to like herself, and it had been a long, hard-fought battle to get there. She didn't ever again want to get lost in a man.

Realizing she was just sitting there staring at herself, she tossed the brush to the dresser, rose and turned out the light. Slipping out of the robe, she draped it on the end of the bed and crawled, naked, beneath the sheet and soft cotton blanket. The night air was sweet and cool through the window. After a minute she peeled back the covers to allow the air to whisper over her skin.

She lay in bed for a long time, in the dark, staring at the patterns the streetlight made on the ceiling and thinking about her life. And she thought a bit about Oren Breen and how she'd felt when he'd looked at her.

The house was quiet when Oren and Harvey came in. Oren was glad, because he didn't feel like talking to anyone. He switched out the light burning over the kitchen sink and moved through the house in the dark. Having lived in this house all his life, he knew it like the back of his hand. He undressed in the dark and got into bed and told Harvey that no one would know they hadn't brushed their teeth. Harvey curled up on the rug beside the bed and was soon snoring.

Oren lay and looked at the slices of silvery moonlight on the walls and thought about Lorena Venable. He thought about how amazed he'd been when he'd seen her standing in the doorway. With her hair in a ponytail and wearing a blue shirt about three sizes too large and black clinging tights, she hadn't looked like the mother of boys who were eighteen and twenty. But she'd still looked like his brown-haired queen.

He thought about how he'd enjoyed talking with her—and about how unusual that was for him. He didn't usually spend a lot of time talking with a woman. He thought about how something inside him had wanted to get close to her.

She'd been surprised when he asked her out, surprised and resistant. He wondered why. Because he was younger? That didn't seem such a big deal to him. It certainly wasn't as if anyone could even tell there was an age difference. She liked him. He really thought she did.

She'd turned him down, but he wasn't ready to simply accept that.

The For Rent sign he'd seen in her kitchen popped into his mind, and a vague memory of the house next to hers came after. The thought that he could rent the house followed, and was met with amusement.

And then it came again, more seriously.

Chapter Four

On most Sundays the entire Breen family would gather for a late breakfast at the home place. Big Jesse had bought a new table that could accommodate everyone; it had three leaves and extended into the living room. When Oren finally got up on this Sunday, Matt and Annie and Big Jesse and Marnie and the little ones, Little Jesse and Mary, were already sitting around the long table. Rory and Zoe and their girls were off to a horse show.

His nephew, Little Jesse, popped from his chair and grabbed Oren around the leg and balanced on his boot, asking, "Can I have a ride?" Oren walked him around the table and lifted his baby half sister out of her high chair when she raised her hands to him.

Still holding both children while he rounded the table again, he kissed first Marnie's cheek and then Annie's. Oren had the idea that it was his duty to lead the world in rediscovering the value of honest affection. And sometimes he kissed Annie's cheek just to remind Matt to pay attention to his wife. His brother often got preoccupied with the mundane details of everyday living and forgot the most important parts. And Matt knew how Oren felt about Annie, and Oren knew Matt knew.

This morning, though, kissing his sister-in-law and stepmother was for himself. He felt the need to touch his family. He mussed Matt's hair, getting a rise out of him, and squeezed his dad's shoulder, getting a squeeze in return.

Little Jesse spied Harvey through the window and ran off outside to play with him, though about all Harvey would do was lie on his back and let Little Jesse roll all over him. Oren hugged Mary and gave her to her dad. Marnie brought him fresh warm pancakes from the kitchen. He knew she'd made them, because they were like cakes. Two things had been foreign to Marnie when she'd married Big Jesse: cooking and the outdoors. For the past months, though, she'd decided to learn to cook, and so far pancakes were the only halfway edible thing she could make. She maintained she would never take up with the outdoors.

He heaped his plate with sausages and blueberries from dishes on the table. The conversation touched on happenings from the barbecue—about how Lola Shatto had gotten mad during the target shoot and everyone had thought that this time she might really shoot Joe, and about Big Jesse's argument with Otto Hunsicker over Otto's ruling that his nephew Irwin had won the horse race, with Zoe coming in second, when everyone had seen it had been a tie, and about how everyone's children were growing up. All of that pretty well got them up to Nick Venable crashing the lawn tractor into Oren's Cadillac, and that had to be joked about for a few minutes.

Then his dad asked, "Was Lorena very upset?"

Oren swallowed a bite of pancake. "She wasn't very happy, but she seemed to take it in stride."

"I'll call her later," his dad said and shifted his now dozing daughter from one arm to the other. "She raised those boys alone, and she's pretty protective of them. Max seems to feel she babies Nick, but I told him that boy is doin' a good job here and makin' a good hand.''

Matt agreed heartily, and Marnie commented on Nick's politeness. Oren mentioned that any man alive was polite to Marnie, because they couldn't help it. She still blushed, after all this time of being with them.

His dad slid back his chair. "What are my heirs' plans for this fine day?''

Annie said she was spending the day on the sofa reading a good book, and Matt said he was putting the tractor barn back to rights.

Oren said, "I'm gonna see about renting a house." And he enjoyed all the surprised expressions. He had a mischievous streak in him that enjoyed setting people off balance. Annie had always said he liked drama.

"Are you movin' in with some woman?" Matt asked right off the bat and not a little testy. He got irritable when threatened with change.

Everyone else just stared at Oren. Annie's face was anxious; she tended to worry about everything.

Oren shook his head. "Nope. I just decided it's time I got a place of my own.''

"*This* house is yours, as much as it is Annie's and mine,'' Matt said, and Annie reached over and laid her hand on his. He was sensitive to being the one their dad had given the house to, but the way Oren and Rory saw it, Matt, as the eldest, was the one who should have it. "We could make some changes to it, if you'd like. We could add on and turn your room into a separate apartment. By golly, wouldn't take anything to do that.'' As he spoke, the idea grew in his mind, and he glowed as if he'd come up with a way to wipe out the national debt.

"There's no need to go makin' this house any bigger than it already is," Oren said, almost a little regretful to dampen his brother. "It isn't more room I need. I just think it's time I got a place of my own."

"Well, then, let's build you a house. We certainly have the land to do it."

"I don't want to build a house."

"Why not? Rentin' is just throwin' money down the drain." Matt leaned both arms on the table and looked intense. He was a very logical thinker, and it was true he was the best in the family with money. "If you don't want to build here, you could buy an existing house, but you'd probably have to go near to Clayton to find one."

"I want to rent for a while."

"Do you have a place in mind, son?" his father asked. His eyes had been studying Oren right along.

"Yes," Oren said with a nod. "And it *is* down in Clayton. Lorena Venable has a house for rent." He got all tense for some reason and tried not to show it.

But the old man could read minds, and a speculative light entered his eyes.

Matt got prickly. "Do you want to quit workin' on the ranch, too? All you have to do is say so."

Oren shook his head and answered patiently. "I don't want to quit the ranch, big brother, and I won't until I'm dead and gone. A prospect you should give some thought to. Since I took over the new computer, you have no idea of just what I've been doin' with our taxes and cattle count. Considering Dad's and Rory's past experience with computers, you'd better find time to take a peek with me."

Matt gave him a half grin and looked somewhat mollified, though he went on grumbling about rent being money down the drain. Annie and Marnie jumped right in and started making plans for all the stuff he would need. His dad sat with Mary in his arms and stared at the table, lost in thought.

So that was that. Oren felt let down. He'd imagined he
would have more explaining to do, more egos to massage,
something.

Thirty years in this house. The door over there to the
kitchen bore the notch from the time when Matt had measured off his height when he was five. His dad had scolded
them about defacing the house, and his mother had then
notched Matt and Rory. That was his only vivid memory of
his mother. And now he was moving out, and it seemed
okay by everyone, except Matt, who couldn't stand to see
money going down the drain.

Then he saw Matt looking at him a little sadly. He smiled,
and Matt grinned. And Oren knew he'd reached some sort
of turning point in his life, and that his brother did understand.

About once a month her father ragged her about always
wearing pants. Apparently the time had rolled around again.

"You know, daughter, I often wonder if you still have
legs. A woman as lovely as you should dress like a woman."

Lorena rose from the dining table and began gathering
plates. "I *am* dressed like a woman. No man would wear
'summer-peach trousers of fluid rayon.'"

Aunt Esmerelda laughed and wove her graceful hands
together. "I think those are wonderful trousers. I had some
just like them, in blue—and mind you, Lorena, back in 1947
I was as thin as you are. Isn't it funny how those styles are
coming back? Mine were rayon, too. Back then we called it
the poor man's silk," she said and frowned. "These days
rayon costs the same as silk. Do you suppose that's considered progress?" Uncle Rennie, who was hard of hearing,
asked what they were talking about, and Aunt Esmerelda
very loudly repeated it to him. "If you'd break down and get
a hearing aid, I could whisper sweet nothings in your ear."

"I'll give you fifty dollars to go buy a dress," her father
said.

"Daddy, you haven't bought a dress in a long time. For fifty dollars I might get half a dress. Would you like me to wear that? Now, who wants an apple dumpling? Do you want an apple dumpling, Aunt Josephine?" She put her face in front of her great-aunt's and spoke slowly. Aunt Josephine was one hundred years old and deaf as a doorpost. She expertly read lips, though, and she smiled and nodded. She still had her own teeth, not all of them, but those she had were her own, and she had a smile that was like the sunshine. Lorena hoped that if she herself lived to be so old, she would have such a smile.

These were all of her relatives who lived in Clayton. Aunt Esmerelda was her father's older sister, but she seemed lots younger somehow. Maybe people always thought of their parents as being older than everyone else. Aunt Esmerelda had iron-gray hair that touched the floor when it was down. She wore it braided, with the braid looped up several times and fastened at her nape. She liked rings, had one on every finger, and long, dangling earrings in her ears. The older she got, the more Mexican she liked to dress. She was fat now but still lovely in the face, and she was as gay as a pink balloon. Her husband was Uncle Rennie. He was as thin and somber as Aunt Esmerelda was big and gay. He did smile a lot, though, mostly as a means of covering up that he hadn't heard everything. He absolutely refused to get a hearing aid because he refused to spend his money. Aunt Esmerelda and Uncle Rennie each had their own money and did not combine it. A long time ago they'd split their house down the middle with a line of masking tape, and each paid to keep his own half.

Aunt Josephine was Lorena's great-aunt on her mother's side. She was a tiny gnome. She could sleep sitting up, and would fall asleep now and again without anyone ever knowing.

Once each season—each spring, summer, fall and winter—Lorena had a brunch for them all. Though, of course,

she saw each of them every few days. In a town the size of
Clayton a person was bound to run into her relatives at the
post office, if nowhere else. Lorena had a love-hate thing
about being so close to family. This was the love part. She'd
entered a phase of her life, with her boys grown and her
parents growing older, that she realized how short life really was and that she had better appreciate these people as
much as possible while she could. She enjoyed sparring with
her parents, enjoyed simply watching them together. She
adored hearing Aunt Josephine tell stories of the family and
listening to Aunt Esmerelda's jokes and observations about
life.

She looked around the table and wished Jaime could have
made it down to join them. It was the first time he'd missed.
She'd bitten her tongue to keep herself from pressing him.
He had his own life, and these older people didn't mean to
him what they did to her. Nick was here because he lived
here and had respect, but soon he would be gone, too.

"Coffee is served." Petra Sandoval, Lorena's mother,
came from the kitchen, bearing the good china cups and
saucers. Only a few strands of gray showed in her mahog-
any brown hair, and she remained an attractive woman.
Petite, she stood straight as an arrow and drew attention
when she entered a room.

Nick came right behind her, bearing the silver coffee
service. He was pale, looking as if something had run over
him and squashed him.

Lorena met his sorrowful gaze with an I-told-you-so one
of her own. Then she took the silver tray from him. "Go
stretch out on the sofa and watch television."

"Don't you feel well today, Nicky?" her mother asked.

"No, Nanna, not too good." He retreated to the living
room. By tacit agreement they hadn't told his grandparents
of his drinking episode. Lorena thought her father had
guessed, but he had remained silent. He savored having
knowledge his wife didn't.

Lorena and her mother served the coffee, so strong and sweet it could stand without a cup, as her family liked it, and her father started in about dresses again. Lorena wore dresses only for ceremonies such as weddings or funerals or graduations. Back when she and Tony had divorced and her father had been pushing her, she had started wearing trousers everywhere as some sort of rebellion against life and her father. Now she was comfortable in them; they were practical, could be lovely, and they were her.

"How about a hundred and fifty?" her father said. "Will *that* buy you a dress?"

"Daddy, if slacks are good enough for Katharine Hepburn..." She left the rest unsaid as she took up the stack of dishes and waltzed out of the room. Her mother idolized Katharine Hepburn, and therefore her father was hesitant to make a comment that would sound like a criticism of the great woman. He couldn't fight a legend, and when Lorena resorted to this response he usually gave up.

Her mother said, "Max, you're worrying about your daughter wearing slacks and not about what it looks like for a man to be leaving her house in the middle of the night?"

"Oh, Mother, this is the nineties. No one cares," Lorena called from the kitchen. Her mother came after, bringing glasses.

"People talk, the same as they always have."

Aunt Esmerelda called gaily, "Petra, just be glad in these days that it wasn't another woman."

"Essie, you are crude," her mother responded. She'd always felt a little superior to Esmerelda, and it galled her no end that Esmerelda didn't have the grace to feel inferior.

She set the dirty glasses beside the dishes on the counter. "People *say* they don't care. And they don't really care and never have, but they talk, always have and always will. You better bet Aggie Pacheco told more than me at church this mornin', and has told everyone on the street by now, and I could put money in the bank on that. I know, I know..."

Oren Breen's visit was innocent, but that isn't what it *looked* like. There's only one thought in anyone's mind when they see a man leaving a woman's house in the middle of the night.''

Lorena began dishing up the dumplings.''And what's that, Mama—that the man didn't enjoy himself enough to stay the night?'' She immediately scolded herself for being smart mouthed to her mother.

Her mother harrumphed and tightened her lips until they almost disappeared. Lorena hated to see that. It always reminded her that her lips were shaped just like her mother's. Right then, involuntarily, she touched her lips.

''You're being flippant, Lorena Maria, and you aren't thinking about how the rest of us might feel, having you talked about as trash.''

Lorena felt properly scolded. In the middle of my life, my mother can make me feel ten years old, she thought. What's wrong with this picture?

Petra Sandoval was petite and feminine, but she was a powerhouse. At times the clashes of willpower between her mother and father could wither Lorena. She often thought that she'd married Tony all those years ago to keep from having to come home between college semesters. She'd had absolutely no self-confidence in those days.

''I promise, Mama. Next time I have a man at my house at night, I'll have him either stay the night or sneak out by the back door.''

Her mother frowned and then made her own sarcastic comment. ''If that's the best you can offer.'' Her mother's dry sense of humor was what Lorena truly admired about her.

Her mother had opened her mouth to say something else when Nicky spoke from the doorway.

''Mom...'' He hesitated and looked from her to her mother with an odd grin on his face. ''Oren's here. He'd like to speak to you.''

Oren is here? And he wants to speak to me? What could he want to talk to her about? She hurriedly wiped her hands on a dishcloth. Her mother sent her an inquiring look, with an arched eyebrow as an exclamation point. Lorena shrugged.

Aunt Esmerelda's eyes were bright with high curiosity, and Uncle Rennie was saying, "Who? Who is it?" twisting around in his chair, while Aunt Esmerelda shushed him. Aunt Josephine's eyes were closed.

"Mama, you'd better make sure Aunt Josephine doesn't fall over," Lorena whispered, grasping at a way to get her mother off her heels.

But her mother tossed that aside with, "Oh, she never falls over," and followed. Thank heaven her strict rules of what constituted polite behavior made her stop and look on from the dining room doorway.

Nicky and her dad were there with Oren in the middle of the living room.

He looked at her, and she looked at him, and the silliest pleasure leaped into her. They shared a warm smile . . . and a private amusement. Speaking without words.

Then she said with all the polite grace she possessed, "Hello, Oren. We were just having coffee and apple dumplings. Please come join us."

He shook his head and cut a quick glance to her father. "I didn't come to interrupt your family meal," he said. His gaze fell full on her again. "I came to see about renting the house...your place next door," he added, inclining his head in that direction.

Of everything he could have said or done, this wasn't anything Lorena could have imagined.

Max Sandoval wanted to know if Oren had gotten a job in town, and Oren told him no, that he just wanted to move in. "There aren't many places to rent up in Wings," he said. "There are two empty houses, but they'd take a lot of work before a person could live in them. It isn't a very long drive from here to the ranch,'' he added, because Max Sandoval kept looking at him.

The old man held a dislike for him and hadn't ever tried to hide that. Maybe dislike was too strong a word, because Oren doubted that Max Sandoval thought much about him, period. But he wasn't one of the old man's favorite people, and Max Sandoval wasn't his, and they both knew it, though neither had ever said it straight out. It was one of those instinctive things.

Lorena sent Nick upstairs to get the keys for the rental house and then introduced Oren to her mother and aunt and uncle. He found Petra Sandoval a coolly polite, very dignified lady. The aunt was bright and friendly, the uncle a small, odd fella. Lorena identified the very old lady on the far side of the table as her aunt Josephine. The old woman was asleep, sitting right there, sunk down into herself but not leaning to one side or the other. Oren said his great-uncle Woody did the same thing. Except for the sleeping old woman, everyone else seemed to be regarding him as if he were a curiosity in a zoo. And he got the distinct impression that Petra Sandoval didn't care for him any more than Max did. He gave her his most charming smile, and she didn't know how to react to that.

Then at last he was walking across to the rental house with Lorena. He felt excited to be with her, as if they were going for a day down to Amarillo, instead of into an empty old house.

Both times he'd seen her before had been in lamplight. There was a big difference between that and daylight. He'd thought her eyes were beautiful, but today they were a warm, glistening brown, like chocolate kisses in the sun. He'd noticed the circles beneath her eyes last night, and the fine lines, too. But today the creamy color of her blouse flattered her, and she had on a bit of makeup, giving her more color and the sophistication she'd possessed that night at the rodeo. Her hair was twisted loosely atop her head, and strands escaped around her face and neck, making her all soft and feminine. She could be taken for a very young woman until a person looked into those cocoa brown eyes. There was a certain knowledge of life in her eyes, and a calmness and surety and amusement, too. Those eyes fascinated him, drew him.

She said, "The yard isn't big, but you'd have to keep it, and a mower doesn't come with the house."

"I'm sure I can get a mower."

They went up on the porch. "It doesn't have a garage," she said, casting him a highly doubtful look. "You'd have to park your Cadillac out in the weather."

She gave the Caddie a long, questioning look, and thinking that the dented door might be among her questions, he said quickly, "It's parked outside most of the time at the ranch, anyway. I never can seem to get it in the garage. Hey... a porch swing. That's great." He went over and pushed it, setting it to rocking.

Their gazes touched, and hers flickered away.

She led the way into the living room. He gazed at her back and thought of what her skin would look like.

The living room was of medium size according to what Oren was used to, with scarred but polished wood floors, large wooden windows, freshly painted, one with an air conditioner stuck in it, and a fireplace on one wall. It was hot and smelled musty from being shut up.

Lorena went across to open a window, saying, "It doesn't come furnished."

"I figure it's time I bought furniture," Oren said and meandered around. The walls were freshly painted, too, a pale tan.

"There's no central air-conditioning."

"The window unit looks pretty new."

"It's two years old." She looked at him as if that was something to truly be considered. Then she moved into the dining room to open more windows.

He followed. "You sure don't see woodwork like this much any longer." He pointed to the crown molding at the tops of the walls. He wanted to get in the good points about the house, since she seemed determined to point out the bad and dissuade him. If he'd been a man of lesser confidence, his feelings might have been hurt. But then, he really wanted this house, no matter how she might feel about it.

"No, not usually." She cocked her head slightly. "You really intend to move out of the ranch house? I thought all you Breens kept it in the family up there."

"The home place belongs to Matt and Annie now, and their family is growing. I'm not ready to build a house, but I am ready to have a place of my own. No offense to my big brother, but he can be a bit bossy—and it isn't too easy to bring a woman home to do some romancin' on the sofa in a house you share with your older brother, his pregnant wife and a three-year-old boy."

She smiled, and man, it was stunning, quick and full and with her eyes sparkling. "No, I don't imagine that would be very easy." Then, as if self-conscious, she averted her eyes and stepped out briskly to show him the rest of the house.

In answer to his questions, she told him it was a bungalow, built back in the thirties, the same era as her house, though not many renovations had been made to this place. She had installed a new furnace and intended to add air-conditioning next year. The bathroom still had a great old claw-foot tub and ceramic tile floor, cracking in places. But the entire house was clean, shiny and neat as a pin. He liked the house *and* the landlady, though he mentioned liking only the house when he asked the rent.

She gazed at him for a thoughtful moment and then told him the people in the house next door had three rowdy children between the ages of three and nine.

He said he liked kids.

She said he would have to pay his own utilities, and that the insulation was poor, which led to high monthly bills summer and winter.

He said he expected he could afford it.

She looked at him, and her face was full of questions. She shook her head and went over to lean against the kitchen counter. She was just about to say something when a voice called out.

"Lorena? Lorena?"

"In here, Mama." Lorena went to meet her mother.

Petra Sandoval, moving as elegantly as if she were crossing the marble floor of a mansion, flowed across the bungalow's living room, bringing with her a young couple who were interested in renting the house. Petra Sandoval seemed very pleased about that. She went on to explain that the couple were planning to be married and were looking for their first place together. "This house is just perfect for a couple starting out, and the neighborhood is all couples and families. It's very quiet and friendly." She looked directly at Oren, and he had the feeling she was mentally taking a broom and sweeping him out.

Lorena didn't look at him, and he was about to speak up when she said, "I'm awfully sorry to disappoint you, but Mr. Breen has gotten here first."

Petra Sandoval and the young couple looked at him, and Oren folded his hands behind him and tried not to look exuberant in the face of their loss. Being polite, he walked to the door and held it, bidding them goodbye and feeling somewhat like a laird in his castle. Petra Sandoval, dragging her feet, though with grace, and looking back over her shoulder, went, too. And Oren mentally took a broom and helped her along.

Oren sauntered back from the open door. "Thanks."

Lorena shrugged and brushed her hair from her forehead. She thought how she might have been in less trouble if she'd rented to the lady who had the three Great Danes and two parrots.

"Okay, Oren..." She assumed the manner she used when speaking to Jaime or Nick. "This house isn't exactly a bachelor pad. I don't want any wild parties going on here that rip up the house and get the neighbors down on me." Or my parents, she thought.

"I don't have wild parties. I don't drink much more than a couple of beers at a time, I don't smoke and I'll stick to one woman at a time on my sofa. Do I pass, or do you need to see my school records?"

She had to smile, couldn't help it. "I'll let your school records pass, but I will need one month's deposit plus one month's rent. I don't require a lease, unless you want one, but generally they don't carry any more weight than the paper they're printed on. The rules are that I pay for any repairs that crop up as a result of natural wear and tear. Any damage you do, you pay to have repaired. The interior has just been repainted, so it stays the color it is for another year, unless you buy the paint and do the work. If you have a problem and can't reach me, call Cecil Doak. He's my repairman, and his number is taped inside the pantry door. Here're the keys. I don't have extras, so don't come to me if you lock yourself out. Call Cecil, and he charges twenty-five dollars to pick the lock."

He said, "I don't need a lease," and paid her in cash.

He'd obviously been certain he was going to rent this place, or else he tended to carry a lot of cash in his pocket, in hundreds.

He grinned down at her with his considerable sexy charm. "I'll try to be a very good neighbor."

His eyes danced with expectations and brought a quickening of life inside her.

She walked toward the door. "Well, if you're not—" she paused for emphasis and looked back "—I can always throw you out."

* * *

Oren Breen wasted no time moving in. That evening Lorena was watering the flowers on her front porch when she saw him arrive. His pink Cadillac was loaded with stuff, seeming to rumble down the road as if puffing under its burden. She wondered how he'd come to wreck the driver's side door. It appeared as if something had hit him, and not a car, either. Her gaze was drawn to the gaping trunk lid tied with twine. His back seat looked as if it had been piled with things from a scavenger hunt. He pulled the car to a stop right at the porch steps and, getting out, waved to her.

"Hi, neighbor!"

"Hello," she replied, a little ruefully. She averted her gaze and went on watering her flowers.

Nick came out of the house and called a greeting.

Oren hollered, "If you feel up to it, ol' son, come help me unload and I'll pay you overtime."

Nick jogged over, saying he wouldn't take the money, and Lorena heard Oren say he would give Nick a six-pack of beer, and then laugh. "What? You don't want a beer?" he teased, and Lorena mentally thanked him for the razzing of her son.

The two of them went to unloading, and Lorena made herself focus on finishing her watering. Still, she kept glancing over, and one of those times she saw a dog lying on the front porch.

She took a second, good look, because it appeared to be more a life-size stuffed toy. A flop-eared basset, either stuffed or dead, and neither of those images made sense.

Uncertain, she tossed aside the hose and ran to cut off the water. She went to the low concrete wall that separated the yards and peered over at the porch of the rental house. It *was* a basset hound, wrinkled skin, black and tan, and sure enough it looked dead, but it couldn't be, because who would bring a dead dog to put on their porch? At that moment the hound opened one droopy eye and looked at Lorena.

Hell's bells, she thought.

Oren came through the front door. "Good evenin', Miss Lorena."

She said, "You didn't tell me you had a dog."

"Well, now, you didn't ask. This is Harvey." Crouching, he scratched the dog behind an ear. "Harvey, say hello to the lady." The dog lay there, one eye focused on her, blinking every other second.

"Oren, I don't allow dogs in this house."

His eyes came around to hers, and his eyebrows rose. "Don't you like dogs?" He said it as if it was a sin he couldn't imagine anyone committing.

Nicky came out of the house. "You don't like dogs, Mom? I always thought you did. We always had a dog when we were kids."

"I like dogs fine," Lorena said, feeling defensive. "But I don't like dogs in my rental house. Dogs tend to scratch doors to pieces and dig craters in the yard."

Oren looked down at the dog and kept on scratching him behind the ear. The dog continued to look, with one eye, at Lorena. Nicky parked his bottom on the edge of the brick pillar and said that Harvey never did much of anything. Lorena said no dog did much of anything, except to get into people's trash and dig holes and scratch furniture and woodwork.

Oren said, "I guess we should have discussed this. You didn't list 'no dogs' in your rules." He met her eyes straight on.

Lorena shifted her feet. "No, I didn't," she admitted. "I forgot. Can't you just leave him out at the ranch? Wouldn't that be a lot better for him, anyway? He'd have plenty of room to run around and...do whatever dogs like to do." She thought of what had happened when the house had been rented for a short time by a couple with two cocker spaniels. Within the space of four weeks every door in the house had been clawed, and holes had been dug all over the backyard.

"Harvey likes to be with me. That's about the extent of his doin'. He's gone everywhere I've gone ever since someone dropped him at our ranch. People do that all the time, you know. They bring the dogs they don't want out and drop them at a likely drive, thinkin' farmers and ranchers will always take in another stray. Thing is, we can only take so many, and then we have to shoot 'em, 'cause it's either that or let 'em starve or start runnin' in packs. They get so they kill, the same as coyotes. And I don't know why people think a rancher can kill a dog easier than other people. Matt has to do it, and he has to drink half a bottle of antacid afterward. This spring he put up this big sign at the entry to our drive." He gestured. "It says, We Shoot All Dogs Dropped Here, So Don't Do It. Guess it works, because we haven't had a dog show up since. We have had a number of kittens, though, because Annie went out and wrote on the bottom, We Do Take Cats."

By the time he finished there was a small grin tugging at the corners of his mouth. Their eyes held, and Lorena did her best not to smile. Oh, my, how he made her feel! She couldn't deny it.

At last she said, "He's your responsibility, and so is any damage that he does."

"Don't you worry about Harvey," Oren said. "He's too lazy to do any damage. Never digs or chews or anything. You won't even know he's around." And he grinned his charming grin.

That night Lorena discovered what Harvey did do, however. He howled. And he sounded like a foghorn that could be heard across the entire Gulf of Mexico.

His call came floating out the windows of the rental house and through the open window of Lorena's bedroom and sent a cold chill down her spine, startling her awake.

Whooff-oooo . . . whooff-oooo.

After realizing what was making the sound, she lay there waiting for it to stop. She was considering what she could throw through the window of the rental house when she heard the window go down, and the howl was cut off.

Lorena pulled a pillow over her head and thought how she'd rented her house to a country cowboy come to town with his howling dog in a pink Cadillac.

Chapter Five

The telephone rang just as Lorena was halfway to the garage. There were few things more irritating in life than to have just shut and locked a door when the telephone began ringing on the other side of it. The other side of the door and through the laundry room and on the wall on the far side of the kitchen, beside the microwave oven. By the time she could get to it, either whoever it was would have hung up, or the answering machine in the den would have picked up.

Still, she stood there, poised to make the mad dash, with thoughts of an emergency running through her head. Though the percentages said it would be her mother, and her mother probably didn't have anything to say that couldn't wait.

It went against her nature, but she went on to the garage and left it ringing. And now all day long she would wonder who had called.

She backed her bright yellow Mustang carefully from the driveway. Looking over, she saw Oren's pink Cadillac, its white top up now. Nicky had left for work at the ranch two and a half hours earlier—which went to show what a ranch hand had to do and what the upper management got to do.

As she slipped on her mirrored sunglasses she wondered if Oren was up, looking out the window, seeing her Mustang. Would he be surprised at what she drove? Impressed? Her Mustang wasn't a classic, but it did have plenty of pizzazz.

She shook her head at her childishness. What in the world had happened to her since meeting Oren Breen? Resisting the juvenile urge to squeal her tires, she very quietly drove off. Just because her Mustang could burn rubber doing zero to sixty in 5.2 didn't mean she had to show off.

At eight o'clock on a Monday morning the town of Clayton was as awake as the bright sun above and humming with life. Aggie Pacheco was sweeping her walk, which she did every sunny day at eight in the morning, winter and summer, regular as clockwork. Joe Hershberger was delivering dairy products to Aragon's Grocery—he was early. Tom Elam was speeding along in his battered red GMC, heading for the feed store, and he was way late for the men's coffee klatch that went on there every morning. Julie Ann Garcia was opening the Klassic Kuts Beauty Salon.

Lorena was heading to the Community Savings Bank. The Moody Blues played from her stereo, and the light breeze ruffled her hair. This morning she wore the latest in men's-style suiting, which consisted of a shimmering white silk blouse, paisley vest and buff-colored sandwashed silk trousers. There were certain outfits that helped her moods. She'd awakened feeling vaguely ill at ease, so she'd chosen this particular outfit and, sure enough, it had helped.

Driving at a snail's pace, she could wave easily at Aggie Pacheco, Joe Hershberger and everyone else. When a person had lived a number of years in a big city, such as Denver, where Lorena had lived, she either embraced the slower, more intimate ways of a rural town or she hated it with a passion. Lorena adored it. Here she waved to neighbors all the way to work. Here she could pay her grocery bill in Aragon's with a check that they dropped into the cash register without jotting down her life history on the back; she could charge her prescriptions at Whitman's Drug, and if she was sick, her groceries and medicine would be delivered to her home.

If everyone knew everyone's business, that was part of the friendliness, too, Lorena mused ruefully. And many times everyone knowing everyone's business could be a blessing. A person never had to feel embarrassed about confessing a need, because it would already be known and neighbors would already be answering it. When Lorena had first moved here, her neighbors had all dropped over, bringing food for those first days, so she wouldn't have to be bothered with cooking, or even going out. When Leo Perkin's automotive garage had been blown away by a tornado and there had been a problem with his insurance, the community had all donated money and time to help him rebuild, and when little Carmela Montano had been lost, everyone had looked until she'd been found.

As Lorena saw it, the only real drawback to living in your small hometown was that your mother knew every single thing you did. And there wasn't a woman alive who wanted her mother to know everything she did.

She parked the Mustang in the bank lot, whipped her purse and brown leather portfolio out of the passenger seat and walked briskly toward the rear door of the building. She waved to Delores Curry, who was at the drive-up window. The window opened at seven-thirty, while the bank lobby didn't open until nine o'clock.

She entered by the back door, which was unlocked. Paul Martinez, the bank manager and her boss, was always the first one to arrive. Divorced five years ago, Paul lived alone and divided most of his time between the Main Street Café and the bank. At forty-eight, medium height, with brown-gray hair, he was an attractive and charming man who didn't lack for female attention. He and Lorena often went to lunch together, and had dated several times. Paul had given every indication that he might like to explore a deeper relationship, but Lorena, while finding him a very nice man, didn't want anything serious with him. She didn't want anything serious with *any* man, not now and perhaps not ever.

Paul was at his big desk, bent over a computer printout. He looked up and smiled, his eyes crinkling behind his dark-rimmed glasses. "Good morning. I brought jelly-filled, fresh out of Pete's oven."

That he knew how much she loved jelly doughnuts was mildly perturbing. It seemed too intimate a thing for him to know, and like something he could use to bribe her. The look in his eyes made her feel vaguely guilty, though she couldn't have explained it.

Lorena made a face. "I just started a diet today." She'd been on a diet for the past ten years.

"You can always start it again tomorrow, or at lunch."

Lorena smiled and shook her head, then headed on, arguing silently with herself about the doughnut.

Prima was already there, too, behind the teller counter with a telephone receiver jammed between her shoulder and her ear. She waved the fingers of one hand at Lorena. Her nails were freshly painted bright red, and she was working on the nails of the other hand as she spoke on the phone. Since receiving the title of assistant manager, she felt that if her boss arrived early, she should, too, but she never did manage to do any work until nearly nine. No doubt she was now talking to her sister; she and Mary Jean talked at least three times a day. Prima and Mary Jean were Lorena's closest friends, though they weren't all that close.

Lorena went into her office, set the portfolio on her desk and opened the window blinds. When she went out to get her coffee, Paul was there.

He filled her cup for her, then handed her a jelly doughnut on a napkin. There was simply no polite way to refuse it, and it did smell so good. Still, the first bite stuck in her throat, because she had the somewhat cockeyed notion that if she wouldn't accept his affection, she didn't have a right to his doughnuts.

Life was often quite complicated, she thought as she went back to her office.

When she sat in her chair and moved her portfolio to empty it of the papers she'd taken home, she saw the telephone message, in Prima's handwriting. *Oren Breen.* The box was checked for her to return the call, and the number was written below. She recognized it as the number for the rental house. Apparently the telephone company had never stopped the service.

After staring at the pink message slip for a full thirty seconds, she rose and went to the doorway. "Prima, when did this call from Oren Breen come?"

Prima put her hand over the receiver. "Just about five minutes before you got here."

"Oh." She thought of the phone ringing as she'd stood in the driveway. "Did he say what he wanted? It wasn't some problem with Nicky, was it—some emergency?"

"He didn't say, but he didn't sound upset or even like it was anything real important. Just said you could return the call when you got a chance. Who is he?"

"Oh...he's one of the people Nicky's working for." Then she added, "He's that guy we saw pulling out of the Dairy Freeze the other day in the pink Cadillac." She didn't for some reason want to mention the George Silva episode, and she bit her tongue against saying anything about his renting her house, which was really silly.

"He's one of those Breens from up in Wings?"

"Yes, one of those."

Prima smiled. "Well, he's one darlin' fella."

"And you're married."

"Doesn't mean I've gone blind. Do you want to go to the Pizza Hut for lunch? Mary Jean would like to join us and get away from her kids for an hour."

"Sounds good." Lorena nodded and went back into her office, staring at the phone message as if it could speak to her. It was just a phone call, probably about a plumbing leak in the house, or something. Why should it unsettle her so?

She sat in her chair and looked at the phone, then tucked the message under her pencil cup. She would return his call later. She had work to do now, she told herself and began pulling the papers from her portfolio.

But the little pink paper seemed to taunt her, seemed to wave at her and call her coward. Finally she pushed it all the way beneath her blotter and felt as if she had shown it a thing or two.

She turned on her computer and connected with Albuquerque, checking stock quotes and verifying figures against those on the papers she'd worked on during the weekend. One at a time the eight other office personnel arrived and exchanged greetings as they passed her door. Prima called "Witching hour!" as she always did when crossing the lobby to unlock the front doors.

A half hour later, when Lorena was contentedly absorbed in her work, a knock drew her attention to the doorway. Oren Breen stood there. He smiled a smile that floated right over to touch her.

He sauntered forward. "Good mornin'."

"Good morning." She swung her chair around and straightened her spine. "I received your message, but I haven't had time to call."

"It's okay. I wanted to come by the bank and open an account, anyway." Easy and relaxed, Oren sprawled in the nearby chair facing her. "Thought that since I'm livin' down in Clayton now, it'd be more convenient to have my bankin' over here, and since you're my landlady, I decided it should be your bank."

"It isn't *my* bank," Lorena said, amused. "I just work here. But speaking for the bank, we appreciate your business."

"That's what the lady out there said, and she gave me this dandy little brass car bank for doin' it, too. I think it's supposed to be a Model T Ford." He held it up. "This is really why I chose this bank."

Lorena said, "We have some other good features, too, in case you're interested in anything as practical as banking services."

"Those'll be nice, but this brass car's the thing. And speaking of cars, you sure drive a hot piece of machinery." His grin was oh, so warm.

"I enjoy it." She almost smiled back. Inwardly she was pleased that he'd seen her that morning and aggravated at herself for that juvenile pleasure. She changed the subject. "How's Harvey's voice this morning?"

Oren straightened and raked his hand through his hair. "Ah . . . that's another reason we dropped by this mornin'. We figured you'd heard him last night, and we thought we needed to apologize for the ruckus."

"We?" Following Oren's gaze, Lorena leaned around her desk and saw Harvey lying on the floor beside it, looking up at her with those droopy eyes. He thumped his tail three times on the floor, and Oren said that was his apology.

She looked at Oren.

He said, "In Harvey's defense, he was only doin' his duty last night and protecting me. It was a snake," he added seriously.

"A snake?" Lorena raised a skeptical eyebrow. "In the house?"

"Yes, it was, and I was there on the floor, in my sleeping bag. Oh, it was only a king snake, but Harvey didn't have any way of knowin' that."

"A king snake . . . on the bedroom floor."

He nodded. "It was nearly an inch thick and about yea long." He measured by spreading his arms. "I'm pretty sure it came in through a crack in the closet between the baseboard and the floor. Anyway, that's how it got out. I saw it disappear beneath the baseboard as soon as I turned on the light. These older houses that are built up off the ground sag and leave holes like that. We've got a few out at the home place."

"Did you see it before or after you shut the window?" she asked.

He gazed at her, and she gazed at him.

Then he said, "Harvey doesn't usually bark like that, but I guess the newness of the place set him off. I do believe he was trying to protect me. He was right at the window, like he was warnin' somethin' away." His lips twitched, and his eyes begged for her to smile.

She tried not to. "Are you a habitual liar?"

"I wasn't lying. No, ma'am. Too much was true to call it lying, and storytelling is only lying when it's meant to deceive for gain. All things considered, I believe the correct term would be embellishin'. And I guess I *am* a champion embellisher. I get it from my father."

His eyes sparkled, and she had to grin.

A rap sounded on her opened door. "Lorena." Paul leaned through the opening. "I'm sorry to interrupt, but we have that meeting with Duran."

Lorena told him she'd be right there. Paul cast a puzzled look downward, and Lorena realized he was looking at Harvey. Then he raised his eyes and looked curiously at Oren.

"This is Oren Breen," Lorena said. "And that's Harvey, his dog."

Both she and Oren stood, and the men shook hands. Lorena said that Oren had just opened an account at the bank and that he had rented her house. They talked right above Harvey, who never did move until Oren stepped to the door and patted his thigh with his palm. Then Harvey rose and lumbered away at his master's heels.

"Does that guy take that dog with him everywhere?" Paul wanted to know.

"I have no idea," Lorena said as her gaze lingered on the man and dog.

She liked his "embellishments." And, Lord have mercy, she enjoyed his flirting with her. She enjoyed the fluttering exhilaration that swelled inside her when she looked at him. When he smiled, when he walked, when he just stood there.

Flirting she could allow. There was no harm in it. But she would have to be very careful to keep from making a fool of herself with Oren Breen.

If he'd been older, maybe... but he wasn't, and she liked her life just as it was.

That evening, again while Lorena was watering the flowers in pots on and around her porch, Oren's laden Cadillac came rumbling down the road. This time a white pickup truck and red Suburban, both bearing the Breen ranch emblem, followed, like a Breen caravan. Nicky was in the pickup truck, and waved gaily to her. When the driver alighted she thought at first it was Jesse Breen. Then he called across, "Hey, Lorena. I'm Matt!"

She'd known Matt and Rory years before. Now she met them again, along with their wives—Annie, who was four months pregnant and lovely like an angel, and Zoe, a pretty, slight young woman who looked almost a child herself. They were a warm bunch, ragging Nicky and patting him on the back, wrapping their arms around each other as they spoke. They said Jesse and Marnie were keeping the kids, so they wouldn't be underfoot while they got Oren set up in his new home. Zoe asked if Lorena would mind them putting blinds at the windows, because Oren didn't want curtains. Lorena said that would be fine, that aside from knocking out walls, the house was Oren's to decorate as he wished.

While the others went to work, Annie lingered to speak with Lorena. "We already miss Oren out at the home place, but he's as excited as a boy to have this place of his own. Except when he went to college, he's always lived at the ranch house. He never was one to hear the call of faraway places. He's plannin' on going down to Amarillo and buying furniture tomorrow." She turned her head to watch the activity. "I guess I just never thought of how it must be for him, living there with Matt and me and Little Jesse—and now another one comin'."

She touched her gently rounded stomach as her gaze followed Oren, who was hefting a box out of the truck. There was a warm light in her eyes. The next instant Oren grabbed Zoe from the bed of the pickup truck and slung her over his shoulder, toting her inside, both of them laughing. Carrying on as the young do, Lorena thought with a twinge of envy, recalling how she used to behave like that. Perhaps she still would, if there was anyone to do it with.

She looked over to see Annie smiling at her. "That's us. We like to have a good time. And we all tease Nick, but he is a very good hand. Jesse and the others have said so on more than one occasion. Matt's awfully glad to have him, because it's hard to get good young hands. The good ones work their own ranches, and the others don't usually know what hard work is about." Then Matt called a question to her from the porch, and she went off, saying her job was to supervise everyone.

As Lorena was going back into her own house, a bright blue Corvette came squealing into the rental house's driveway, stopping with a powerful jerk about an inch behind Oren's Cadillac. The driver's door swung wide, and a woman with voluminous red hair popped out with the energy of a cork from a bottle. It was the woman who had been with Oren at the rodeo. Lorena paused, watching from the hidden shelter of her screen door. The woman called, "I've brought dinner!" and very gracefully bent to bring two large sacks from the car. "Jada! My favorite woman!" Oren called from the porch and stepped down to help her with the bags. As he took them he kissed her cheek, and she patted his rear.

A sharp, sudden flash of jealousy touched Lorena. She closed the door behind her, having to stop herself from slamming it. She wasn't really jealous of the woman—Jada, he'd called her—and Oren. No, that wasn't it. It was just that seeing them like that pointed up how alone she was herself.

She'd dealt with that before, she thought with a sigh, and she could deal with it now.

The activity in the rental house went on until ten o'clock that night, when everyone left at once. The sudden quiet was startling. Lorena was in bed, reading. She thought of Nicky. During the week he spent nights out at the bunkhouse on the Breen ranch. He probably hadn't come to say goodbye because he'd thought she wouldn't want to be disturbed. She did prize her quiet time, maybe a little too much. Again a bit of loneliness touched her, and she pushed it aside as she'd learned to do. Everyone in the world had their bit of loneliness; it was a part of life.

Several minutes later, very faintly, the romantic country sound of Johnny Lee came floating up to her from the rental house. Oren's house. Somehow she'd thought he would change his mind about renting the house, but he hadn't, and it didn't appear, after all they'd hauled in that evening, that he was going to.

Over the following few evenings her new neighbor had quite a few visitors, most of them women. Lorena chanced to see that two were young and blond, very stylish and looking quite a bit alike; they came together in a fancy pickup truck. A beautiful, elegant in a natural way, auburn-haired woman came in a white convertible Cadillac. Annie and Zoe returned and with them the buxom redhead, Jada. Then there was a young woman with shiny black hair past her waist, who came in a faded and rattling twenty-year-old truck, and a tall, stately, steel-haired woman, who reminded Lorena of Aunt Esmerelda, who arrived in a limousine, with driver. The woman couldn't have been from Clayton.

All these females came with their hands full, no doubt with housewarming gifts. Lorena had wondered if the buxom redhead was Oren's girlfriend, but by all appearances there were plenty of females in his life.

All these women didn't go unnoticed by Aggie Pacheco, who reported in detail all the comings and goings at Oren's house to Lorena's mother, who in turn telephoned Lorena.

Lorena listened with interest to the tales of a few women who had arrived during the day while she was at work. Then she said, "Mama, those two women in the Suburban are his sisters-in-law, and Nicky told me the woman in the white Cadillac is Jesse's wife, but that's neither here nor there. Oren is a young man with many friends. It is none of my business—or anyone else's—how many people come and go over there. They are quiet and not bothering anyone."

"I didn't say they were. I was just saying that the man has quite a reputation where women are concerned. Even Jesse told your daddy that women have always been attracted to Oren, and that he has a way of getting them to do things for him. You had certainly better be careful, Lorena."

Lorena said, "Well, he's paid his rent in full and he's quiet—" though Harvey's foghorn bark *had* woken her two nights out of three "—and clean and friendly, so I can't say he's taken advantage of me, and what else he does isn't any of my business."

The goings-on at Oren's house might not have been her business, but whenever Lorena heard a vehicle drive up out front she found herself going to the window to peek out to see just who was coming to visit Oren now. She began to tally up the number of men versus the number of women. It ended up being about two females to each male, and there were a lot of repeats that she didn't know how to figure.

Just as interesting and fun as checking out Oren's visitors was checking out Aggie Pacheco's various methods of snooping while trying not to appear to. Aggie couldn't see well enough from behind her window, so she would come out on the porch with her broom, or into the yard with her shrub clippers. If this kept up, she was going to have both a bare broom and bare shrubs. Once she got confused and started sweeping the grass. Joe Sanchez, a widower who'd recently retired, found the women visitors interesting, too. He stood in his doorway or sat in the orange metal chair on his porch and watched, not bothering to hide his curiosity. Sometimes he gave a wolf whistle of appreciation at a woman, and if she looked around he waved to her.

Lorena had to admit to enjoying all her spying immensely, though she was certainly glad no one could see her nosy behavior. It had to be said that Oren's presence had livened up the neighborhood considerably. And then she thought, what kind of commentary was that about the state of her own life?

Well, so what if her life wasn't anything to write about? She'd chosen it, after all. She liked her quiet life. She liked being solitary, too. She could do whatever she wanted whenever she wanted. She didn't have to rearrange herself or her habits for anyone, and that was just fine.

His initial reason for wanting to rent the house might have sprung from his interest in Lorena Venable, but from the time Oren began gathering his things to spend that first night in *his* house, he was thoroughly wrapped up in creating his first very own home.

All his family contributed, so he didn't lack for necessities like dishes, pots and pans and linens, and with what friends brought, he considered himself a rich man in both material possessions and friendship.

He took a number of pieces from the home place—his bedroom set, of course, and stereo, and the one freestanding glass-door bookcase. He brought things that meant a lot to him, like the plant stand that had been something special to his mother, and the set of photographs of Breen ancestors that he'd had restored and mounted in antique frames. He brought a number of his own photographs, too, and Marnie and his dad gave him three really nice Western prints, signed and numbered. As a special gift, Marnie brought over a rodeo picture she'd taken—a black-and-white study of a bronc rider. He and Marnie had a love of photography in common.

He and his dad spent a full day down in Amarillo, and managed to find a sofa and chairs he liked and an area rug and lamps, too, for the living room. At an antique store right there in Clayton they found a great old trunk to use as a coffee table.

It was grand, having all that time with his dad. The past year his dad had been pretty busy with Marnie and their new baby daughter; he'd had little time to really talk with Oren. They talked a lot that day. And, though he hadn't meant to, Oren let slip that he was attracted to Lorena Venable.

"I kinda figured that," his dad said. "There's a lot there to be attracted to. I've only seen her a couple of times in the last year or two, but she struck me as a mighty lot of female."

"She doesn't like it that I'm ten years younger than she is."

His dad's eyebrows rose. "Hmm... guess she is older. Years go by fast. Well..." He grinned. "Might be good for you to meet a woman who doesn't fall at your feet."

"I don't feel improved upon one bit, I'll tell you that."

His father laughed, then looked thoughtful. "How do you go about catchin' a fish?" He took on his wise look, and Oren waited. His father knew more about people and life than anyone he knew. "You sure don't go chasin' after it. Leastways, that isn't the most productive way to go about it. You dangle your bait and wait for the fish to come to it. If you have the right bait, and are quiet and patient enough, you'll get your fish."

Acting on this bit of advice, Oren deliberately didn't seek Lorena out the rest of that week. He did, however, watch for her return from work each evening, which it turned out she did each day promptly at six, and he managed to be out back so he could call hello as she walked from her garage. And when he saw her bedroom light come on each evening, which it did just after ten o'clock, he made certain he opened his window and played some romantic music loud enough for her to hear. Twice he managed to be out front when she left, too, and waved gaily. The first time she waved hesitantly, the second she waved and smiled.

When Sunday rolled around Oren awoke late, with no special place to go or special thing to do, and was suddenly very aware of the quiet house. All week long he'd been too busy and had had too many visitors to get the true feel of living by himself. However, this morning here he was, alone.

It was still cool, and the air conditioner was quiet; he turned it off every night and opened his windows. Right that moment the loudest sound was Harvey snoring. Oren lay there and absorbed it all—the smell of coming heat, the stillness, the aloneness.

Back during his college years he'd shared a room with another guy and had often been alone. Then, a number of times in the recent past, he'd been at the home place by himself when Matt and Annie were off on a trip somewhere. But this was totally different. This was his own home, where he lived alone. And it was in town. The sounds were different. Along with Harvey snoring, he now heard someone, far off, running an electric saw. A car passed on the street. A horn honked up on the highway. There were no cattle lowing or sheep bleating. And the noisiest thing in the house was still Harvey.

He thought how back at the home place Little Jesse would be chattering, dragging toys around, and maybe Zoe and Rory's girls, Glory and Mercy, would be singing. Lately they'd taken to singing the hymn "Rock of Ages," which seemed a highly unusual song for little girls of four years. They'd gotten it from the radio, which at this time would be going—that or the television. And voices would be coming from the kitchen and dining room.

For about half a second he experienced a sharp longing for the home place, and considered throwing on his clothes and driving out to have breakfast with the family. But then he thought that was stupid. After all, one of the reasons he'd wanted to move out to this house was for the privacy and peace and quiet. He'd moved because it was time to make changes in his life, so he would just enjoy lazing around for a few hours. Sitting on his new sofa, propping his feet on his new coffee table.

Perhaps he could enjoy visiting with Lorena Venable.

That brought him out of bed with some enthusiasm. He started to put on his jeans, then stopped. He could walk around in his underwear if he wanted, and so he did, just to get the hang of it. Not since Annie had come to live at the home place had he had this freedom.

He let Harvey out the back door, popped a sausage biscuit in the microwave oven and then walked quickly to the front windows to check out Lorena's driveway. Ah-hah! No cars parked there. He stopped at the phone and thought about calling her, then decided to shower and shave first. He sure hoped she would still be home when he was ready. He would be awfully disappointed if she wasn't.

He had a great excuse for seeing her, he thought as he hurried to retrieve his sausage biscuit. He needed to give her his new phone number.

He was shaving, with half his face scraped, the other half still covered with cream, when he heard what sounded like Lorena out in the yard just beyond his bathroom window.

Chapter Six

He couldn't see through the window glass because it was that opaque frosted kind, but it was open a few inches, and he peered through. The window was small and set high up in the wall, so he had to get up on his tiptoes to see anything other than the roof of Lorena's house. What with the small opening and the way he was peeking, he imagined he looked pretty funny from the other side, all nose and eyeballs.

But Lorena's attention was on a cat walking along the three-foot-tall concrete wall between the houses, and she was mumbling to it—or, more likely, to herself. Her hair was pulled up into a ponytail, and she was wearing very baggy denim overalls and a bright pink muscle shirt. She didn't look at all like the sophisticated banker he'd visited at her office. But she still had that queenly air.

She walked along her side of the wall that separated their yards. Actually, the houses at this point were only about twelve to fifteen feet apart. If Oren had been a good spitter he could spit to hers, his father had said with the great disdain of a man who had the high plains running in his veins.

She said quite loudly, "Harvey, don't you dare get after that cat," and Oren jumped.

He saw Harvey then. He had his front paws up on the wall and was sniffing. He wasn't about to chase the cat; he was too lazy and too gentle. The next instant the cat hopped from the wall into Lorena's yard and disappeared from Oren's sight. Then Lorena went down, and he saw her reappear—or, at least, he saw her backside. She was on her knees, pulling at a grate in the siding that covered the foundation of her house.

He turned back to the mirror and hurried to finish shaving. He wanted to find out what she was doing, wanted to speak to her.

But then Lorena let out a scream. He jumped and nicked his jawline. Tossing the razor into the sink, he swiped at the bit of blood on his chin, then ran into his bedroom to grab his jeans, hopping and stumbling as he tried to put them on while racing to the back door. He burst outside just as he realized there had never been another scream.

"Lorena? Are you okay?" he called as he hurried around the corner of the house, doing a little hop-tiptoe on his bare feet in the prickly, summer-dried grass. He peered over the wall. She wasn't there. But there was a gaping hole into the crawl space beneath her house, and the picture of her lying under there, on the dark earth, knocked unconscious, flashed across his mind.

Just as he was vaulting over the wall, here she came from the back of her house, running with a hoe gripped in her hands. "It's a snake," she said breathlessly.

She knelt and looked under the house, then took up a flashlight she had there and shone it inside. Oren bent and peered over her shoulder. Couldn't see anything but dirt, though. She pointed and said that it had been right there at the edge of the foundation.

"What kind of snake was it?"

"I don't know," she said testily, as if he'd been irresponsible to ask. "A snake snake."

He couldn't resist saying, "It's probably the same one I told you about." And he couldn't help noticing the firm, shapely muscles of her bare arms and shoulders, and that her skin was a nice blush color.

Her head came around, and she gave him a dark, unamused look. "It's a snake, and I'm not goin' under there with it there, that's for sure."

"Why do you want to go under there?"

She told him about the calico cat having had kittens two days before, and how it wasn't her cat, was just a stray, but that she and Mr. Sanchez fed it, and that she was certain now that it had bedded those kittens underneath her house, and she wanted to get them out.

"Who's Mr. Sanchez?"

"Oh . . ." She gestured toward the street. "Joe Sanchez. He lives over there, in the house with the orange metal chairs on the porch."

"Oh. Why do you want to get them out—the kittens?"

A question that earned him a you-are-a-foolish-child look. "To make certain they're okay."

"Mother cats are real good at takin' care of their young. She chose a place under there that's comfortable and easily protected."

Another you-are-a-foolish-child look. If Oren hadn't had such a thick skin, he would have taken offense.

Then she told him that she'd once had a dog that had her puppies in a hole underneath the porch and, believe it or not, the stupid dog didn't move the litter when it rained, and three of them drowned. "And that snake could be after those kittens, you know," she said very practically.

Oren figured it had something to do with being a woman and a mother. He said, "You haven't had very positive experiences with pets, have you?"

"No, I haven't," she said smartly.

He told her to give him a minute to get his shirt and boots on and he would go under after them. She said she could do it, but when he came back she was still sitting there, on her knees, staring into the hole. A warmth stole into his blood when he looked again at her bare shoulders and arms. He loved to look at women's arms that had shape to them. It seemed only right that Lorena should be so perfectly made—since he'd thought of her as his fantasy woman.

"Let's let Harvey go under and scare the snake away," she suggested.

"The snake could bite him." Oren hunkered down beside her. "Let me have the flashlight."

She held the flashlight away. "The snake could bite you. Aren't you worried about that?"

"I have more sense than Harvey."

"That's not an encouragin' thing to say about your dog. What good is he?"

He motioned for the flashlight, and she handed it to him. "He gives me a lot of laughs." He got down to slither underneath the house, just like a snake, he thought.

She wanted him to take the hoe. "You may need it to kill the snake."

"I don't kill anything I don't absolutely have to."

"What if it's a rattlesnake?"

"Then I might have to kill it, but I'll probably just come screamin' out of here, so don't crowd this hole."

He took the flashlight and searched around. He really didn't want to come upon the snake; snakes made his skin crawl. Rory used to have a pet garter snake, and once he had sneaked it into Oren's bed. Oren had gotten mad enough for his nose to gush that day—but so had Rory's after Oren had busted him.

He thought he heard kittens mewing, and when he went a little farther he was certain. Also about that time he heard fierce hissing. He swept the light around and located the snake. It was just a bull snake, a big one at about four or five feet long, rising and puffing and flicking his tongue. Bull snakes made a big show of being dangerous, but they weren't. They were good to have around because they ate rats and mice.

"And newborn kittens," Lorena said.

He couldn't argue with her about that. She was probably right. He took the hoe and tried to scrape up the snake, but he slithered away, which was all the same to Oren. He went farther beneath the house, and Lorena poked her head after him. He found the litter of kittens when the mother jumped down from a hole in the insulation and landed right on his head, about giving him a heart attack. He was thankful not to have yelled and made a fool of himself.

Feeling around, he located the hole, then probed upward and one by one pulled the kittens out, twisting and crawling backward to hand each one out to Lorena. The whole time the mother cat was jumping all around him and on him, mewing her disapproval. She would have been a match for that bull snake.

There were four kittens. Twice Lorena made him make certain he hadn't missed any. She put them and the mother cat into a box she had, then took them into her house. Oren went right along, not officially invited but swept along by the camaraderie he and Lorena were sharing. He thought this was great bait dangling.

Lorena set the box in a corner of her laundry room, brought milk for the mother and then sat cross-legged on the floor. Oren crouched down beside her, and together they admired the kittens one by one, in the manner of proud grandparents.

They picked names: Tubbs, for obvious reasons, and Little Guy, for the runt, and Othello.

"Othello?" Oren asked with curious doubt.

"Yes," Lorena said. "I've always wanted to name something Othello."

"Well, Screamer sure fits this one," he said, holding one that was black and white and looked like Sylvester, the cartoon cat. Its meow was loud and sharp to the point of almost drowning out the others.

He looked over to see Lorena staring at him. Her lips twitched, and she began to laugh.

"What is it?"

She shook with laughter. Finally she managed to get out, "Do you always go around with shaving cream on half your face?"

"Oh...that." He wiped his face with his hand and came away with dirty shaving cream. He wiped that on his shirt-tail. "I was shavin' when I heard you scream. Cut myself, too. Any blood there?"

She peered at where he pointed and shook her head. Then she gazed at him, her brown eyes large and round and studying. She smiled, almost shyly. "I'm sorry I scared you. Screamin' like a banshee when I'm startled is one of my worst habits. The boys used to like to sneak up on me, just to hear me do it." Her gaze flitted away. "It was awfully nice of you to come check on me. And I sure do appreciate you gettin' the kittens. I don't like to get into small, dark spaces. Well, actually, I don't mind small, dark places...it's more places with low, heavy ceilings and dirt and spiders and snakes."

Oren felt pretty heroic about the whole thing. And he was feeling pretty good, looking at her bare shoulders and arms, too.

Lorena suggested he wash up in the laundry sink, while she went to get a towel to line the kittens' box.

She told Oren that he could have first pick of the litter, and he said his landlord didn't like him to have pets. Then she said she knew a place with a sign that said they took cats and maybe they could palm a couple of these off on those people. His excitement about her didn't do anything but grow, with no fading in sight.

However, he sensed a reserve come over her, slowly but surely, as she poured two glasses of lemonade. By the time they took their lemonade out on her deck she had once again brought up her careful guard.

Lorena sat straight in the slatted wooden chair, both feet on the floor, and reminded herself about being careful where Oren Breen was concerned. It was in her to throw herself at him with great abandon, and for heaven's sake, she had to keep a level head about this.

Her attraction to Oren was no more than a temporary temptation, like the temptation to eat an entire package of Oreo cookies—oh, so sweet when indulging, and oh, so regrettable afterward. She knew that well, because she had once eaten an entire package of Oreos.

Her mind thought of it as The Oreo Cookie Episode, in big black print. The episode had consisted of her eating, at one sitting, an entire giant package of Oreo cookies. Her mortifying binge, she'd always thought of it. At the time she could justify it—she was greatly depressed and underweight. She even managed to find a good reason for doing it—it would make her feel better. People have such odd thoughts when they are tempted.

While she'd been stuffing those cookies in her mouth she had felt better, but soon afterward she'd been sick as a pig on sour mash and thoroughly ashamed of herself for being so stupid.

Getting involved with Oren would be just as stupid. And more than likely, any carrying on with Oren would leave much more residue to deal with than eating a package of Oreo cookies.

Still, she didn't tell him to go home; she couldn't, after he'd been so kind to help her. And she had to admit that she greatly enjoyed sitting there on the back deck and talking with him.

"You make a mean lemonade," he said. He propped his boots on the railing, as comfortable and relaxed as he would be in his easy chair in front of the television.

"Thank you. Fresh lemons through a juicer, nothing special."

His grin was easy, too, and he put her in mind of a long, warm and wet spaghetti noodle. A very sexy spaghetti noodle—but she wasn't supposed to be thinking like that.

"How did you come by your Cadillac?" she asked him, focusing her thoughts on something besides his body.

He shifted his legs, graceful and easy. "Bought it from an old man down in west Texas. He'd bought it new and had kept it in his garage all these years, took it out on Sundays."

"You're embellishin' again," she said, highly skeptical. "Sounds like one of those little-old-lady-drove-it-only-on-Sundays stories."

He grinned at her. "No. I swear." He held up his palm. "It came from Charlie Perea, a guy my dad knew. Dad used to go huntin' down on Charlie's ranch. Charlie was one of the old ones, native to the area, who ran sheep. In the fifties, oil was found on Charlie's place, and one of his indulgences was to buy the Caddie. Went all the way to Dallas to get it back then. Brought back the car and a new young bride. He kept the car a lot longer than he kept the bride. I was sixteen when I first saw it. Man, I thought it was the greatest thing! Charlie put it in his will that the car would be sold to me out of the estate on his death, if I wanted it. That made his son-in-law plenty mad, and maybe, if I'd been a more generous fella, I would have let the son-in-law have it. But I just couldn't pass it up. Charlie hadn't kept it polished the last years, and the heat had dried the leather seats pretty badly. I had it painted, and managed to recondition the seats. I put in seat belts and new air conditioning... new top, too. Would you like to go for a spin?"

That surprised her. And she surprised herself by saying yes.

"Great. I'll just go over and get my keys and be back in a jiffy."

He hopped over the low concrete wall, and Lorena ran inside. It was an innocent enough thing, she told herself as she got her purse and took a glance at herself in the mirror. A simple drive. He wanted to show off his car, which was a perfectly human trait, and she wanted to see it, which was also a perfectly human trait. Innocent, simple, harmless fun and nothing more. And she wasn't changing clothes or putting on makeup or anything else. She would go just as she was—faded denim overalls and tank top, hair in a ponytail. There wasn't time to change, even if she'd wanted to. At the last minute, though, she paused in the downstairs bathroom and applied a dash of lipstick—to protect her lips.

Oren was waiting for her. "You drive," he said and handed her the keys. He'd combed his hair and put on a fresh shirt.

"Oh! Yes, I'd like to." She bit her lip and looked at the key. It was awfully warm...from being in his hand. "I can't stay away long," she cautioned. She didn't want him to be getting ideas, though her mind didn't define exactly what ideas he was supposed to get. "I have household accounts to catch up on."

Oren said, "There's a photography show on PBS I'd like to catch myself."

"Oh." He was thinking about a TV show. That was rather disconcerting.

Oren was opening the car door for her when Lorena's mother's sedan pulled up. Her mother honked the horn, and Lorena thought, *Rats!* Disappointment stabbed clear to her toes, and she clutched the key. She'd been looking forward to driving the car, she really had.

Her mother had Aunt Esmerelda and Uncle Rennie with
er. "Lorena!" her mother called, and waved as she
lighted.

Lorena cast Oren an apologetic glance. "Hello, Mama,
.unt Esmerelda, Uncle Rennie."

Esmerelda called a gay greeting, and Uncle Rennie gave
is half wave, coming more slowly behind the two women.
smerelda greeted Oren with enthusiasm. "I'm Lorena's
unt Esmerelda . . . this is my husband, Rennie."

"I remember," Oren said. "Nice to see you again."

Lorena's mother was more frosty, if polite. Lorena
ouldn't recall a time her mother had been impolite, no
aatter what. "Were you two goin' somewhere?" she asked.
I do hope we haven't interrupted." Lorena knew darn well
er mother was very glad to have interrupted.

"No . . . nothing important. Oren was just showing me his
ar."

But Oren said, "We were about to go for a ride. Would
ou all like to join us? We could stop up at the Dairy Freeze
or hot fudge Sundaes." And he *winked* at Esmerelda.

Esmerelda said, "I take to that idea, young man!"

Lorena could tell her mother wasn't overjoyed, but Es-
aerelda wasn't asking for anyone else's opinion and just
ashayed away to the Cadillac. Oren quickly followed to
elp her into the rear seat. Her mother said she didn't want
o sit in the back and be blown to pieces, and Oren insisted
orena go ahead and drive as planned, so when it was all
ettled, Lorena was behind the wheel, with her mother in the
aiddle and Oren at the edge. Harvey was in the back be-
veen Esmerelda and Rennie. Rennie was rather squished to
ae side, because he was afraid of dogs.

Lorena drove through the middle of town and headed
orth. The Cadillac purred along, seeming to float over the
oad as only cars of yesteryear can. Lorena would have en-
oyed driving it if her mother hadn't kept bracing her foot
n the floorboard every time Lorena went to stop and

sucking in her breath at corners and snapping out little bits
of advice, such as, "There's Louie Peebles. Watch him, he
doesn't see you... Don't go so fast through town... You're
jerking the wheel, Lorena. I just about ended up in Oren's
lap."

"Will you hush up, Petra?" Esmerelda called from behind.

"I'm not sayin' anything. I was just tryin' to help."

Lorena got tighter and tighter and finally she pulled over
to the side of the road. "You drive now, Oren."

His eyes met hers, and he didn't say a word, simply un-
folded his long legs from the car and came around. Lorena
hopped out and told Aunt Esmerelda to move over. Harvey
was put up front.

"He doesn't slobber, does he?" Lorena's mother said to
Oren.

"No, ma'am. He sleeps."

"Does he go with you all the time?"

"Mostly. He thinks he needs to take care of me, and I feel
sorry for him left alone behind."

"That's . . . thoughtful of you."

Oren's gaze met Lorena's in the rearview mirror, and they
shared a silent amusement. How rare a man he was, she
thought, not to be bothered by any of this.

Oren drove back through town and out again on the
highway. Lorena relaxed, enjoying the wind in her hair and
grinning with Esmerelda. Her aunt sat up straight, gracefully unwound the fuchsia scarf from her neck and allowed
it to flutter in the breeze. She looked very grand. There was
something about riding along in the big car that brought a
lightness to the heart, and by the time they got to the Dairy
Freeze, Lorena's mother had mellowed enough to give the
remains of her sundae to Harvey. By the time they returned
to Oren's house, she had warmed considerably toward Oren.
She beamed at him as he held the door to her car and helped
her into the seat behind the wheel.

"I am most appreciative of the drive and the treats, Oren" he said, employing her most genteel Southwestern lady manners.

"I enjoyed the company, ma'am." And he gave her his most charming grin. "We'll do it again soon."

"Oh . . . yes, that would be nice." Her mother batted her eyes and looked coquettish.

Lorena watched with not a little amazement. And then she was standing there waving goodbye as her mother drove away. Oren waved, too.

She looked over at him. He looked at her, crossed his arms and tucked his hands up into his armpits.

"Nice family you have." He looked rather satisfied with things.

"Thank you." He'd been flirting with her mother. He'd deliberately charmed her *mother*.

He glanced at his watch. "Well, guess I'll be goin'. Don't want to miss that show. Let me know how you get along with the kittens."

To her amazement he turned away.

"Yes . . . I will."

Realizing she was standing there staring after him, Lorena took off in long strides up her own walk. She wouldn't allow the disappointment that sliced through her. She wouldn't. It had been an innocent, simple drive. That was all she'd expected, and that was all it had been. And she hadn't hoped anything!

Oren was quite satisfied with himself. He thought it safe to say that Lorena's mother liked him now and that Lorena was thinking about him. He hadn't wanted to leave her there at the walkway to her house, but he'd done so in the interest of dangling the bait for a little longer. Lorena wasn't a woman to be pushed or to make decisions in haste. If he was going to get anywhere with her, it had to be on her terms.

She would first have to want him and then have to admit that to herself.

Over the following week Oren made certain to "run into" Lorena a number of times. He made a trip to the bank and naturally, since it was the neighborly thing, stopped by her office just to say hi. Seeing her yellow Mustang in the grocery-store parking lot, he quickly pulled in, too, and did a bit of shopping himself, coming upon her in the produce section. At lunch on Wednesday he found her at Jake's Ribs eating with her friend, Prima. He was alone, so of course Lorena asked him to join them. When he pulled in beside her at the gas station and said, "Howdy, neighbor," she smiled and answered, "We must stop meeting like this." Then, as if embarrassed by her boldness, she averted her face and went about her business.

On Friday the town of Clayton and the surrounding communities began the Fourth of July celebrations. Oren sounded Nick out and discovered the young man had a date with Corinne Hunsicker, which meant he would be out nearly all night long, because Corinne liked to party, and the holiday was made for the young.

Friday morning Oren went over to see Lorena, hitting on the excuse of discussing making some changes to modify the pantry into a darkroom for developing his pictures. She said she didn't mind, as long as he made it back into a pantry before he moved out.

He lingered, commenting about the holiday and all the goings-on. "Dad's havin' another big barbecue, at his place this time," he said. "Heard your parents are goin'. Are you?"

She shook her head. "No. I'd rather stay around here. I don't care much for the crowds in town, but I like to see the fireworks."

So he knew she would be home, and he intended to be, too.

Around six o'clock he pulled a grill from the shed, set it on the back walk and lit the charcoal. He had hot dogs grilling by the time Lorena came out to water her plants.

"Good evenin'," he called to her up on her deck.

"Hello." She gazed at him, and a grin touched her lips.

"What is it?"

"I've never seen a man in a cowboy hat and boots using a backyard barbecue grill before."

"I don't like to be barefoot, and the hat keeps me shaded." He lifted and repositioned it for effect.

"Smells good," she said.

"Come on over and join me. I've got potato salad and beans, too."

She hesitated, moving from one sneaker to another.

"Beats cookin' yourself, or goin' out to the café." He gestured toward town.

She smiled. "You talked me into it. Give me a minute."

Oren watched her go, then sprinted inside to check the beans he'd put on the stove: one pan of hot pepper beans and another of brown sugar, to suit her taste. Red wine was chilling, glasses were ready—bless Annie's soul for the wineglasses—and all the necessary condiments, sliced fresh tomatoes, chips and salsa were on the counter. None of this was what he termed high-toned food, but it was what he thought of as food for the soul. Music! He wasn't certain of her taste, so he popped a CD of Spanish music into the stereo.

Lorena hurried inside. The mother cat—Queenie, she'd named her—came rubbing around her legs, almost tripping her. Lorena hurriedly fed the cat, then she checked her makeup, put on fresh lipstick, ran a comb through her hair and drew it up atop her head. She looked casual but nice. She refused to consider why she was going to all the trouble.

She popped out onto the deck and looked over at Oren's backyard. He stood there poking at the hot dogs on the grill.

"Do you need anything? Ice?" she called.

"Nope. Got it all in hand." He went across to help her over the low concrete fence. "Do you like hot dogs? They're about my favorite thing to eat. Matt gets all bent out of shape, because he says we make our living by raisin' beef, and the sale of steaks is desirable. I do buy beef hot dogs, but I've never cared much for steak, myself."

She nodded. "Me, either." He was still holding her hand, and she tugged hers away. "I like hot dogs... scorched, if you don't mind."

"Just the way I like mine," he said and smiled happily.

In his kitchen she found everything ready and waiting. He even had a very good wine. She laughed at that.

"What's wrong with wine with hot dogs?" he said. "Is there a rule I don't know about?"

"I imagine there are quite a few."

And he said, "When the man buys the wine, I guess he can eat whatever he wants with it."

She agreed and thought he was a singular man. He made a meal of hot dogs an occasion. It was the youth in him, youth that loved celebrations. For an instant she was very glad, for he'd rekindled a youthful spirit inside her.

He poured her a glass, then raised his in a toast. "To summertime."

"Yes... summertime."

It had been a long time since she'd had a meal made for her, except by her mother, of course, and then she generally pitched in. They filled their plates in his kitchen and then returned to sit on the back stairs, which were in deep shadow now. The birds were singing their evening songs. Mrs. Feldman was taking in her day's washing, and Mr. Gardenia was watering his prize tomato plants.

With his fork Oren pointed at the tomato slices on his plate and whispered, "I sneaked these tomatoes from his plants."

"Mr. Gardenia's?" Lorena said in surprise. She stared at the ruby red slices on her plate. Stolen goods.

"Shush!" Oren was chuckling. "I didn't like the ones at the store, and Mr. Gardenia's looked so good I couldn't help myself. I didn't think he'd miss two tomatoes."

"Not if they don't happen to be ones he was growing for the county fair or something. Look! He's searchin' his plants."

"Well, don't point!" He grabbed her hand. Their heads together, they tried to stifle their chuckles.

Lorena asked, "Why not go tell him, if you don't think he'll care?" She speared a piece of the tomato and savored it—forbidden fruit and all.

"I wasn't that certain. He is rather sour."

"Take it from me—he'll care."

They laughed together and ate the tomatoes. Occasionally their arms brushed and thighs touched, gazes locked. Sunset came softly.

"It's a good summer," Oren said. "The kind we get once in fifty years, Dad says. We've had enough rain, and temperatures haven't been scorchin'."

"Summer is my favorite season, really. I never mind the heat." She looked over to see Oren's eyes warm and thoughtful upon her. She averted her eyes and played with a nub of thread on her jeans. Still, she felt his eyes on her, as truly as if he were rubbing her neck with his fingers. She wished he was, and that was a heady thought.

"What other favorites do you have?" he asked, and his voice was sultry. "Do you like chocolate?"

"Yes. Oreo cookies, most especially. And popcorn... and distinctive cars...."

"And horses," he added for her.

She nodded. "What about you? What are some of your favorite things?"

"Oh, summer evenings, country music, distinctive cars...and lovely women." He said the last with meaning in his eyes.

Lorena looked away and fed Harvey her last bite of hot dog.

"So, what happened with you and Nick's father?" Oren asked.

She chuckled self-consciously. "You can be direct, can't you?"

"I wanted to know."

She sighed. "That was an awfully long time ago."

"How come you two didn't stay married?"

She shrugged. "Because I discovered Nicky and Jaime's daddy had a penchant for his blond secretaries. Or maybe more to the point, he didn't need me once I'd helped pay for his education and he was an up-and-coming attorney. Oh, I didn't mean to sound so bitter. I'm not anymore. And who's to say that Tony didn't have reasons for what he did?"

"Everyone has reasons. Doesn't mean they don't hurt, or make them right."

"No, it doesn't."

"You never married again?"

She shook her head and looked off to the lights coming on in the Gardenias' kitchen. "Once is enough...and I had Nicky and Jaime. Have you ever married?" she asked, changing the subject.

He shook his head. "Nope."

"Why not?" She expected to hear a rather sad story of lost love.

Instead he said, "Never met anyone I wanted to marry."

"No one?"

"Why is that so surprisin'? You haven't in all the years you've been single, either."

"But at least I tried it. Seems like out of your large selection you would have tried it."

"I don't intend to *try* it," he said rather intensely. His gaze, too, was intense. Searching.

"No one means to *try* it. But I guess, after all, that's what it is." She picked up their plates. "I'll help you with the dishes before the fireworks start."

But when she set the dishes on the counter he took her hand. "Let me show you what I've done with your house."

She opened her mouth to refuse, but he looked so eager. She couldn't bear to hurt him. It was his house now, she told him, allowing him to tug her along into the living room, where two lamps burned low. Spanish music filled the air. Oren told her how he and his father had chosen the sofa and chairs down in Amarillo, and how he thought the "ol' man" had great taste. She agreed. Everything had been put together with care, colors of the Southwest in a masculine but warm room. However, it was all the photographs adorning the walls that captured her attention.

"You're very good," she said, studying a picture of men branding cattle. It could have come right out of the eighteen hundreds. "Oh, my..." She stopped at a photograph of a young girl cinching her horse, getting ready to ride barrels; all the excitement and fear were there. And there weren't only photographs but a few pencil sketches, too. From picture to picture she went, admiring, questioning. He was pleased, of course, and shy, too. It was the shyness that surprised her and made her heart turn tender.

"I'm adequate," he said, though he admitted to turning down assignments from a couple of national publications.

"Why?" she asked. "Why not sell these, go into photography full-time? Surely you could make a good living."

He shrugged. "Then it becomes work, remember?" he said. "Why would I want that? I'm one of the rare, fortunate souls who doesn't have to work to put food on the table. I have a trust fund and investments that, while not a fortune, are adequate."

She hadn't known that. "People must work at something, preferably something they like."

"Why?"

"Because . . . well, to give meaning to life, I guess."

He shook his head. "The meaning of life is in here," he said and touched his chest.

Lorena looked long at him, wondering. Harvey barked at the door, and Oren went to let him inside. Following more slowly, Lorena began to put the dishes in the dishwasher. There were already dishes in his sink, and she put those, too, into the machine.

"What did you burn in this pan?" she asked, lifting a small saucepan from the stove. Whatever had been in it had been cooked at least the night before. "If you'll soak it in vinegar it'll come clean, and you need to do it before it sets for days."

She took it to the sink and had water running in it when his hands came and turned off the water, then gripped her wrists.

"You don't need to clean up for me." His face, intense, was only inches from her own, and his eyes held hers. Male strength emanated from him. "I am not one of your sons, Lorena."

The words confused her, and his manner hurt. "I know that." She pulled her hands away and reached for a towel.

"Do you? A number of times it hasn't seemed like it, so I want to make it clear. Not only am I not one of your sons, but what I feel for you isn't in the least sonlike." A warm sensuality slipped into his penetrating gaze.

Instinctively she turned away. She smoothed out the towel, then smoothed it again. "Oren, I'm flattered." She laid the towel on the counter and repeated impulsively and emphatically, "Heaven knows I'm flattered." Honesty had always been her long suit, and her downfall.

"Good," he said before she could say another word, and in any case she didn't know what else to say. His tone lightened. "Then how about going out with me tomorrow night?"

Of course it didn't surprise her. But it did frighten her. She shook her head. "I appreciate the offer," she said with careful patience, "but no." Keep it light, she thought.

"You shouldn't answer out of hand. I'm offerin' a proper supper over at the Portobello in Raton." He folded his arms and tucked his hands up under his armpits. His stance, his manner, challenged her. "Do you have better plans?"

"Yes, as a matter of fact. 'Destry Rides Again' is showin' on television, and I want to see it. And I plan to quilt, and there isn't anything I like much more than workin' on a quilt. Even supper spent with you, as charmin' as you are, Oren Breen."

He grinned a good-natured grin, though the light in his eye was definitely sensuous. "Oh, I bet I could make time spent with me rival time spent alone with your quilt."

She shook her head. "No, thank you, Oren. Now, if there isn't anything else, I'd best be going. Thanks for supper. It was a treat."

"How about goin' to the movies with me Sunday night?"

She shook her head and started for the front door.

He followed. "How about Monday night? Wednesday?"

She kept on going, stepping over Harvey, who was lying in her path. She was fleeing, and not so much from Oren as from the grasping hands of temptation.

When she reached the door he said, "Is it because you don't date men at all? Or is it that you just don't like me? Or because I'm younger than you?"

She stopped and turned slowly to face him. She didn't know what to say, and explanations were always so awkward. But she needed to deal with it.

"As a matter of fact, I don't date much. I'm very content with myself. And I like you, Oren, but the fact is, I'm not simply one or two or even five years older than you. I was forty this past February, which makes me over ten years older." She raked her fingers through her hair and held up a hand when he would have spoken. "That is a big difference between us, a difference as wide and deep as the Grand Canyon, and one I just can't overlook. I don't want to deal with being mistaken for your mother, Oren. And add to that the fact that I just don't want to get involved with any man. I'm happy with *me*." She stabbed her chest with her finger. "I just don't want any of it."

His jaw tightened, but she couldn't read his eyes. "Okay. I get the picture. But I want to point out that while I may be ten years younger than you, Lorena, I'm hardly a boy anymore." He let that sit there, bold and heavy. Then his lips twitched. "And you could hardly, under any circumstances, be mistaken for my mother."

Chapter Seven

After Lorena had left, Oren noticed his nose was bleeding. It just trickled a bit, like his temper. He grabbed a paper towel and dabbed at it and thought how it was silly to be angry. He'd been turned down for a date before. It wasn't any big deal.

But he wasn't turned down often. And never by a woman he'd pursued the way he was pursuing Lorena. Come to think of it, he had never pursued a woman the way he was pursuing her.

Anger and disappointment washed over him again. He'd really thought she would go out with him and had imagined taking her over to Raton for some fine Italian cuisine. The atmosphere at Portobello's was quiet and intimate. It was the kind of place with candles on the tables and a guy who strolled around playing a guitar. Real class for this part of America.

It didn't help his ego any that she considered him a kid.

He guessed he hadn't handled it so well. He shouldn't have said anything about the way she sometimes treated him like a boy. But when she did that, it irritated the daylights out of him. He couldn't help being ten years younger than she was—and he didn't see that it was such a big difference at their ages. He was thirty years old, not nineteen. His father was thirteen years older than Marnie; it didn't bother them.

Not feeling like finishing the cleaning up, he tossed what dirty dishes were left in the sink, turned out the kitchen light and went into the living room, where he switched on the television. He sprawled on the sofa and flipped the channels, watching each for about ten minutes but not really seeing anything. When he noticed the sound and flash of fireworks outside the window, he tossed the remote control aside in disgust, called for Harvey and went out to the Cadillac. The soft summer night enveloped him. The night lit up with fireworks. The sounds of the Feldman children watching in their side yard came to him. Lorena's bedroom light was on. Her window was still closed, though she usually opened it before turning in. Odd that he knew that and had never set foot in her bedroom. He simply knew that each evening, just before the light went out, she appeared at the window and opened it.

Turning firmly from her house, he decided to drive out to see the family. Or else he would just drive, anything to put space between himself and Lorena and the damn happy fireworks, when he felt low as a sinkhole. As he started the engine he thought it rather ironic that now that he'd gotten a place of his own, with a sofa of his own, the one woman he wanted to romance there didn't want anything to do with him.

Lorena heard Oren's car start. Hurriedly she set aside the small plastic bowl of Oreo cookies, scooted off her bed and went to her window. She peeked out, not wanting him to catch her looking. There wasn't any need. The Cadillac was already heading away down the street. Fireworks lit up the sky, and she looked away from them, back to the Cadillac.

She watched it pass beneath the streetlamps, its red taillights growing smaller, and for an instant it was as if she were watching a scene from a sixties' television show—"77 Sunset Strip." Oren would be too young to recall that show. She watched the Cadillac go all the way to the corner and turn out of sight. Fireworks bloomed again across the night sky.

With a sinking heart Lorena returned to sit against the pillows on the four-poster bed. She took up a cookie. She didn't have a whole bag—she'd controlled herself. She'd counted out six, then added four more to make ten, put those into a small plastic bowl and then tucked the rest into a big plastic container and stuffed it way back in the corner cabinet. Now she was eating each cookie very slowly, taking them apart and licking out the cream with the tip of her tongue. The indulgence, which included eating them in bed and getting crumbs on the crocheted spread, was helping to soothe her. It was simply a plain fact that a person could mull over her life much better while eating cookies.

All Lorena could think of was that she'd made a mountain out of a molehill over Oren's invitation. He had asked her for a dinner date, not to fall in love with him and end up in a hot affair that would result in both their hearts being broken and her feeling like a fool. All of that had been added in her own mind.

Most probably, if she had gone to supper with him, they would have had a nice time, and that was all there would have been to it. Probably he would have been satisfied and never asked her again, and she would have gotten over her interest in him. That was usually how those things went.

The telephone rang, and she let the answering machine get it. Oh, mercy, but she was in a fine state. She was certainly glad Nicky was going to be out late.

Her mother had always told her she was overemotional and made too big a deal out of every little thing. Once her mother had told her that in front of Tony, and then the next big fight she'd had with Tony, he'd flung the overemotional label right in her face. She had never forgiven her mother for giving that handle to Tony.

The years had yielded for her the realization that what some people, such as her mother, labeled overemotional was really the ability to feel things deeply. Lorena had spent so many years trying to hide and deny her deep emotions, believing them something to be ashamed of, that she'd reached the point of not knowing *what* she felt. For at least two years she had known Tony was running around, and she'd tried to convince herself that the wise thing to do was to ignore it, that she was above going crazy about it, that if she just didn't get overemotional he would quit and stay home with her. Ha! How good it had been when she'd finally boiled over and let him have it—the it being steak au poivre she had dumped on his head, in a restaurant, a very exclusive five-star restaurant that he'd told Lorena he couldn't afford to take her to, where he was dining with a lady friend.

It had been about then that Lorena had begun to learn to be glad for her emotions, because they enabled her to truly live. Except sometimes, like now, when they got her all confused and wrung out.

The thing was, what an emotional person sensitive to each nuance knew was that there were dinner dates and then there were dinner dates. A dinner date with Paul Martinez or most any other man was just sharing a table, a meal and a few hours of conversation. But a dinner date with Oren was . . . well, it was more.

She was interested in Oren Breen. *Very* interested.

And he had to know it, because of the way she acted every time he asked her out. That was what actually mortified her. He must know she was attracted to him.

She was forty years old, for heaven's sake!

Though, on closer examination, her age had nothing whatsoever to do with her ability to appreciate the attributes of a charming, attractive man.

It was, she thought, as much who she was as how old she was that separated them. Many a woman wouldn't be bothered by their age difference. But she was. She wasn't the type to get involved with a man ten years younger than herself. Was she? No, she wasn't. And not having had any kind of interest in a man in—she thought back—at least eight years didn't make anything easier. The last time her heart had beaten fast for a man had been for Gary Waddell, a philosophy professor with the habit of analyzing everything. When he'd finally gotten around to asking her to go to bed with him, she'd been beyond the notion. And now, after all these years, she had practically forgotten all about relating to a man. She'd thought all this was behind her.

By the time she finished her last chocolate cookie Lorena felt much more relaxed and in control of her life. She changed into cotton pants and a loose shirt, then went downstairs and petted the kittens while their mother took a short trip outside. The calico was a good mother and didn't leave her babies for long. Suddenly Lorena had a picture of herself sitting there, kittens in her lap, all alone. The house seemed very quiet. The house of a grandmother, which she could be any time Nicky or Jaime took a notion.

She got up and went around turning on lights and the television in the den, where she settled to watch a comedy and work on her quilting. She had to put on reading glasses to do her quilting, because a year ago her perfect vision had started being interfered with by presbyopia. It happened to people in their forties. A person might look thirty or, in the case of good plastic surgery, twenty-five, but a person's eyes knew the truth. She pushed her lenses down her nose so she could look over them at the television. It was Jimmy Stewart weekend. "Destry Rides Again" would be on tomorrow night, and tonight the movie was "Harvey," which brought

Oren's dog to mind, which brought Oren to mind. Lorena thought how Jimmy Stewart was one of her favorite actors and how Oren's favorite actor was probably someone like Arnold Schwarzenegger, or Tom Cruise. Jaime and Nick loved their movies.

When the movie was over, Lorena set her quilting aside, folded her glasses and set them on the arm of the chair, then went to her bedroom and worked with her weights for thirty minutes.

But when she quit, she still thought of Oren Breen's firm shoulders and lean hips and sky-blue eyes. It seemed her mind was like a starving dog who'd gotten hold of a good, meaty bone and wasn't going to let go.

The next day Lorena got up early and treated herself to a shopping spree in Amarillo. She visited the beauty shop, and in addition to having her hair done, she also had a complete facial and manicure. She purchased a new cosmetic set, perfume, designer jeans, a linen pantsuit for work and an evening pantsuit set of sandwashed silk with a cropped-jacket-style top. It was very expensive, and she had no idea where she would wear it, but purchasing it was one of the seemingly impractical things she did from time to time that was really practical, because as a matter of mental health a person should do the impractical once in a while.

When she arrived home she saw Oren in his backyard, playing a game of catch with the rowdy Feldman children—three of them, the youngest a chubby three-year-old in baggy shorts. Oren waved to her at the same time that five-year-old Suzie Feldman tossed the ball, and the ball passed him and came over in Lorena's yard. Running awkwardly with her packages, she hurried to get it for them and toss it back, throwing it as neatly as she could. Oren called her the next great pitcher for the Giants.

Lorena saw him drive away not long afterward. From her bedroom window she watched the Cadillac, its pink surface dusted golden by a Western sun. "Cowboy in a pink Cadillac," she whispered to herself.

Turning from the window, she went to the closet and took out the evening pantsuit, gazed at it for a long minute, then went down to get herself all ready to watch "Destry Rides Again."

The following morning, while she was making waffles for Nicky, she saw Oren sitting on his back steps. Impulsively she grabbed the garbage bag and took it out. He was looking her way when she turned around from the cans. She waved to him.

"Nice mornin'," she said and lingered there on the deck, thinking she shouldn't but unable to stop doing it.

"Yep." A slow grin came over his lips, and he held up a tomato.

She laughed and hurried back into the kitchen. She wondered if she should give him a chance, if he would ask her to go out again. Oh! She was being foolish.

Monday afternoon he dropped into her office at the bank. "Had to stop in for some money, so I thought I'd just say hello," he said from her open doorway. At first he looked hesitant, as if expecting her to growl at him.

She leaned over to look around her desk at the floor. "You didn't bring Harvey?"

He grinned and shook his head. "He's waiting in the car for me to bring out our latest car bank." He held it up. "I didn't need to open another account, so they let me buy this new one you all got in. I'm gonna collect them all."

"How nice of them to let you buy it," Lorena said, chuckling. Oh, his eyes were so blue and warm. "We had another model about four months ago... let me see. I may have one here. It was an early Chevy, I think. Here it is. Add this one to your collection."

He took it, and his grin bloomed, "Well, I sure do thank you."

They gazed at each other, and it was suddenly there between them, the curiosity and anticipation and attraction, all of it bold as a full moon. The question was there in his eyes, too, and unable to deal with it, Lorena averted her gaze and said it was better for him to have the car than for it to be taking up space in her credenza. After he'd left she felt as if she were empty inside.

Tuesday evening, as she was watering her plants, Lorena saw the two beautiful young blond women she'd seen that first week arrive at Oren's. She looked from them down at herself, at her sweaty arms and baggy, water-splashed overalls. She wasn't competing, she told herself firmly, and went on to finish the watering. A few minutes later Oren and the young women came out his front door.

"Hi, Lorena," Oren called and waved the hat in his hand. His hair was damp, his shirt and jeans crisp, and his boots would put eyes out with their shine. And his smile was wide.

"Good evenin'." She included the blond girls, for that was what they were, in her greeting. She felt about like Ma Kettle next to them. As she watched the three of them get into the front seat of the Cadillac and drive away, she thought they wouldn't even have known who Ma Kettle was. Tossing aside the hose and turning off the water, Lorena went inside to cook herself a baked potato for dinner. She ate it in front of the television, then put on her glasses and took up her quilting.

Wednesday, when she and Prima were on their way to lunch, they saw Oren coming out of the flower shop with a bouquet. Prima saw him first and said, "Look! Look! Isn't that Oren Breen?" Lorena saw him and the flowers. "Lucky girl," Prima murmured enviously. "I don't remember the last time Carl brought me flowers."

Lorena's heart sank to her toes.

She didn't see him Thursday, and he hadn't returned home by the time she went to bed, nor was the Cadillac in the driveway when she left for work on Friday. She asked herself why in the world she was paying so much attention to Oren Breen's comings and goings. But she knew why, and it was foolish.

Then, while she was having lunch with her mother at Jimmy's café, she looked up to see Oren enter. He stopped to speak to Jimmy at the cash register, and she returned her attention to what her mother was saying about the church's annual craft sale. The next minute Oren was standing beside their table.

"Good afternoon, ladies."

One glance into his sparkling eyes and Lorena shifted her gaze to his shirt, his belt, her mother.

"Why, hello, Oren," her mother said with an unusual warmth. "How have you been?"

"Fine . . . and yourself?"

Her mother said fine, and Lorena had to say fine, and so everyone was fine. Oren had dropped in to pick up hamburgers to take out to the ranch, and while he waited, Lorena's mother suggested he sit with them. He drew over a chair, straddled it and had Jimmy bring him a soft drink.

Lorena was very glad, but she wasn't about to show it, and besides, it was all so awkward in her mother's presence. One of those times when small-town life really was difficult.

Mostly Oren and her mother carried on a conversation, until Oren asked Lorena how the kittens were.

"Growing," Lorena said. "Their eyes are beginning to open, but they can't see much yet. You'll have to come over to see them." She met his gaze then.

"I'll do that," he said, looking directly into her eyes.

She wondered what in the world she could have been thinking.

Jimmy called, and Oren rose to leave. His gaze was intense when he told her goodbye.

"Have you dated him yet?" her mother asked.

Lorena choked on her iced tea. "No, Mama. He's just renting my house. There's nothin' going on between us."

"I didn't say there was." Her mother's gaze was amused and speculative.

"You certainly have done an about-face," Lorena said. "You didn't like the idea of him renting my house, and now you have us dating."

"I don't have you doing anything," her mother said. "But I'm not blind. I can see when two people are attracted to each other."

"Oh, Mama, Oren likes to flirt, you yourself know that. He likes women." She spoke very nonchalantly; she'd always been able to hide her feelings from her mother. "He is ten years younger than me and has had the attentions of plenty of women."

Her mother waved a hand and surprised Lorena by pulling a pack of cigarettes from her purse. "You know, Lorena, if you follow your heredity, you have at least fifty years left yet on this earth." She put the cigarette to her lips and brought out a lighter.

Lorena frowned. "I thought you'd stopped smoking."

"I've decided to indulge in one a day. I have so little fun anymore, Lorena, don't begrudge me this." She blew out a stream of smoke. "It's almost an affair—and you should consider having one. With a man, I mean. Don't raise your eyebrows at me. Fifty more years is a long time for you to be alone and celibate. What kind of memories will you have? The problem for a woman your age is that there are so few men from which to choose."

"Thank you for that, Mama."

"You might as well face facts. You are hitting middle age. Eligible, good men of your age or older are very, very few. And most of them are dumpy and inactive. While you are a woman in the prime of your health and sexuality." Her mother puffed slowly, gracefully. "It is a physical fact that while men of your age are slowing down, a younger man has the ability to keep up with you—in bed and out of it. There's no need to turn red, Lorena. I've known about sex for a long time.''

Lorena shifted on the vinyl seat. "Yes, but you've never talked about it, and I'd just as soon not." She spoke low, almost whispering. "We've never had the sort of relationship where we talked about sex." Lorena had first learned about sex from Aunt Esmerelda.

"It *is* in poor taste to be so bold about sex, no matter what the mores are today. However, this is between you and me, and I feel I made mistakes in the past that I should not repeat in regards to explaining things to you."

"Mama, I'm forty years old and have been married. I know about *things.*"

"You need my older-woman point of view. The bald facts are that women far outlive men. I'm one of the lucky ones to still have your daddy, even if he does pay more attention to his golf game than he does to me." There was tight bitterness in her tone. "All of my friends are widowed, and all of them are alone, except Jacinda, who married last year, to a man fifteen years younger. And know what she said to me the other day? She said that she didn't intend to bury another husband, if she could help it, and that she wanted a little sex before she died. That bears thinking about, Lorena."

"I'd just as soon drop this conversation," Lorena said.

"I've said all I need to."

They sat there in silence while her mother finished her cigarette. Lorena walked her mother to her car. Impulsively, feeling a little awkward, she put her arm around her mother.

"Thank you, Mama . . . for caring."

Her mother patted her hand. "I *am* your mother. I just want you to be happy."

That evening, as she again sat alone in front of the television, with her quilting in her lap and her glasses halfway down her nose, Lorena considered all that her mother had said. She had said she wanted Lorena to be happy. And that was what Lorena wanted, too. That was why she'd returned to her hometown, why she'd remained single and hadn't thought of marriage or even an affair with a man in all these years. Because she was happy, with herself, with her life. She didn't need the complications of a man, and she certainly didn't need to fall for a man ten years younger, who might be considering her some type of conquest. Oh, perhaps he would truly mean well, but surely he wouldn't want anything permanent, and an affair... well, an affair was so messy. Someone always fell out of love first, and then one of them had a broken heart, and it would probably be Lorena. Oh, man and woman things were too complicated, and that was why she'd given them up and why she didn't want to go through them again.

The following afternoon was Saturday, and she was watching a NASCAR race on television with Nicky. She was in her bare feet and had just polished her toenails with crimson and was admiring them when Oren knocked at the door. She knew it was Oren the same way she would have known it was Nicky or Jaime or her father. She let Nicky get it.

Nicky invited him in, and Lorena gave him a polite greeting but didn't look him in the eye. He apparently hadn't come for any reason in particular, and, settling himself on the sofa, he became interested in the race.

Lorena, curled in one of the chairs, didn't say anything and still didn't look him directly in the eyes. Having her son right there certainly did help her resolve not to act stupid. She was wearing her baggy overalls and bright pink tank top—which, after all, were her most comfortable clothes, and what did it matter that she wasn't more fancy? She acted perfectly nonchalant, with one leg thrown over the arm of the chair.

Realizing she'd shifted her position about a dozen times and was about to bounce her leg off, she rose to go to the kitchen to make popcorn. She had to get out of the room.

But Oren said, "I'll help," and rose, too.

"Making popcorn is a one-person job. I don't need any help, but thank you."

He came right after her, though. "I can make our drinks. Can't have popcorn without somethin' to drink. Besides, I'd like a look at the kittens."

"They're out in the garage."

"You stuck them in the garage?"

"I didn't *stick* them—I moved them. It's a nice garage, and I propped the door up with a brick, so Queenie can come and go as she needs to. She doesn't care to be trapped in the house so much. You can go on out and see them." She went about the business of getting the pan and oil.

"I'll see them later," he said. "Do you put butter on your popcorn?"

"No...it's fattening, and it makes Nicky sick." She should have offered to do it for him, but she didn't.

He said, "Good, I don't like butter. Where do you keep your glasses?"

"Right-hand side of the sink." She turned on the burner beneath the pan and got the jar of popcorn, not allowing her eyes for one instant to stray over to Oren. Still, she was *very* aware of his presence.

Nicky called excitedly from the living room, "Kyle Petty is fightin' for the lead, Oren."

Oren sprinted back for the living room, and Lorena breathed a sigh of relief. However, within three minutes he was back. "Petty took the lead, but anything can happen with half the race yet to go. Which bowl is mine? I like a lot of popcorn." He began filling the glasses with ice.

"Then yours can be the biggest bowl." She kept her gaze on the pan.

He opened the refrigerator door. "What would you like to drink? Looks like you have Coke, orange juice and whatever this red stuff is."

"Fruit punch, and that's what I'll have. Nicky likes Coke."

He moved to the counter at her back, and she heard the ice cracking as he filled the glasses. She dumped the popcorn into the big bowl, filling it. "There you go. You can go sit down. I'll bring Nicky's when it's ready."

Instead he brought the bowl with him and stood at her right arm. "Mmm-mmm, this is great. You're one fine popcorn maker. I like a lot of salt, though." He picked up the saltshaker and went to town. "Do you work out? You have great shoulders and arms."

The back of her neck prickled, and her heartbeat skittered. "Umm...some. Nothing that would win me any titles, and I still have trouble liftin' the garbage."

"Well, it's enough," he said in a low tone.

She could feel his eyes on her, and she kept her own focused on the pan of popping corn, which was thumping loudly. She shook it hard.

He bent, resting his arm on the island. He was close enough for her to smell his sexy after-shave. She knew he had that bit of a grin on his face, though she didn't look at him. He asked, "Have you ever used a popcorn popper?"

"Yes, and I prefer how I grew up doing it—in a pan. In those days only rich people had popcorn poppers."

"Oh, yeah...back in the Stone Age."

He kept looking at her, but she refused to look at him all the while the corn in the pan made a staccato sound. When it finished, he handed her a bowl, and she poured the popcorn into it. At last, as if all on their own, her eyes shifted, and she looked at him. Sex was bold and hot in his eyes.

He took the bowl from her, picked up a piece of popcorn, stuck out his tongue and placed the popcorn on it, then chewed slowly. "You make great popcorn," he said.

He stayed to watch the entire race. A number of times their eyes met. Lorena tried to deny she felt anything, that anything was happening, but in her heart she knew that the air between them was electric with feeling. If Nicky noticed, he didn't let on. It had been her experience that males who were watching car racing rarely noticed a tornado taking the house, as long as it didn't take the television, and for this she gave thanks. She would just as soon keep her foolishness to herself.

Late Sunday Oren was driving into town from the ranch, going by way of what was popularly known as Purgatory Road. It was an unlined county road that serviced the Bernal and Drumm ranches. Old Cleeve Drumm had gotten the road paved nearly half a century ago, before most of the others around, when he'd been a state senator.

Oren was heading south, daydreaming and half listening to Reba McEntire singing from the radio, when a car came flying toward him. He didn't recognize it as Lorena's lemon yellow Mustang until she was already passing. He had just enough time to wave and get a glimpse of her with those big sunglasses on her face. She waved back.

Where is she going?

Oren put on the brakes, tires squealing on the patched blacktop. Harvey would have landed on the floor except that Oren had him belted in. The long Caddie wasn't exactly easy to whip around in the road, but he did a three-point turn and pressed the accelerator, and the big engine swelled with power. He caught up to the Mustang and pulled out to come even with it, waiting for Lorena to look at him. He motioned, pointing ahead, and pressed the Caddie ahead by a few inches then dropped back.

She stared at him through the side window, her eyes hidden by those absurd sunglasses. He tried again, pressing ahead and dropping back. *Come on, darlin', have some fun.*

The next instant the Mustang shot ahead, and the race was on!

Chapter Eight

There she was, racing down the road. Both hands on the wheel, her heart beating ninety miles an hour, and her spirit soaring with the eagles. This was something Lorena knew about. She was a hell of a driver, thanks to her uncle Sherman and her natural affinity for speed.

The road disappeared so fast beneath her that the potholes and patched places looked the same—a gray blur. The Mustang flew, seeming to skim the bumps. Sometimes the bumps bounced the Caddie and Mustang within inches of each other, and sometimes they bounced them nearly off the road, but Lorena didn't give an inch. And she would have won, too, if that cow hadn't gotten in the way.

On a road flat as a griddle it was easy to see a cow before getting anywhere close to it. Lorena didn't slow when she first saw it, because she figured it would move. But it didn't. She had to slow up, doggone it, because that cow was more on her half of the road than Oren's. The Cadillac nosed ahead.

Then, yippee! that cow moved to the middle. Lorena was certain she could get around it now, but when she aimed to go around her side, the stupid cow darted in the way. There was no time to stop. She braked cautiously and veered off the grassy slope alongside the pavement. When the rear wheels hit the grass they started sliding and bouncing, rattling Lorena from her heels to her teeth. When she felt herself tilting she figured she was going to turn over and thought maybe she was about to be dead and how it would serve her right for indulging in such foolishness. Then she came to a stop.

She stared at the dash and felt as if she'd just been round and round in a clothes dryer and then spat out. The engine purred softly, Billy Joel's throaty voice came softly from the radio and the air-conditioner fan hummed. Through the sun-glared windshield Lorena saw that stupid cow still up there in the road, staring at her. It was a Hereford, and it was observing her as if observing a jackass.

Oren came running and jerked open her car door. "Are you okay?"

She nodded. "Yes," she said with a big sigh. "I didn't even pee my britches." Still slightly addled, she gave voice to the first thing that came to mind.

Oren reached in and switched off the key, then removed her sunglasses. His hands shook. He searched her face, as if looking for brain damage. His eyes were a deep, startling blue. "You sure you're okay?" He reached for her hand.

He was worried about her. *Oh, Lord, he's worried about me.* "Now you're worried?" she teased dryly, totally discomfited by his gaze. "You were the one who started it, you know."

He blinked and backed up quickly as she swung her legs out the door. The late-afternoon heat enveloped her as she stepped, very ungracefully, out of the slanting car.

He took hold of her arm to help her, saying, "And you're the one who took off like a bat out of hell." Then he started to laugh.

The next instant he was laughing so hard he held his arm across his lean belly. It made her chuckle, and then she went to laughing, too. It was crazy—two adults racing down Purgatory Road as if there was no tomorrow.

She told him that if he'd made her hurt her car, she was going to kill him. He answered that he hadn't made her race him. He was laughing so hard now, he had sat down right there in the grass.

She walked around the Mustang, checking it out. "You started it, so it's all your fault," she said, which was a weak accusation but all she had. "I can't believe I did this. I risked my car. Do you know what one of these things costs? It has leather everything, lumbar seats, computer controls for goodness' sake."

"My Caddie can't simply be replaced by a phone call to the factory, you know, and I just had that door fixed. It was at great risk, too. Especially the way you were drivin'."

"Oh, you're just sore because I was winnin'." She saw one of the rear wheels had dug deep in the ground from where they'd had heavy rain the night before, but the car didn't have any dents or anything. She looked across at Oren and saw him gazing sexily at her. Pleasure washed over her.

"You're one hell of a driver... for a woman," he qualified, mischief all over his face.

She put her hand on her hip. "Sonny, I was racin' this road when you were in first grade. I had a '65 Mustang with an engine my uncle Sherman had bored out, and I beat all comers in my sophomore year—until Daddy found out and took my keys. Then I went to racin' horses. At least that was legal, though I could still have gotten killed." For a few brief, cocky minutes it all came back to her, the parts of her spirit that had been covered over, buried beneath disappointing romances, raising two boys, getting her own education and paying the orthodontist and the mortgage company.

Oren had to grin as he watched her. She stood there, all fiery, with the sun shining red highlights on her brown hair and dusting a hazy gold on her bare arms. In a paisley vest and faded Wranglers, she didn't look at all like a sophisticated businesswoman, nor like the mother of grown sons, but like a hometown country girl, and this was the side of her that Oren knew went deep and wide and that he liked best.

His eyes lingered on her, and then he hefted himself off the ground and hurried over to the Caddie for his camera. Harvey rose up on the door, and Oren lifted him out, then bent and retrieved his camera case from the rear floorboard. Earlier he'd been taking pictures of the youngest Breens: Little Jesse, and Zoe's twins, Glory and Mercy, and his half sister, Mary Regina. He adjusted the camera as he walked back to Lorena.

"You're gonna take a picture of this?" she said, disbelieving.

"Sure. Save it for posterity." He put the camera to his eye and aimed.

"Don't you dare!" She held up her hand, as if to stop him.

"What's wrong? Don't you want evidence that can be shown to your sons?" He snapped a picture of her protesting, with the Mustang in the background. "We can capture it. Old Lady Loses Grip."

"Old lady!"

He caught a shot of her outrage, then grinned, an idea sparking inside. "Well, you're the one who's been insistin' you're over the hill." If she wanted to dwell on her age, he would, too.

She fumed. "I never said I was over the hill, buddy. I was simply pointin' out that you were a mere babe," she said saucily, posing with one hand on her hip and her other on the Mustang.

Oren snapped shots, saying, "That's right. You pointed out that you're a hell of a lot older than I am."

Their gazes locked, and for long seconds it was there in her hot brown eyes, just as he felt it inside himself. They connected, touched without words. And Oren knew damn well he wasn't mistaken. He knew damn well he wasn't the only one thinking about being buck naked and tangled in the sheets, which was what the picture would be if one could be snapped of their feelings.

She shifted her eyes away, as if retreating, and raked back loose strands of hair. "You bring out the worst in me, Oren Breen."

And he answered, "That could be argued. I think I bring out the best."

Her brown eyes met his. Emotion, like heat up from a road, shimmered between them.

Abruptly she turned away, gave a small shake of her head and drawled, "Oh, right—and I end up almost killed and with my car stuck in a rut." She reached inside the Mustang.

"Aw...you can come closer to being struck dead by lightning in your bed than you were with that race. And your car isn't stuck. It isn't wet enough for it to be stuck."

She straightened, with the keys in hand, and he followed her to the rear of the Mustang.

She opened the trunk, saying, "How many people have you ever heard of struck by lightning in their bed?" She had a small cooler in her trunk, and she brought forth two cold canned Coca-Colas, handing him one. Hers she pressed to her forehead.

He popped the tab of his and said, "Matter of fact, I do know of at least one man killed by lightning in his bed."

"Oh, by all means let's hear this one." She slammed the trunk lid, propping her buttocks on it.

He joined her. "It's true. Pell Worsthorne was killed in his bed by lightning. Not only that, but he was the third of three men from the same family over in the Oklahoma panhandle killed by lightning, and all in the same year."

She cast him a highly skeptical glance, then drank deeply of her Coke. He watched her stretch her neck and slide the moisture-beaded red can up and down it. Her skin was like smooth cream. His eyes traced down to the scooped neckline of her tank top, then flitted over to the curves of her bare shoulders.

Averting his gaze, he crouched, poured cola in his palm and called Harvey over for a lick. He continued, "Pell's oldest brother was killed when a bolt of lightning struck a calf he was carryin' over his shoulder just as he slipped through a barbed wire fence, and a cousin was killed while drivin' a wagon and team home from the general store when a storm came up. The lightning hit the wagon and fried him and the horses."

"You're makin' that up, Oren Breen."

"No, I'm not. My aunt Ina's second husband—or maybe it was her third—anyway, she was married to Pell's nephew. Pell was in his bed, but his bed was on the front porch, so you can see how it could happen. And Aunt Ina said he had a steel plate in his head from the war. Probably was a magnet for lightnin'."

She crouched down beside him. Their eyes met. Hers twinkled, but she wouldn't let herself smile. She nodded at Harvey. "He really likes that stuff."

"Oh, yeah...here you go, fella."

Lorena cupped her hand and gave some to Harvey, too. She was close enough for their knees to brush, for him to catch the scent of her, which was sweet and feminine. The heat came up from the ground and seemed to wrap them together.

Her gaze met his, then skittered away, looking out at the grassland. Her caution around him was so tangible he could have bottled it. He asked her what she was doing out there, and she said she was going to visit her horse—that mare she'd bought from Rory twelve years ago. The mare was in the pasture up at her grandfather Bernal's old place.

"Would you like some company?" he asked.

Her brown eyes came back to his, and he watched her deliberating.

"Sure," she said at last. And, though she tried to hide it, she smiled.

The Mustang came up out of the rut, just as Oren had said it would, even though he stood behind in case she needed a shove. He waved her on, then he and Harvey hurried over to the Cadillac to follow.

Her grandfather's old place was about three miles past the Drumms' new brick home. Oren had said he'd stop in at the Drumms' to tell them about the stray cow if he couldn't reach someone there on his car phone. Apparently he did reach them by phone, because he stayed right behind her.

She pulled to a stop in front of the rusty stockman's gate, retrieved her old Western straw hat and put it on as she got out. Oren came toward her, tall and lean and grinning, Harvey trotting at his heels. The gate was latched by several strands of baling wire. Oren stepped in front of her and undid the wire as only a man who's familiar with the intricacies of baling wire can. His forearms sticking out of his rolled shirt sleeves were strong and tanned, and he smelled faintly of sultry cologne and pleasant male warmth. His eyes were starkly blue in the shadow of his wide-brimmed hat, and they brought a slow, sweet burning deep inside Lorena. She was as aware of Oren's nearness as she was of the perspiration trickling between her breasts and dampening the waist of her jeans. And, however foolish it might be, she was oh, so glad to have him with her.

To cover her nervousness she talked, telling him about her mother leasing the place to the Drumms now, and how they

fed her Molly along with their stock. She whistled and called
Molly, saying, "Here, girl," the way she would call a dog.
Oren didn't think the mare would come, and Lorena bet him
a dollar she would. She called several times as they walked
up the lane toward the old adobe house.

The sun was low in the western sky, leaving long shadows
and giving everything—the grass, the fence posts, the old
abandoned house—a golden wash. She and Oren walked
side by side, close enough to clasp hands if they'd wanted to.
Swinging at her hip, Lorena's hand darn near buzzed with
the thought. The breeze played over the grass and over the
bare skin of her shoulders. She thought about how Oren had
liked the look of her shoulders, and she thought very irrev-
erently about how she liked the look of him all over.

No one had lived here for nigh on fourteen years now, she
told Oren. That was when her grandmother had passed away
and her grandfather had gone to live at the Guardian Care
down in Tucumcari. The old house, five small rooms and
still solid, though with its windows long gone, sat in the
middle of three fenced acres. A gate far in the back stood
open to a section of land that rolled away to the north, but
the horses and cows kept here didn't stray far from the
house, because this was where they were fed twice a day. The
only tree was a half-dead chinquapin oak that clung to life
between the house and the roof of the storm shelter. Her
grandmother had planted the tree the second day she had
come here and had watered it faithfully by bucket. There
were two falling down sheds way in the back and one still
usable, if rickety, horse-drawn wagon. A hay rake and several wagon wheels were rusting away in a pile.

"I used to bring Grampa out here to visit," she said as she
stepped onto the low, weathered front porch and looped an
arm around the square corner pillar. "Because of his health,
they didn't like him to come so far, and sometimes I'd drive
all the way down there from Denver, and they wouldn't release him to go. So I'd help him sneak out. Once they caught

him climbing out his window." She chuckled, remembering.

"Sounds like rebellion to me, and I didn't know bankers did things like that." Oren stood on the ground in front of her, his head tilted upward, his eyes as sparkling blue as the sky above.

She averted her gaze to her boot. It was dusty. "I wasn't a banker then. I was workin' for a collection agency, and that's where I learned all the tricks of skipping out of places. But I guess bankers will do stuff like that, because I'd do it today. Grampa used to say he could die on the trip up here just as well as he could die sittin' in his antiseptic room at the care center. The times I brought him up here were times he was almost dead, and he'd get here and come to life again. Daddy's been after Mama to sell this place, but she and I hold out against him." She pressed her cheek to the rough post and gazed off south. "Sometimes I come out here to find some life, too." She'd never admitted that to a soul.

"It's a fine spot, even if it could use some trees," Oren offered honestly as he looked in all directions. The view to the north and south went for miles and miles, as far as the eye could see.

Nearly every move Oren made was as slow as Methuselah, Lorena thought as she watched him lower himself to the edge of the porch and scoot his back against the opposite post. He had to be the sexiest-moving man she'd ever laid eyes on, with a lazy, sexy way that said he took all of life in stride and enjoyed it, too.

He took hold of his faded denims to ease them as he bent one leg and planted his boot on the cracked floorboards, while letting his other boot rest on the bare ground. Harvey flopped down against his leg, and Lorena looked away, hiding a smile at the thought: two of a kind. And then another thought came whispering. They were both steady, reliable. That brought her eyes back around to him.

He grinned. "I do believe you're about to owe me a dollar."

"Don't be countin' your money too early, fella." She called Molly again, this time cupping her hands around her mouth. She listened and called again. The unmistakable sound of hoofbeats reached their ears. Soon Molly appeared over the small rise.

"I told you so," Lorena said with superiority, and motioned with her palm up. Then she turned and pushed through the creaky front door, returning with an old white enameled dishpan half-full of sweet feed, and grinning with high satisfaction.

"I think I've been cheated," Oren grumbled, getting to his feet as the gray-spotted mare came trotting across the yard.

Lorena shook the pan at Molly. "There you go, darlin'," she said as Molly dug her nose into the grain.

"Rory would say you're spoilin' her rotten."

"She deserves it. She was a great horse for both Jaime and Nicky. Nicky was just six when he began riding her, and one time the saddle came loose as they were trotting around the arena. Molly girl here just trotted herself over to the side and pressed up against the wall to hold Nicky and the saddle in place until somebody came to help her out." With her free hand she caressed the mare's forelock and velvety gray cheek.

"As I recall, Rory really liked her, too." Oren spoke close behind her.

Another step and his chest brushed her back. Almost imperceptible but every cell in her body was attuned to him. A tingling went through her. She stilled, to the point of breathing lightly.

Oren continued, "The mare wasn't broke when he got her. She was just a brood mare out of the pasture, but she never did dump him. When he first tried her around barrels, he couldn't believe how fluidly she could circle those things. Made us all come out and watch."

His voice was low, and she could feel his chest move as he spoke, feel his breath on her nape. Her blood grew warmer.

She stroked Molly's warm, velvety cheek. "She isn't all that fast, never was, but it was the smooth way she could turn barrels that won."

Molly kept rooting in the pan and jarring Lorena back against Oren. He was like a solid wall behind her; he didn't move. She didn't want him to.

"Do you still ride her?" he asked, his voice a caress over her hair and neck.

She nodded. "Occasionally." It was difficult to sort her tangled thoughts. "She's twenty, but she has plenty of good years yet. I could sell her for top dollar."

She caressed the soft hair behind Molly's ear. Her pulse pattered in her ears. Oren was warm against her back.

"But you can't bear to," he said and stepped away, off the porch and down beside Molly.

"No... I'd worry if she'd be well taken care of."

As Molly searched for the last bits of grain in the pan, Oren ran his hands over her. "Does she ride without a saddle?"

"What difference should that make to you? You *are* a bronc rider."

"And I know enough to be prepared. Besides, I'm a *retired* bronc rider." He cast her a wry look, then returned to Molly. "Here, girl, let's see how you do. You really ought to earn your feed."

He grabbed hold of the mare's black mane and hoisted himself atop her back, smooth as silk. Lorena was reminded of being a kid; all ranch kids did this. Molly's head came up, and for a brief moment she seemed to study the matter. Next she decided she didn't like it, and the next second she went to bucking.

When a rider is on a horse bareback there isn't much he can do if the horse decides to get ornery. There just isn't a handhold, except for the mane, but that doesn't keep one's bottom in place. Oren was great for about two seconds, then off he went.

Lorena sprinted off the porch. "Oh, Oren! Are you all right?" She knelt and reached her hands out to him, then drew them back, uncertain. He was already setting himself up.

"My pride's bruised more than anything."

She got his hat and brought it to him. "Are you sure?" She dared to brush the dry grass off his back. "You sure you didn't break anything?" She felt almost sick.

But he shook his head and straightened. "I'm fine…but it sure isn't the same as when I was twelve."

"Well, you're a long way from twelve, you know."

"I know." He looked deep into her eyes.

Lorena, suddenly embarrassed, got to her feet. She guessed he wasn't hurt, so her heart could settle back down. She turned to Molly, who was surreptitiously watching both humans while she contentedly munched grass at the base of the house. "Molly, girl, you were naughty. Now just come here."

Lorena took hold of the mare's mane. The mare pulled away, but Lorena tugged her back. "There's a halter just inside the door there," she said to Oren.

Oren brought the halter, with a frayed lead rope attached. "Why didn't you tell me you had this?"

"Because you didn't ask," she said very sweetly.

He shook his head. "You're a hard woman, Lorena Venable." His tone was husky, and his eyes were warm.

Lorena put the halter on the mare and brought her to stand near the porch. "I'll get on, and you hold her."

"Why don't I get on and you hold her?"

"Because you're bigger and stronger and can hold her better than I can."

She thrust the lead into his hands and slipped atop the horse. Molly got taut all over. Oren spoke soft words to her and stroked her neck. Then he led her around the yard for a short while. Lorena could feel the acceptance flow into the horse beneath her thighs. She took the lead from Oren and directed Molly around the yard.

Riding a horse bareback was wonderful. The mare was warm and damp beneath her legs, and Molly being so fat made her soft to ride. Lorena waved at Oren, who stood with his arms crossed and his hands tucked up under his armpits. He grinned at her and told her to do tricks. She came back and stopped beside him, then held out her hand.

"Come on . . . just like when we were twelve," she said.

He took her arm and hoisted himself up behind her. Molly braced herself under the extra weight but took it all patiently. She'd showed her stuff, so she had saved her pride. Oren's arms came around Lorena. The fronts of his thighs brushed the backs of hers, his chest pressed against her back, his breath caressed her hair.

"Just like when *you* were twelve—I was only about two," he teased, his voice low and sensual.

And Lorena laughed. All that seemed very far from this moment.

She directed Molly toward the back gate at a comfortable, rambling walk. They went down a low hill and up a rise, turned and headed to flatter land. They laughed and held each other when Molly decided she wanted to trot. Oren's arms were around Lorena; their bodies bounced, rubbed, and caressed each other with every step Molly took. Lorena thought she had to be crazy to be doing this. But Oren was against her, and, oh, my, she couldn't help but feel his swelling low against her backbone. He pulled her against his chest, and she reveled in it. How wonderful it was! Wild and crazy and wonderful. She hadn't felt so alive in years. Suddenly it seemed the sun was more golden, the sky more blue.

And then she felt herself sliding. "Oh! Whoa!" She grabbed Molly's mane, but Oren's weight had already shifted and pulled her with him. Like a film in slow motion they slipped gently to the ground. They landed with breathless laughs, legs entangled.

Lorena lay there trying to catch her breath, staring at the sky. Oren's legs were heavy on hers but she didn't care.

"Are you all right?" he asked.

He rose on one elbow, and she gazed up at him. He was grinning. She nodded and laughed all over again, then told him he'd done that to her on purpose.

"Yeah, and you had fun," he told her.

And then his grin seemed to slip away. His blue eyes turned almost turquoise. Fiery like the sky around the setting sun. Lorena gazed at him and wanted him to kiss her.

Slowly his head came down to hers, blocking out all light. Panic fluttered like a bird in her chest. But desire was much stronger. And she thought, *Just this one time.*

The kiss was hesitant, tentative, each of them testing the boundaries. Emotion swelled inside Lorena like ocean waves, and then, when Oren parted her lips, those emotions crashed and flowed to every part of her. His arms came around her, and her arms went around him. Deeply and demandingly he kissed her, and it was sweet and drugging. When he lifted his lips to take a breath she wrapped her arms around his neck, pressed herself against the rock hardness of his body and went back for all the warm, heady, delicious forbiddenness of it. And it was good.

Suddenly reality came rushing back. Lorena jerked away, gasping for breath. She saw Oren's chest heaving, too. They stared at each other.

Lorena trembled with a weakness so sweet that just about all she could think of was throwing herself on Oren. *Oh, Lord, what he must think!*

Oren reached for her, but she shook her head and held up her hand. "We might as well stop this right now." She pushed herself up from the ground.

"What's wrong? You certainly enjoyed it, and so did I." And his expression dared her to refute him, which she couldn't, of course. *Enjoy* was a mild word to describe what she'd felt, and that was the truth of it, she thought as she went to retrieve her hat.

More slowly, he lifted himself up off the ground. Lorena brushed at herself, trying to get her thoughts under control. Every part of her wanted him, but she had to deny herself that.

"I don't indulge in quick affairs, Oren. No matter how tempting." There certainly wasn't any use in pretending their kisses had been casual, or that she wasn't tempted.

"Neither do I," he said slowly, flatly.

She didn't know what to say to that. Fears that she could never admit to him, much less begin to explain, swirled inside her, battling with her desires. She watched him step toward her, until he stood only inches away.

He put his hand up, caressed her cheek and slipped her hat from her head. Gently, oh, so gently. And the tender desire on his face was more than she could bear.

She pushed him away. "This is all just crazy."

"Will you tell me why?" he demanded.

She stepped backward, while he came forward. "Oh, don't be dense, Oren. You know perfectly well why."

"I don't." He stopped and gestured with her battered old hat. "I really don't know why in the hell you're backin' up at every approach I make. I've made it clear that I'm interested, and if you think it's just for sex, let me say very plainly, I'm not out just for some quick sex. I could get that elsewhere, and I don't mean to be braggin', but it's the truth."

That sat there between them for a long moment. "There's a lot more to it than that," Lorena said at last.

He shook his head. "From what I see, we like each other and we have a lot in common. I like sharp vehicles, you like sharp vehicles. I like animals, you like animals. I like small country towns, you like small country towns. I like popcorn without butter, you like popcorn without butter. What's crazy about any of that? Seems about as normal as normal can be."

"If you think a relationship is as simple as sharing popcorn, you really are a child."

He reached out, gripped her arm and shook her. "Quit throwin' that up at me. By God, I may be younger than you, but thirty is hardly a boy. And it isn't the number of years but how they're lived that makes the man...or the woman."

His glare was white-hot, and his strong fingers dug into her flesh. Then he threw her arm away and cursed, grabbing his nose and turning his back.

Puzzled, she gazed at his lean back. His shoulders were tight beneath the fabric of his shirt. "What is it? Oren?"

He shook his head.

"Oren?" She raced around him and saw the blood. "Oh, God, your nose is bleeding!"

"No kidding." He held his arm out like a weapon to keep her at bay. "It'll be okay in just a second."

"Here . . . I have a tissue." She dug it from her pocket. It was shredded from being pressed between the layers of sweat-dampened fabric. She held it out to him anyway, stretching her arm because he seemed to want her to stay away. He took it and pressed it to his nose.

After a few seconds she said, "Is it really all right?" Images of a brain hemorrhage flashed through her mind.

"It's fine . . . stopped now." He dabbed at his nose.

"Do you do that often? Have you seen a doctor?" She was still thinking about brain hemorrhages.

He cast her an impatient look and tossed away the tissue. "I get a little nosebleed sometimes when I get mad. I've always done it. Maybe that sounds like a childish thing to you," he said sarcastically, "but all I can tell you is it's a family trait. My great-uncle Norvel did the same thing up until he died at ninety-nine. We Breens are a long-lived bunch, even if we remain immature by some people's standards."

"Oh, Oren, I didn't mean..." She raised her arms, then let them drop and faced him squarely. "I'm sorry I hurt your feelings. I just don't know how to handle this at all. Good Lord, all I can think of is how when I was in high school and datin', you were entering first grade."

"It isn't like you're old enough to be my mother," he said sharply. "If it was twenty—hell, even if it was fifteen years—maybe I could see a problem. Or if we weren't where we are in life. But I'm thirty, more or less established, and you're forty and free, and we both know what we're about. And it isn't abnormal or unheard of, either—look at Elizabeth Taylor."

She sighed, then raked back her hair. "I can hardly be compared to Liz Taylor. If I looked like Liz I'd have moved to Hollywood a long time ago."

"Looks? Is that what bothers you? Let me tell you, lady, you don't have any problems there."

Lorena thought how she needed improving, because right there in the midst of their argument the compliment touched her. "Oren, I do like you—yes, I'm attracted to you," she said plainly at his expression. "I can even understand what you're sayin'. But I can't see it all just like that... so simply. And there isn't any reason to start something that has nowhere to go."

"Have you made up your mind to that—that it has nowhere to go?" His eyes bored into her.

"Where do you think it can go?" she asked, turning it back on him.

His face gentled. "It can go anywhere we want, but only if we give it a chance."

His voice, his words, echoed inside her. He made such sense. It was crazy, yet he stood there making such sense.

"When you're forty, I'll be fifty. When you're sixty, I'll be seventy."

He gave a slow grin. "Do you always project like that—worry about ten years down the road?"

"Yes," she said seriously. "I do it a lot. It's a trait of mine. Good or bad, it's me." And by heaven, she wasn't bending herself out of shape for anyone, not ever again.

He shook his head and licked his lips, thinking. Then he took his characteristic spread-legged stance, folding his arms and tucking his hands up beneath his armpits. She knew he was gearing up. He said, "When you first tried to ride a bike, while you were wobbling along and scared to death, did you stop because of fear that you'd fall?" He let that sink in and then continued. "When you first drag raced on Purgatory Road out there, did you worry about the end of it? When you first raced a horse on barrels, did you worry about the end of the race—or ten years down the road, when you wouldn't race any longer?"

She just stared at him.

He asked, "Do you regret ever doing those things? Would you have missed the experiences for anything?"

"No," she said quietly.

He asked, "Ten years from now, will you regret passing up what we might have together?"

And she thought, *Oh, yes, I might.*

He stepped closer, though he didn't try to touch her. They gazed at each other.

She said, "Have you ever seen '77 Sunset Strip?' "

He looked puzzled and shook his head.

"Did you ever own a hula hoop?"

He frowned sadly and shook his head.

"I don't suppose you know who Ma Kettle is?"

A bright grin came across his face like the dawning sun. "I sure do," he said, "and you're a lot younger than those movies."

She breathed deeply. It was crazy, totally impractical. She was going to end up hurt.

He said, "If you think we aren't already involved, you might as well think again." And he held out his hand. The setting sun cast its coral glow over him. His gaze was steady.

She tried to hold to her good sense, but it was crumbling like sand along a wet riverbank. She put her hand in his. "Haven't you ever heard of passing through the friendship phase first?"

And he drawled, his voice full of sex, "Oh, lady, we passed the friendship phase that first night in your kitchen." He tugged her to him gently, offering her the chance to say no.

But she didn't.

She went into his arms, her heart pounding. She allowed him to press himself against her. Her blood warmed rapidly, deliciously. She wrapped her arms around his neck and met his kiss, opened her lips and her soul for him. She forgot being older, she forgot being a mother, she forgot being scared. She became simply a woman enamored of this man.

Chapter Nine

They left Molly on the range and walked, hand in hand, back to the old place. They sat on the porch and watched the sun sink out of sight. Oren sat with his back propped against the post, one leg bent. He held Lorena nestled between his thighs and leaning against his chest. He held one of her hands with his. By mutual agreement they didn't touch any more intimately, didn't kiss again. Still, he was tight and very aware of Lorena against him.

He knew he could have had her right here, knew she wanted it as badly as he did. But suddenly he was more aware of her vulnerability, and he experienced the powerful compulsion to protect her. This wasn't the time or place for them to come together. Not only was this place lacking in amenities, but Lorena was right when she'd chided him about bypassing friendship. The time wasn't yet right for them to make love. Or, perhaps closer to the truth, it was for him, but it wasn't for her.

"I have more reputation than actual experience," he told her suddenly. She turned her head and looked at him. "I haven't been celibate, but I'm not anywhere near as promiscuous as my reputation. And I haven't been with a woman since last year, when there was a lady I was involved with…but it didn't work out." He felt pretty tongue-tied with it all.

But tender understanding filled her eyes. Then she looked away. "There has only been one man in my life since Tony…and that was eight years ago, and it wasn't much of anything."

Her eyes came back to his, and they gazed at each other for a long minute, and then Oren couldn't resist kissing her, very lightly and chastely, seeking to show her how he felt. She smiled at him, hesitantly at first, but then fully, like the sun coming from behind a cloud. Man, she had the prettiest smile he'd ever seen. It lit up her face, made it seem almost translucent.

She leaned forward and laid her head on his knee. "My dad calls you a cloud-head."

"So you've said. Well, I've never been overly impressed by him, either."

"I'm my parents' only child."

He digested that, thought he read between the lines and decided there wasn't much he could say to it. Instead he said, "I was interested in you the night I saw you at the rodeo."

Her face flushed. She returned her cheek to his knee. "I was interested in you then, too."

"What about the night I visited you in your kitchen?"

"Then, too," she said in a bare whisper.

"I knew that," he said, and she slapped his leg. He stared at her bare arms, the curve of her cheek. "You know, I kid around and I cut up, and a lot of times people don't take me seriously. I know they don't, and I use it." She gazed at him, listening intently. "Most of my friends are older than me, always have been. I guess Mom dyin' when I was just a kid and me spending so much time with my dad and Matt and Rory made me grow up fast. Matt, mostly. I was always hangin' out with him and his friends. But I have fun playin' these days with Little Jesse . . . and Glory and Mercy. Seems like I don't fit anywhere in between.''

She brought her palm to his cheek, understanding in her eyes. "When I was a kid I didn't get to play much like other kids. I had chores, and Mom and Dad weren't big on wastin' time playin'. When a person is an only child they spend a great deal of time in an adult world. I sometimes feel that my childhood just raced right past me. Sometimes I think I miss it."

She dropped her hand, and he caught it, gave it a squeeze.

A minute later she said, "Prima—you know, the teller you always flirt with—she saw you comin' out of the flower shop with a bouquet the past week." She kept her cheek on his knee and didn't look at him.

"Oh, she did?"

She didn't say anything.

"I picked up flowers for Matt for Annie." And that she'd asked him indirectly tickled him to death. He couldn't help chuckling, and she smacked his leg again. She cared! She cared enough to be jealous!

After the sun had set they drove over to Raton to get pizza. He suggested Raton because some inner voice told him she would rather not go where they were likely to run into a lot of people they knew. And when he suggested they leave one of their cars at Royal's gas station she said she'd as soon take both cars. "It's five miles out of the way to Royal's from here," she said. But he suspected that for some reason she wanted to drive herself, that she was still protecting herself, but he let it go. He was too busy being excited about being with her.

They ordered a large, thick crust pizza and chatted across the softly lit table. He saw the child within the sophisticated woman, the part of her that liked the crust of the pizza best, liked to stretch the strings of cheese and sat on one leg or the other rather than put both feet on the floor. Her brown eyes were shiny and warm, like clear pekoe tea, and at times shy, sexily so, and they drew him like a warm fire on a cold night. For this time they were alone in their own world.

Oren had never talked with a woman the way he did with Lorena. The only other woman he could talk a lot to was Annie, but there were a lot of things he couldn't say to Annie, her being who she was and he being who he was. He talked a bit to Jada, too, but mostly he and Jada joked and flirted with each other. With Lorena he really and truly talked, about everything, and they didn't run dry on any subject.

At ten she said she needed to call Nicky, because she'd told him she would be in for the evening, and he would be worried. "I like him to call me when he changes his plans," she said. "So I try to do the same for him."

Oren could see her at the phone in the alcove. Her head was bent and partially turned away. She didn't talk long.

He watched her returning across the restaurant toward him. His eyes skimmed over her bare, shapely shoulders and the bit of cleavage that showed, then on down to her feet. The wanting rose in him.

"Did you get him?" he asked as she slid into the seat across from him.

She nodded. "He'd planned to come in early tonight—to visit with me, as a matter of fact, which he made certain to point out. I reminded him of the times he's changed his plans." She grinned wryly.

Oren kept his mouth shut about asking if she'd told Nicky just who she was with. He didn't think he would like the answer.

She wouldn't stay but a few minutes longer, because she said Nicky was waiting for her. Oren walked her to her car, and at her door he kissed her, a long, deep kiss. He was encouraged by her response, encouraged and made hot. He pulled away with an effort and saw her into her car, making certain she was buckled in.

He followed her car lights all the way home. And the thoughts he had put him in knots. It came as something of an amazement to him. He had never felt this way about a woman. Suddenly he wanted to protect her, take care of her, love her. He kept thinking about what his dad had said would happen when he fell in love. "Nothin' like it, son. It ties you into knots... but they're such sweet knots."

Lorena gave a little honk as she went on to her driveway. He quickly pulled the Cadillac far into his own and called for Harvey to come on and hurry up, going around to his backyard, where he could speak to Lorena as she came from her garage.

The bright light from her back deck shone over into his yard. She was looking his way as she crossed from her garage.

He called softly, "I enjoyed tonight."

And she returned, more softly still, "I did, too."

"I'll see you tomorrow."

"I have—" Nicky greeting her from the door cut off her words. "No, I'm alone," she said loud enough for Oren to hear. "I was just saying hello to Oren."

Nicky stepped out and looked over. "Hi, Oren," he said, and waved.

Oren waved back. Lorena called good-night and then went inside with her son.

"Feel about like a guy sneakin' around with the neighbor's wife," Oren muttered to Harvey as he unlocked the door.

His house was dark, empty. He went around turning on lights, and switched on the radio, but after about five minutes he switched the radio off again. He was in no mood to hear sexy love songs.

After a shower he lay in his darkened room. The light was on in Lorena's room, and it fell across into his. Her window was a little higher than his own, with window blinds cut so that light filtered downward, but he couldn't see into the room, and if he could have, all he would have been able to see was the ceiling. He'd tested this out several times since he'd moved in.

The light went out in her room, and he lay there in the dark, thinking about her.

There had been times in his life when he'd been attracted to a woman and hadn't restrained himself. The women he'd wanted hadn't restrained themselves, either. Once, a number of years ago, his brother Matt had told him that there was more to a relationship with a woman than what went on between the sheets, and Oren had come to know the truth of that statement. In all his life he'd never been in love. He'd been waiting and hoping, and he lay there wondering if he'd finally found what he'd been waiting and hoping for.

However, for Lorena, those years stood between them, as strong a barrier in her mind as a concrete wall.

Those years didn't mean anything to Oren. If she was concerned about looks, he thought she looked just fine. Hell, she looked great. On close inspection she had fine lines about her eyes, and maybe she didn't look twenty-five, but she wasn't twenty-five. That was why he was attracted to her. She was a full woman, with all the blessings of a full woman. And she was certainly as sexy a woman as he'd ever in his life met.

None of these thoughts was conducive to helping him go to sleep.

Oren awakened early the following morning, reached for the phone and called Lorena. He got a jolt when Max Sandoval answered.

"I'll get her," Max told him gruffly.

"How are you this mornin', beautiful?"

"Fine, and you?" Her voice was guarded.

"Great. Are you gonna be occupied all day?"

"I have a meeting in Amarillo today. Mama and Daddy are driving down with me." She seemed very reluctant to talk at all, and this irritated Oren.

"Well, I guess I'll catch you another time."

"Okay."

So much for that, he thought as he hung up. She hadn't wanted to talk because of her parents and Nick; that much had been obvious. And that certainly didn't make a guy feel wanted.

He told himself he had to be patient if he was going to get somewhere with Lorena. She would back off quickly if her family gave her trouble about him. He wasn't certain how Nick would feel about it, but he didn't think it took a genius to know that Lorena's dad would kick up a fuss. Max Sandoval didn't like him and never had. While Oren was trying to win Lorena, it would be best if ol' Max didn't complicate things.

The following morning, before Lorena had left for work, Oren again telephoned her. "Good morning, beautiful. Did you miss me yesterday?"

She laughed, warm and easy this time, and he knew she was alone. The knowledge made his blood as warm as her voice.

"You have an ego as big as Mount Rushmore," she teased.

"It's what makes me so lovable," he said.

"Well, as lovable as you are," she said primly, "I'll have you know that I was too busy to miss you yesterday."

"Are you trying to put me in my place?" he countered.

"Yes, but I think it doubtful that I can."

"Oh, sure you can—just invite me over to your bed."

Her only response was a chuckle.

"Okay, since that is out—what are your plans for today?"

"I have to work. Some of us do that, you know."

"Well, since that's what you're gonna do, I guess I'll do some of that myself. But I can drive back down and have lunch with you."

"And when do you get any work done, between drivin' back and forth to the ranch?"

"Oh, there's plenty of time. A few hours, anyway. How about it?"

Quickly Lorena weighed and measured, then said yes and told him she would meet him at Jimmy's Café. She often talked business with customers over lunch; this would appear to be nothing more.

That evening he—and Harvey—came over. Harvey sprawled near the kitchen door, while Lorena and Oren made supper, a simple meal of omelets and corn bread and fruit salad. Oren made Harvey his own omelet.

Afterward they sat in the den and watched television, she in her chair, Oren on the floor with his back against her chair, and Harvey next to Oren. Lorena made certain the window blinds were closed, and she was very aware of being alone with Oren. Very aware of his dark glossy hair and firm strong shoulders and faint men's cologne. She was also very aware of his hand occasionally caressing her leg, while she stitched on her quilt. She couldn't have given a good report on the television programs they watched, she had a hard enough time keeping her stitches straight. At first she resisted putting on her glasses, but then she thought that was simply adolescent and irresponsible. She had to wear glasses, and he might as well see that.

He said he was mildly myopic and had glasses that he didn't often wear, but that he was finding it harder to read road signs, so he would have to start.

He went home after eleven, when she reminded him that she had to work the next day. She told him to go the back way and led him through the kitchen.

He paused in the laundry-room doorway. "There isn't a back way. There isn't any gate."

"You've never had trouble stepping over the wall before."

"Harvey does," he teased, gazing sexily down at her.

"Go the back way, because Aggie Pacheco across the street will see you in the front, and I'd just as soon she not be spreading it around church. It irritates my mother."

"I'm sure that makes some sense. But, you know, Mis Pacheco is much too preoccupied with Mr. Sanchez to pay us much attention these days."

"You're kiddin'?"

He shook his head. "He was headin' over to her place when I came over here. What's wrong—don't you pay proper attention to your neighbors' lives?"

"I've always tried not to."

"Not me. This city life is quite interesting."

He bent and kissed her quickly, then embraced her and kissed her deeply, lifting her right off her feet. "Thanks for supper and the company," he said with a grin. Turning abruptly, he left her standing there aching for more.

They saw each other often over the following three weeks. They had lunch together again at the café and nearly every evening during the week he came for supper and hours of watching television and talking. They talked a lot, and this was as great a novelty as a pleasure to Lorena. She and Tony had rarely talked; she and Gary had talked theories of life. For the past years she'd been very much alone without long conversations with anyone.

They talked about everything from the habitat of coyotes to how high gas prices would rise. Oren didn't try to change her mind on certain issues, as her father, Tony and Gary always had. He would say, "That's one way of lookin' at it." Oh, he was a diplomat, and she told him he should go into politics. He said that took too much energy.

If there was anything that troubled her about Oren, it was that he seemed to lack ambition for more than simply being happy. He wasn't lazy, but he seemed to do only what pleased him, and this, while certainly no sin, didn't fit with the concept of life that Lorena had been brought up with. It seemed irresponsible.

On the second weekend Nicky was kept out at the ranch through to Sunday morning, and Lorena suspected Oren had had a hand in it.

"Not I," he said, raising his hand in a pledge. "It was Matt who wanted those cattle rounded up and moved. I simply said I didn't want to ride with them, and that Nick was perfectly capable of doing it in my place."

With Nick gone from home Saturday night, Oren talked Lorena into going to Las Vegas for a steak dinner and dancing afterward. It was a legitimate excuse for them to be in each other's arms, and they both knew it. The unspoken knowledge added to the forbiddenness of it all.

They danced every slow dance, held on to each other, gazed into each other's eyes. Their bodies moved against each other seductively, rubbing and caressing with their chests, bellies and thighs. Sharing with their gazes the delight in the quickening of their pulses, the sweet, heady desire slipping through their veins.

Lorena also had a glimpse into Oren's social life, because he knew a goodly number of people at the dance club, the majority of them women. Once, when she was returning from the ladies' room, she found him talking to a knockout of a woman with long black hair and wearing a form-fitting cat suit. He introduced the woman as Lisa Lujan, and Lorena thought the name fit. And if she had been a betting person, Lorena would have bet that Lisa Lujan wasn't pleased to see Oren with her. That there had been something between the younger woman and Oren was a fact Lorena knew by a woman's intuition. She didn't ask Oren about it, though.

At least three times while they were dancing, women called and waved to him. Lorena felt self-conscious, even jealous, an emotion that irritated her. But to her surprise and gratification, Oren made certain she, and anyone else who might be interested, knew his attention lay with her. She had never in all her life felt so romanced.

Outside Clayton, Oren stopped at Royal's to drop Lorena at her car. Before getting out, he pulled her close and kissed her again and again, until Lorena felt her restraint fraying like a taut, worn thread. Oren saw her to her car and made certain she fastened her safety belt. "Drive carefully," he said good-naturedly, and she felt guilty for hiding that she was dating him.

The next evening, with Nicky upstairs in his room and after Lorena had turned out her light and was in bed, she heard a noise at her window. It was Oren, throwing cereal from his window. There, in the warm summer night, clothed only in a cotton robe, Lorena exchanged whispers with him across the short distance that separated their houses.

"What are you wearin'?" he asked suggestively.

"My robe," she said primly. They were flirting with passion, and it was such fun. She hadn't felt so alive in years.

"And what else?" he asked.

"Imagine," she teased.

While they were at their windows they saw Mr. Sanchez coming out of Aggie Pacheco's house. "I'm not telling my mother," Lorena said. "She'll have to find out on her own."

"You're a gossip hoarder," Oren accused, chuckling.

"Shush!" Lorena warned and pointed upward to Nicky's room.

"Aw... there isn't a son alive who'd believe his mother would be flirtin' with her neighbor out her window at night."

The sexual tension between them grew daily, and Lorena couldn't seem to keep herself from finding excuses to touch him. He was definitely doing the same, though much more openly. He made no secret of wanting Lorena.

Once, after a particularly hot embrace, she pressed her hands against his chest. His rock hard chest. "Oren ... I'm not ready for this," she said.

He gazed at her for a long moment, the wanting clearly there. She thought she had to be crazy. He said, "I'll wait until you are."

He didn't ask her to explain herself in any way. He simply said he would wait, and the light in his eyes took her breath.

Then he kissed her again, long and sweet, and stepped out into the night. She almost called him back. Her voice stopped in her throat.

He said he would wait until she was ready, she thought. A part of her was certainly ready right that minute, no doubt about that. But the other part of her was scared to death.

What if Oren was simply indulging in a fling with an older woman? What if, since he'd lost his mother at a young age, she was simply a mother figure to him? What might he think of her naked? What kind of future could they possibly have? What might he think of her in a few years, when she really started to age? What would her family say? Specifically, what would her father say?

Oh, there just seemed so much against them. How could they have a future? If she had any common sense left she would put a stop to this now.

But she found that thought unbearable. Oren was a special man. He was the gentlest man she'd ever met. He couldn't stand to kill anything, even going so far as to capture crickets and put them out of the house rather than kill them. He laughed easily, and he didn't have a critical bone in his body. What she'd taken for irresponsibility, she was now beginning to believe, was his accepting way of looking at life. Oren had the marvelous ability to accept himself as

he was, and to accept everyone else just the way they were
too. He made people feel good about themselves. And he
made her feel so alive.

She could easily love Oren Breen, if she let herself. Maybe
she already did.

Oren and Lorena never actually discussed keeping their
relationship a secret, but that was exactly what they were
doing. A number of times one of his family had asked him
where he was going or what his plans were, and he'd had to
bite back that he was going to visit Lorena. He did it because to tell someone was to have it passed around and
eventually get to Nick, and Oren well knew Lorena wouldn't
be happy about that. It was wearing on his nerves, not to
mention his pride, but he kept telling himself to be patient.
When Lorena was certain of her own feelings she would tell
her parents and sons and everyone else. If he tried to force
the issue, she might just call it quits, and he sure didn't want
that.

One Sunday morning, when he came out of his house and
saw the Feldman kids playing all over his yard as well as
their own, Oren asked them if they wanted to see some kittens. He was devious, he thought as he and Harvey and the
kids trooped over to Lorena's house, because he wasn't
above using the kids as cover so he could very innocently go
over to Lorena's.

When no one answered the front door he and the kids
went around to the back. The garage door was closed, and
Oren wondered if Lorena had driven off without him seeing. Then he saw her in the glassed-in laundry room. "We
came to see the kittens, Miss Lorena," he said, opening the
door.

He saw immediately that she'd been crying, though she
sniffed and smiled at the kids. "I have them in here," she
said. "Come on in, kids."

They all, even Harvey, crowded into the room. The kids got down on their knees and tentatively petted the kittens, whispering, as if in a nursery. The kittens had grown by leaps and bounds; they had their eyes open and were wobbling around.

Lorena got down on her knees, too, and helped each child hold a kitten, even little three-year-old Barclay, though she pulled out a tissue and wiped Barclay's nose first. That's when Oren noticed there were only three kittens.

"I thought you said there were four kittens, Mr. Oren," Suzie said.

"We lost one," Lorena said.

"How can you lose it?" Suzie asked.

"I think what Miss Lorena means is that it went to heaven," Oren said.

At that Suzie told her brothers, "He means it's dead."

Oren saw Lorena blinking rapidly.

The kids spent a good twenty minutes with the kittens, and then Oren managed to ease them out the door. He returned to Lorena, who'd moved into the kitchen and was pouring a cup of coffee. She was near tears again.

"Somethin' got in the garage," she said with a sniff. "The kitten wasn't sick or anything. It was fine yesterday, and I found it dead today, lyin' way over in a corner."

"It was probably the male cat—the daddy of these. They'll kill the babies if they can, tryin' to get the female back for themselves. It's nature's way."

"I didn't know that. How awful. I thought they'd be safe in the garage. I really didn't want a litter box in the house, and Queenie seemed so unhappy in here, wanting out and then wanting in. Once she tried to take the kittens out, so I thought the garage would be better. I made certain the door was only open a crack, so no dog could get in, and the box was up off the ground. Oh, I just didn't know." She teared up and wiped at her eyes with the back of her hand. "I don't know what's wrong with me. I hardly ever cry. This is silly...it really is." Then she blubbered, "It was Othello," and started sobbing.

"Aw, it's okay...come here." He reached for her and pulled her close, stroking her hair while she sobbed softly into his chest and mumbled things he couldn't possibly understand. He thought how she had about the worst luck with animals of anyone he'd ever known.

He wished he could fix this for her as easily as he'd fixed her faucet the other day. The most he could do was comfort her, and he did that to the best of his ability, which was considerable, though he wouldn't have bragged the fact aloud.

Oren liked comforting a woman, probably because he liked holding a woman. He thought how silky her hair felt and how good she smelled. And how small and warm and soft she was against him.

He stroked her back. Her blouse was of loose, flowing silk, and he could feel the warmth of her skin beneath. And a small bra strap. He moved his hand farther downward, pressing her against him. He nuzzled her hair, savoring the scent of her perfume, something sweet and sultry that stirred his senses.

Her nose burrowed into his neck, and her sobs turned to faint whimpers. He found her ear with his lips. Her breath caressed his neck and his pulse picked up like a horse getting the scent of a race. He kissed his way across her cheek, tasting her tears. Her face came up slowly, imperceptibly, until their lips were nudging. With tentative anticipation he sampled her lips. She sampled his.

"Oren..." she whispered with longing. And again, "Oren..." with fearful caution.

This encounter was different, hotter, more explosive, and they both knew it.

He nipped her lips, tasted their sweetness with his tongue. He whispered, "It's okay...I won't...I promise...just enjoy this right now. Please.'' He thought if he didn't get some relief he was going to shatter.

In answer, she sighed with great pleasure and melted against him. Relief washed over him and lasted about three seconds.

Her trusting ardor sent desire pounding through him like a herd of horses. He cupped her hips and brought her against him and rubbed. She moaned, and he went all out kissing her. He broke to draw a breath, then had his head pressed back to her again, her hands tugging at his hair. And that set his blood on fire.

By instinct, directed by passion, he inched her back until she came against the counter. The sensual sound of their raspy breaths and his heart beating in his ears overcame every thought. His hands fumbled their way beneath her loose blouse and connected with her skin—warm, silky-soft skin. She arched against his hand and slipped her own hand down under his collar. Her feverish touch set him on fire.

He lifted her up on the counter and pressed into her, and her legs came around his waist. Her scent and breath and heartbeat enfolded him. He found his way with his mouth underneath her blouse and to her midriff. She moaned, tightening her legs around him and moving against him. He was riding along on the wave of passion, the wind blowing in his ears, the sun blessing him from above and Lorena caressing him all over. As he unclasped her bra, some part of his brain reminded him of what he'd promised her and that he'd reached the ragged edge of restraint.

That reminder slowed him, and the slamming of the front door stopped him.

''Mom?'' Nick's voice rang out.

It was like a bucket of ice water sloshing over both of them.

Oren jerked upward, and Lorena fought to get her blouse back down. In a flurry of motion she twisted and hopped from the counter.

"I'll speak to him," Oren said, trying to rake his hair into place, while Lorena fled around the refrigerator and into the bathroom. If he hadn't felt so painfully frustrated, Oren was sure he could have laughed.

Lorena was mortified.

She wet a cloth with cool water and pressed it to her cheeks. She thought how what had just transpired could very well debunk the theory of her being a mother figure for Oren.

Oh, good heavens! What would Nicky think? Hurriedly she tried to cream the mascara smudges from beneath her eyes. Would he guess? She stared at her reflection. She looked okay...except her lips were puffy and her color high. She looked like a woman who'd just been made love to.

Oh, my, but it had been wonderful. She felt as if she'd been soaring on the wind.

She pulled a compact from the drawer and dabbed powder on her face. She didn't need to be looking like a woman who'd just been made love to—she needed to look like a mother, she thought, as she heard Nicky's and Oren's voices from the kitchen. Suddenly she wanted to cry again. Her emotions had been on edge all week, like nerve endings coming awake.

Oren stood easily leaning against the counter. Lorena met his amused gaze, and her eyes skittered quickly away as her cheeks burned. The picture that might have met her son came full into her mind.

Nick had his friend, Shelley, with him. They had come to watch a car race on television. With this in mind as he got cold drinks from the refrigerator, he wasn't about to notice anything odd about Lorena.

He did say, "Oren told me about Othello, Mom.... I'm sorry. I know you've gotten awfully fond of those kittens." He gave her a quick hug, and then he was digging into the cabinet for chips.

"I wouldn't mind havin' one of them when they're old enough, Mrs. Venable," Shelley said, cuddling Tubbs against her cheek.

Lorena said, "I'm not certain I'm going to give any of them away." Suddenly she felt very possessive of them. She was an emotional mess, she thought. And it wasn't all to do with losing Othello, either, she realized as she again met Oren's gaze. He leaned against the counter as if quite satisfied with himself.

"Mom...do we have any cheese sauce?" Nicky asked, his voice muffled because his head was stuck in the refrigerator.

"I'll find some. You all go on in the living room." She spoke sharply.

Nicky cast her an odd look, then backed away, taking Shelley and their drinks into the other room.

Oren bent beside her at the refrigerator. "I'll help."

"I can get it myself."

She felt his gaze commanding her to look at him. Slowly she did. He smiled and raised a jar of cheese sauce.

"We used the last of what was in the refrigerator Wednesday night. This was in the cabinet."

She breathed deeply and straightened. Very gently he leaned over and kissed her forehead.

They all watched the car race. Nicky and Shelley sprawled on the sofa, and Oren settled into the recliner, while Lorena took her customary big chair. A number of times she and Oren exchanged discreet, intimate glances. His eyes twinkled merrily, and he cocked his left eyebrow slightly. Lorena's face grew warm each time she recalled what they had been doing when Nicky had arrived. The thought that her son could have walked in on them brought a wave of panic over her, followed by thankfulness and heavenly pledges never to be so foolish and irresponsible again.

But her pledges sounded empty. She realized that for the first time in years she had fallen head over heels for a man and seemed to have little control over her actions.

And to think she'd thought she'd finally reached the age of mature good common sense.

The following Monday was the first evening Lorena had spent alone in weeks. When she came home from work Oren's car was gone, and he hadn't returned by the time she made her supper. There was no reason for her to be angry that he hadn't called, she told herself firmly. No reason for him to call. She didn't have any kind of hold on him. They hadn't made a commitment to each other... not really.

She kept looking for him until bedtime, and after she'd gotten into bed she lay there, listening for the Caddie... or a telephone call. At last, unable to sleep, she brought Queenie and her kittens up into the bed with her. They all seemed perfectly content, and their purring helped Lorena to finally sleep.

First thing the following morning she looked out her bedroom window. Oren's Cadillac wasn't there, and his house appeared still. Where was he? Why hadn't he called? Had he decided to drop her? Oh, my Lord, had something happened to him?

She wondered, as she had often during the previous weeks, if Oren had told his family anything of their relationship. She doubted that he had. By unspoken agreement they'd kept their relationship from everyone. So if anything had happened to him, no one would know to call her.

By the time she came home from work she had decided to call the ranch. She had to know if he was all right. And then, when she drove down the street, she saw it—his Cadillac parked in his driveway.

Barely slowing, she turned into her own driveway, stopped with a jerk in front of her garage, grabbed her purse and portfolio and hopped out, intent on running to the phone to call him.

But there he was, sitting on her back steps, with Harvey at his feet.

She stopped and gazed at him uncertainly. Perhaps he didn't want her any longer; perhaps that was why he'd been away. So she remained, in the middle of the driveway, her heart hanging by a thread.

Slowly, like a strong blade of grass, he straightened. And then he grinned.

She raced forward to throw her arms around him. He grabbed her and held her close.

"Now this is a greetin' a man can get used to."

And they both laughed.

He'd brought a shopping bag full of goodies to make their favorite dinner—hot dogs and beans. He said he'd been out on the range with his brother Rory, that he'd called Sunday night and left a message on her machine. She said she'd popped over to her parents' house, and the machine hadn't registered any calls.

"How strange!" She went to check. The light still held steady. But in pressing the review button she found Oren's message.

"The machine was reset," she said when she came back into the kitchen.

He looked over his shoulder from where he was already slicing the tomatoes and raised an eyebrow.

Her heart constricted. "Nicky must have listened and reset the machine."

His eyes met hers. "I didn't say anything incriminating...just that I was going to be gone for a couple of days."

"You called me beautiful."

"Oh, yeah...and that's incriminating as all get-out. Don't look so worried. He probably just forgot to tell you." He put down the knife. "Would it be so horrible if he found out about us? Are we going to keep playin' this game for the rest of our lives?''

She looked at him and had no answer. She didn't want to talk about it. Not now, not tonight, when she was wanting him so badly.

She said, "I missed you," then looked quickly away, shyness suddenly overcoming her. Inside she was thinking, *He's here!*

They were quiet as they ate. Thoughts of him holding her, of holding him, of the bedroom twenty feet away, kept flickering through her mind like an old-time picture show. She wasn't a young girl anymore. And she was in love with this man. How much, she wasn't certain. More to the point, she didn't think "how much" mattered, for at her age she knew it took more than love to make a lasting relationship.

She had trouble meeting his gaze. She found her eyes returning again and again to his hands. They were so tanned. The hands of a hardworking man. Very male hands, yet she recalled how gentle they could be when holding the kittens, when stroking her cheek.

"What did you and Rory do?" she asked.

"Doctored a few cattle and just generally rode around. Camped up at the north ridge. We hadn't done it in a long time."

There was more, she could tell by the look in his eyes. He'd stayed out to be alone, away from her and what was happening between them, and she knew it as well as if he'd said it.

"Let's get this cleared away," Oren said suddenly, and stood. "There's a John Wayne movie on the television."

"I thought you said you had the entire set of John Wayne movies on videotape."

"I can always watch one."

While she chopped up scraps for Queenie and the kittens, he put the dishes into the dishwasher. They both reached for the dishcloth at the same moment, and their hands touched. Neither let go.

Lorena slowly raised her eyes. Oren was gazing down at her. His eyes were the color of a mountain lake in summer, and just as inviting. His hand reached out, slipped to the back of her neck and pulled her to him.

His kiss was hard and deep, and she sank into it. When at last they took a breath, his name broke from her lips. "Oren," she whispered. And again, "Oh, Oren."

He kissed her once more, hungrily, and when he next lifted his head she raked her hands up into his hair and pulled him back to her yet again. The feeling was sweet and intoxicating, dragging her along on its crest.

She found herself pressed between the sharp counter and his hard male body. He kissed his way down her neck, and she held on to him, trembling.

She whispered breathlessly, "Do you—?"

"Yes!" he broke in with a ragged whisper of his own, sending heat waves down her body.

His hands were hot upon her flesh, moving up and down her spine. She couldn't stifle her whimpers. She'd forgotten how it could feel. *No, I didn't know it could feel like this.* She let control slip away.

When he asked her with his eyes, she took his hand and started for the bedroom, her eyes averted, because she suddenly felt shy and embarrassed and uncertain, even though she didn't stop.

The next instant she was swept up into his arms. She chuckled, gloriously, and buried her face against his neck. With swift, long strides he went through the house. She could feel the powerful movement of his muscles.

He slammed the door shut with his foot and reached the bed in three strides. Light from the street lamps sliced through the window and struck his face with a silvery glow. The passion she saw there shook her to the core.

Quickly, with kisses and caresses, they shed their clothes. Lorena had an instant of embarrassment, of hesitancy, but that slipped away as desire took over. She savored the hardness of his muscles, the smoothness of his skin, the wonderful maleness of him against her femaleness. The sultry, seductive scent of him wafted around her like thick smoke. He slid his body the length of hers, and she slid the length of him, delighting in the sensations. Over and over they rolled, then back again. When he whispered, "You're beautiful!" she began to cry. He kissed away her tears.

She wanted him, badly, but he would not be rushed. His hands and his lips played upon her body, bringing her higher and higher, letting her float down, and then taking her upward again. And then, when she couldn't stand it another second, he took her all the way to paradise.

He held her in the crook of his arm while his body settled itself. Her skin was damp against his; her heart beat against his side. With each breath her scent came to him, tantalizing and comforting at the same time.

She pushed herself upward, looked at him with wonder, a Madonnalike smile on her lips. "Thank you," she whispered, a reverence echoing in her tone and reflecting in her dark eyes.

"Oh, thank you." He kissed her, then ran his hand down the curve of her body, which glowed in the light from the streetlamp. He couldn't take his eyes off her.

"I feel like . . ." she began, and he couldn't see her blushing, but he knew she was. "Like I gave you so little."

"But you gave me a lot . . . you surely did." There was no doubting that. Maybe that was why this had been so different. She had a giving sort of fire inside her.

"Stay the night."

She didn't have to ask him twice. They pulled back the spread and sheets and settled themselves beneath. He held her and explored her skin with his palm. She began to do the same to him, and pretty soon he was getting aroused again. When he reached the edge of sanity, he held her tightly against him, put his fingers beneath her chin and tilted her face to the dim light.

"I'm in love with you, Lorena." The words felt clumsy on his tongue.

Her arms came up around his neck, and she pressed her face to his, her entire body trembling. "Oh, Oren . . . I love you, too," she said in a hoarse whisper, her tone a mixture of exultation and fear.

She held him, and he held her. He stroked her hair and kissed her face, and she cried and mumbled something, and he told her not to talk, not now. For now, nothing else mattered. Then he told her that he loved her again, because he couldn't help himself.

The following morning they both awakened late. Oren tried to get her to call in sick or at least late, but she wouldn't; she said something about a meeting she had to go to, and hurried into the shower.

More leisurely, Oren rose and gathered his clothes. He took the opportunity to look around her room. It was frilly, all woman, in colors of white and rose and what he called blue-green and Marnie always said was teal. It was excessively neat, like Nick's room upstairs, except when he opened the closet. The riotous mess in there made him feel a lot better. Every time his eyes lit on the bed he recalled what had gone on there, and he smiled.

When she came out of the bathroom, in her pink robe and with a towel around her wet hair, he was waiting for her in the bed, with his back propped against the pillows. He grabbed her hand and pulled her down atop him, kissing her soundly.

"I won't be able to get to work if you keep this up," she said, her eyes heavy with passion.

"That's the idea." And he kissed her again.

When she looked at him, her eyes were even hotter, but still she pulled away and rose. He watched the movement of her body beneath her robe, watched her loosen the towel and let her hair fall down to her shoulders.

She dug some lacy things from a drawer, then glanced over her shoulder at him. "Some of us have to work, you know." And she went back into the bathroom.

He rose and went to the door, where he leaned against the frame.

"For some people, working is life. For others, living is working."

She was combing her hair, and her eyes met his in the mirror. "I like my work. I always have."

"I like mine, too."

"You don't do much," she said skeptically.

"Doesn't mean I don't like what I do and that it isn't my work. I try to see to things that other people forget—like pointin' out beauty and finding smiles and always havin' time for a word."

"And you're certainly very good at all that, Mr. Breen." Her voice echoed with true admiration.

"Thank you, ma'am."

He continued to watch her. She opened a drawer and began to pull out makeup. She said, "Are you just gonna stand there and watch me?"

"Yep. I've never seen what a woman does to herself in the mornin'. Not from start to finish, anyway. And I like watchin' you, darlin'."

She told him to go make coffee, so he did, quickly returning with two cups and catching her slipping into her panties and bra. It was a good sight. He told her she was beautiful, and she blushed and told him to quit being charming, it wasn't going to get him anywhere. But he knew she liked it, and he sure liked the sight of her.

Then he asked what had been stirring in his mind since last night.

"The annual Wings Founder's Day celebration is this coming Saturday. My family always goes. Dad always enters the chili cook-off, Matt cooks ribs and Rory races a horse. I would like you and Nicky to join us. I would like you to be my date," he said, making certain she understood.

Her brown eyes met his in the mirror, then flitted away. "Jaime's comin' home. I thought I told you. He'll be here for the weekend, and Mama and Daddy have been makin' plans for us all to spend the weekend with them, so they can have time with Jaime, too."

"Then bring everyone along. As I recall, in the past your parents always made a point of comin' to Founder's Day, because your dad likes to rag my dad about the chili."

She bit her bottom lip, then walked past him into the room and over to the closet. He saw the resistance in her shoulders.

He said, "You'll sleep with me in your bed, but you're ashamed to be seen with me in public." Anger simmered in his gut.

"I am not!" She whirled and stared at him.

"Then let's discuss why we've been hidin' these past weeks."

That stood there between them, solid as a brick wall.

He saw a flicker of pain in her eyes, and her lips trembled as she said, "Because if no one knew, it wouldn't hurt so bad, if we decided it wasn't working . . . or if you realized you'd made a big mistake with me. This way I'd have no explaining to do. I'd be a fool only to myself."

Her words washed over him like heavy rain. He looked away, flinching from them; then he looked at her once again. "I'm tired of slippin' around, like we're doin' somethin' wrong. As far as I was brought up, there has never been a sin in two people fallin' in love."

Her eyes lingered on his and shared the moment of truth. She said, "I'd love to come to the Founder's Day celebration with you." Love, vibrant and warm, seeped over her features as she came to him, wrapped her arms around his neck and kissed him thoroughly.

Chapter Ten

Oren stood there, framed in the doorway, a long and lanky figure, his brown hair shiny, his jeans creased sharply, his hat in his hand, and looking at Lorena the way every woman wishes the man she adores would look at her.

"Hi," he said.

"Hi."

His eyes sparkled, and the memory of making love with him, of his body hard and strong, galloped like bright white horses across her mind. They'd had only that one time together. Wednesday night Aunt Esmerelda had come and stayed late, and on Thursday Jaime had arrived, and there had been no time since for privacy. That fact seemed to vibrate between them.

"You look beautiful."

"You look mighty handsome yourself."

His eyes sparkled at her for another full second. Then he stepped forward and kissed her quickly.

Footsteps down the stairs sent them apart and ramrod straight.

"Hi, Oren," Jaime said cheerfully. The two had met the past Thursday and seemed to take to each other; both were easygoing. They shook hands now, and motherly pride swept Lorena as she looked at her son. Her eldest was as tall as Oren, a man now, handsome enough to turn heads, polite and charming. She wondered fleetingly how he'd come to be this way. Had she really had a hand in it?

"We're ready to go," she said. "Let me just get my hat. Jaime, go in the kitchen and get the picnic basket for me, will you?"

"I told you you didn't need to bring anything," Oren said, still lingering in the doorway.

"Everyone brings something to Founder's Day." She stepped away to the table beside the stairs and looked in the mirror to settle her new hat on her head. Today she'd worn a skirt version of pants—a denim riding skirt, which was cooler than tight jeans, and a rose-colored peasant blouse that ruffled around her bare shoulders.

Nicky came down the stairs. His gaze met hers for a bare instant before flicking away.

"Hi, Nick," Oren said.

Nicky nodded. "Hi." He said to Lorena, "I guess I'll see you all out there."

Lorena nodded. "Okay, babe." She moved to give him a kiss, but he quickly sidestepped and headed away to the back of the house. Lorena called to him to make certain the kittens were shut on the laundry porch.

"Nick isn't comin' with us?" Oren asked.

"No…he wants to have the convenience of his own truck, so he can come and go." Of course, she knew it was more than that, but Nick hadn't spoken of it, so she wasn't going to, either. There was always the chance she was being too sensitive.

"Your mom and dad still plannin' on comin' out later?"

"Yes," she said with a nod. "In time to share supper. Daddy said Jesse told him around four o'clock. Mama says it's too hot to stay all afternoon. 'Course, Daddy says it's too hot for anyone to go at all."

So it was just the three of them—and Harvey, of course—driving out in Oren's car. Oren took her arm and walked her around to the passenger side, settling her in the seat and closing the door with gentlemanly flair. Jaime set the basket in the back beside a sniffing Harvey and jumped over the side into the seat.

Nicky pulled out of the driveway. He kept facing straight ahead, as if he didn't want to look at them. No one else was likely to notice, but, as his mother, Lorena knew it was his belligerent expression. Hurt sliced through her.

Oren reached over, took her hand and squeezed it, and she squeezed his in return. She had many fears that she couldn't explain swirling in her heart—but she was very glad to be with this man.

From the back seat Jaime said, "This is some car, Oren. Do you have extra insurance on it as a classic?" Majoring in finance at college, Jaime was selling insurance during the summer break. He was such a go-getter, Lorena thought she wouldn't be surprised if he turned out to be a millionaire by the time he was twenty-five.

Being the first weekend in August, it was hot, but that didn't stop people from turning out. The little town of Wings was a bustling, crowded place. Cars lined the black-topped country road and were parked helter-skelter off into the empty fields. An enormous banner proclaiming Wings Founder's Day was stretched from Cobb's Drugstore across the road to a pole atop Kelly's Tavern and Lemonade Parlor. Awnings abounded, rippling in the strong breeze, providing shelter to those cooking and those selling craft items and those simply sitting and visiting.

Oren took Lorena's hand and led the way, with Jaime walking on Lorena's other side, bringing the picnic basket, and Harvey, tongue lolling, padding at their heels. Lorena tightened inside. What would Oren's family think of her relationship with Oren—of her coming with him, hand in hand? She might have let go of his hand, but Oren held her firmly.

As they approached the green-and-white awning that shaded a long table and benches, Lorena recognized Annie Breen, very pudgy now with child, sitting in a chair. Zoe and Rory and Marnie were there, too, with children playing around them. Nicky stood with Bobby Tafoya, and there was an older man at the table, obviously an old cowboy, whom Lorena didn't know.

Oren pulled her beside him beneath the awning, and she was met with smiling, welcoming faces. The introductions and greetings all around were warm and friendly, as if these people didn't find her and Oren such a strange combination. Her gaze met Oren's, and she saw pure pride and joy glowing in his brilliant blue eyes. Her heart swelled up and spilled all over.

But then she glanced at Nicky. There was an oddly pained expression on his face. Lorena had to stifle the urge to reach out to him.

He turned away to say something to Bobby, and a minute later he called to Jaime to come "cruise" around, as he put it. "See ya later, Mom," Jaime said and touched her shoulder as he passed. Nicky said nothing. As the three of them sauntered away, their laughter and the name Corinne floated back to those remaining under the awning.

Rory chuckled. "I saw Corinne this mornin'. Dale Quevedo was with me, and he dropped his mama's apple pie and then stepped on it for lookin' at her. That doesn't bode well for what may happen with those three boys there. Let's just hope that Corinne doesn't have the same effect on Bobby and Nick that she did back on Oren's birthday, or we all better look out."

The others laughed. Lorena asked, "Just who is this Corinne, and exactly what effect did she have on Nicky and Bobby on Oren's birthday?" The memory of Nicky coming home drunk flashed across her mind.

Eyes swiveled to her and then to Oren. Oren said, "Corinne Hunsicker, one of Otto Hunsicker's ten daughters. She used to be sweet on Rory." Rory blushed, and Zoe playfully pounded on him. "'Course, Corinne, she just likes the fellas," Oren added.

"So... what happened the night of your birthday?"

Oren shrugged. "Oh, the usual when it comes to males and females. The whole reason Nick got into the shape he did that night was because he and Bobby were showin' off for Miss Corinne Hunsicker. Come on, let's us go do some cruisin', too." He took her hand and tugged her up. "We'll see y'all for supper. Stay here and rest, Harvey. You look all tuckered out."

Off Lorena went with Oren, hand in hand. Quite suddenly she laughed. His eyes came around to hers, and they laughed together.

The sky was a vivid blue, the breeze was light, and Oren felt like a man with the world in his hand as he showed Lorena, his queen, around his community and introduced her to his friends and did his best to give her a good time. His good time consisted of simply being with her. That she seemed more than happy to be with him was icing on his cake. Every time he looked at her, he recalled how hot and pliable she had been in his arms. Judging by the gleam in her eyes, he thought she had to be recalling that wondrous time, too.

They went to the Caddie to retrieve Oren's camera, and then headed to where his dad was passing out bowls of his chili, along with five other chili cooks doing the same. Experience had taught the organizers of the day's events not to make an official contest of the chili cooking, because certain male contestants who entered each year tended to get upset if they lost. The year Otto Hunsicker, a loser, threw Treat Lopez, a winner, through Cobb's Drugstore window was the last year of any official competition. Now the chili cook-off consisted of chili cooks showing up and cooking their recipes as a point of pride and fun, and maybe a few mild arguments.

Lorena raved over Big Jesse's chili, just as she was expected to. When he hauled off and kissed her, Lorena was sure surprised. Oren caught it on film. He took a number of shots of his dad and the other chili cooks.

Afterward, she and Oren wandered from booth to booth, looking at the many crafts, baked goods and doodads for sale. Oren bought her a big pink balloon, and they each had their portraits done by a sketch artist. The sketches turned out amazingly well.

Miss Loretta, the postmaster, was the fortune-teller this year. She sat beneath an awning in the tall-backed mahogany-and-velvet chair that belonged on the church pulpit. She was dressed like a gypsy and had her red-and-white hair, which Zoe had dyed for her, hanging down on her shoulders. She was most definitely the best fortune-teller they'd ever had. She made Oren go stand several yards away, and told Lorena's fortune with cards and by looking at her palm. Lorena wouldn't tell him what Miss Loretta had said, and neither would Miss Loretta when he had his fortune done. His fortune was that he was going to gain wealth and fame before he was thirty-five—or maybe he was going to go broke. Miss Loretta said she wasn't a very good card reader. She looked at his palm for a long time, then told him the time was ripe for romance in his life. He told her it always had been.

Kelly was in the dunking booth, and Oren and Lorena both gave tossing the balls a try. Lorena sank him once, and Oren sank him each of his four throws. Oren told him it was for a good cause. All the money raised from Founder's Day went to the fund for building a community building. The work was supposed to begin this fall.

Lorena's parents were there when they went back to join the family for supper. Oren felt Lorena's hand stiffen in his when they approached. He saw her staring at her father, and old Max, with his face looking as if it had been set in concrete, stared at both of them. Lorena seemed to draw away from Oren. He thought for a minute she was going to drop his hand, but she didn't. He wondered if he should let go of her, but he didn't. Old Max might as well accept things right now, he thought. And then Lorena's eyes came around to his, and she squeezed his hand.

However, Petra Sandoval's approval remained solid. Oren felt pretty good about that, until he watched her and old Max for a bit and realized a great deal of her approval stemmed from old Max's disapproval. Well, whatever the reason, Oren thought her manner preferable to old Max's. All through the meal Max scowled at him. Oren was grateful to his dad, because Big Jesse did his best to keep Max's attention. But once Oren happened to see Max looking as if he was about to come over the table at him, and he realized he had his arm draped around Lorena. Oren removed it. There wasn't any need to press things.

As soon after the meal as he could, he spirited Lorena off. He was polite and asked Nick and Jaime to come along to the horseshoe games. Not that he really wanted them to come, and Jaime obviously understood this, as he declined. Smart young man, that Jaime. Nick appeared to decline simply because he was being morose. Oren purposely didn't intend to give Nick's poor mood any thought. He was too involved with enjoying Lorena.

Oren had always loved the game of horseshoes. Lorena had never played, so he gave her instruction, which entitled him to have his hands and body all over her. Joe Shatto winked at him over that, and Oren just grinned. They cheered Rory on in the horse race—he came in third—and then they watched the elementary school kids' pie-eating contest. That was held at the side of Cobb's Drugstore, and afterward Oren managed to steer Lorena around to the back of the building and into the lattice shed built beneath the stairs. It was cool and shady there, and he could steal a few kisses. But a nest of wasps sent Lorena scooting out of there.

As the cool of sunset came, a country-western band began to play, beginning the dance that capped off the day's festivities. It was held in the parking lot of Kelly's Tavern, which had been paved three short months before. The stage for the band was a flatbed hay trailer. Light came from the parking-lot lamps and colored Christmas lights strung from pole to pole.

Lorena was dancing with Oren to a spirited, toe-tapping tune when her father, tugging her mother along, came up.

"Your mother and I are going home," he said, raising his voice above the music.

Her mother added, "Your father has pooped out on me. Oren, would you mind giving me a go-round before we leave?" She lifted her hands to Oren.

His eyebrows rose with mild surprise, and then he smiled good-naturedly. "My pleasure, ma'am." He whirled her away.

Lorena edged her father to the side of the dancers. He scowled and said, "You and your mother are intent on being fools today."

"There's nothing foolish in having a good time, and Mama looks like she's doin' exactly that." Purposely ignoring her father's intended meaning, she tapped her toe to the music and grinned as she watched her mother dancing with Oren. Her mother had an inborn grace that didn't need perfect steps.

"You didn't tell me that you were Oren's date for the day."

"Yes, I did, Daddy. I told you on Thursday."

"The way you told it, I thought he was extending the invitation from his family." Her father's face was set.

"I'm sorry if you misunderstood. He invited me to come with him today and my family to join us."

Her father looked at her sharply, then faced forward, waiting like a statue until Oren escorted her mother back toward them.

"Whew...you wore me out, Mrs. Sandoval," Oren said.

"I appreciate the dance, Oren. I do so love to dance." She shot her husband a pointed look, but he ignored her and said a terse good-night.

Oren cast Lorena a questioning look. "Your dad doesn't seem too happy about something."

"He's not, but he'll get over it." She grinned and squeezed his hand. She was having too wonderful a time to let anything spoil it.

He leaned close. "If I'd known you'd handle him this way, I would have come on a lot stronger a lot sooner."

"Have you really been worried about my father?"

"Well, he is a tough old bird. Retired or not, I figured he could arrange to have me put in jail."

She chuckled. "I imagine he still could."

"I'd better hurry up and get all I can before he does it, then." He kissed her quickly, while his eyes danced with promises. "Your mother really did dance me dry. You wait here, and I'll go get us a couple of drinks."

He went off to the refreshment booth, and Lorena remained on the side, watching the dancers.

Jesse whirled past with his wife, Marnie. The two obviously enjoyed dancing and were a striking couple. Lorena thought how Oren had said Marnie was thirteen years younger than Jesse. The years were not visible on Jesse. Perhaps it was because he was so happy.

Mary Jean waved as she danced by with Tom Ortega. Beyond them, Jaime was dancing with *the* Corinne Hunsicker and seemed to be having a grand time. From the little Lorena had seen of Corinne that day, the young woman certainly appeared to be a charmer of men. Lorena looked for Nicky but couldn't see him.

Suddenly a woman was walking toward Lorena—it was the voluptuous redhead she'd seen with Oren that first night and later at his house, when he'd called the redhead his favorite woman. Lorena had seen her several times that day, flitting all over. In a flouncy red dress and high-heeled sandals, she wasn't someone to be missed. She seemed to have a lot to do with running things. Lorena was surprised to find that up close the woman was obviously a lot older than she appeared from a distance. At least Lorena's age or better.

The woman smiled and stuck out her hand. "I've been hoping for a chance to meet you. I'm Jada Cobb. I own Cobb's Drugstore over there." Her smile was radiant and appeared genuine.

Lorena shook the woman's hand. "Hello. I'm Lorena Venable."

"I know. I asked Jesse." The woman's green eyes inspected Lorena thoroughly, but for some reason Lorena had a little trouble taking offense. "I've been wonderin' what could be keepin' Oren so busy these days. He and I have been doin' some photography together—he's been teaching me. Or he had been, up until a couple of months ago. I figured the only thing that could keep him occupied this long had to be a woman." Her green eyes sparkled with cool mischief. "In case you're wonderin', I'm an old friend of the family. I've known Oren since he was just a kid."

Lorena didn't know what to say to that.

Jada Cobb's eyes seemed to dance. Then her gaze shifted beyond Lorena, to Oren, who came toward them bearing a soft drink cup in each hand. There was a vaguely uneasy look in his eyes.

"I see you two have met," he said, his face mildly flushed. He handed Lorena her drink.

"And no thanks to you," Jada returned, and arched a carefully formed eyebrow. "Why didn't you introduce us earlier? Afraid I'll tell Lorena all the sins of your youth?" There was a decidedly intimate gleam in Jada's eyes.

Oren said, "Well, somethin' like that. What will it take for you to keep quiet?"

Jada's laugh was full and melodious. "I'll think of somethin', honey." She looked directly at Lorena. "I'm truly glad to have met you, and I imagine we'll be seein' more of you. Take care of her, Oren. You have a special lady here." Her hand, with long red nails, very gracefully gave his arm a gentle squeeze, and then she waltzed away.

"She's just an old friend," Oren said.

"Might I guess a very old and *good* friend?"

His mouth quirked into a grin. "Yes…a very good friend, but not like you're thinkin'. And dare I hope that you're just a mite jealous, darlin'?" He lifted his cup to his lips and gazed at her very sexily over the rim.

"Should I be?" she returned with deliberate coolness, and drank from her own cup. After a second she had to add, "She certainly looked at you like someone looks at a lover."

And he laughed. "I'd love you to keep on being jealous. Makes me feel pretty good. But I suppose I should tell you the truth, which is that Jada looks like that at a number of men—not just any man but ones she considers her good friends." He turned more serious and looked out at the dance floor. "She's been a good friend to all of us, but if there was anyone special to her, it was Matt. But that was a long time ago."

Lorena followed his gaze to see him watching Matt and Annie, gazing into each other's eyes, dancing slowly.

"Why didn't you introduce me to her earlier today?" She looked at him out of the corner of her eyes.

He gazed down at her. "I'm not really sure. I just didn't want to deal with it, I guess. I didn't want anything to spoil things for us today."

She reached up and touched his cheek, forgetting that they stood there with hundreds of people. And suddenly she had to blink back tears.

He took the cup from her hand and thrust it and his own into the hands of a man walking past. Then he swept Lorena into his arms and out among the dancers. His palm was warm in hers, and his other pressed the small of her back. His eyes were intent, hot upon her, and there was a kiss there, deep in their depths. Lorena smiled, thinking of intimate things. Oren returned an intimate-thinking smile of his own. And in the midst of the crowd, they were alone.

Lights shone from nearly every window of Lorena's house, and Nick's blue pickup was in the driveway, when Oren pulled to a stop in front.

"I thought they were taking Corinne Hunsicker home," Lorena said. "How in the world could they have gotten here ahead of us?"

"I believe it was Nick drivin' Jaime, who was takin' Corinne home, and no doubt in that situation three was most definitely a crowd. And besides, I was drivin' awfully slow."

"Yes . . . you were."

A slow smile spread her pretty lips, and he shared it. He knew that Lorena, just like himself, was thinking of things a lot more sensual than where everyone was at that moment.

Her gaze drifted down to his lips. She said, "I had a wonderful time today."

"I did, too." He took her hand and rubbed his thumb on her fingers. He wished they were out, parked off Wings Road, in the dark and all alone.

She said, "I'd kiss you, but it isn't easy to be kissin' a man while knowin' your sons have a perfect view."

He nodded and grinned. "I was thinkin' the same thing. Next time I'll remember to put the top up."

She grinned, too, then looked down. "Oren . . . I have to tell you something."

Every cell in his body tensed when she said that, out of the blue. She looked up at him again, and he waited. He saw a struggle going on in her eyes, and he prayed she wasn't about to break off with him.

"All these weeks, when I haven't wanted to tell anyone about us, a lot of it was uncertainty about how I felt . . . how you felt. Wondering what in the world I was gettin' myself into and knowin' it wasn't gonna set well with my parents. Thinkin' I was being crazy." She breathed deeply and swallowed past the lump in her throat. "But I realized today that not wanting to tell anyone, that keeping our relationship a secret, was like when I found out I was pregnant with Nicky. I kept that a secret, didn't even tell Tony for a month after I found out, because it was so special to me, an experience that remained extra special as long as I could hold it to myself. That's what I've been doing with us. You're the best thing that's happened to me since I had my sons. You make me feel things I didn't know I could feel again. I've just wanted to hold what we have to myself and savor it, without having it touched by anyone else. It wasn't shame over you, or us . . . never that. It was a treasuring."

She peered up at him almost hesitantly. He felt emotion wash over him like a powerful wave, saw the tears in her eyes and felt as if there were tears inside himself. He knew what it had cost her to reveal herself. And he realized suddenly that the past week had produced a shift between them. At last Lorena had come to see him as a man. A man she could lean on, could take from and give to.

Slowly, gently, forgetting about being in plain sight of others, he kissed her. Her body trembled against him, and it was hard to break away.

But sitting there with her wasn't helping him one bit, so, purposefully, he drew her from the car and walked her to the house. "I don't need to tell you I wish I didn't have to leave you here."

"I wish you didn't... but this is where reality sets in." Both her voice and her gaze reminded him, as if testing. "What are you doing tomorrow?" she asked when they reached the door. "Mama and Daddy are comin' for brunch before Jaime leaves. Would you like to join us?"

He shook his head. "I'd rather keep my skin, which your father is bound to be after. Besides, I promised Dad and Jada that I'd help with the cleanup back in Wings."

Then he kissed her again, a kiss that promised deeper things. And as he opened the door he whispered close to her ear, "And anticipation is half the fun."

Anticipation.

It washed over Lorena like water over pebbles in a stream. Now that she'd crossed the biggest hurdle and begun making love with Oren, she couldn't seem to keep her mind from thinking of it all the time.

She was like a young woman in love, she reflected with amusement.

Oh, my, but she wasn't so young any longer. However, she was undoubtedly totally in love. And it was the grandest time of her life.

The following morning, as she prepared brunch for her family, she was strung tighter than a banjo string. When Oren sneaked into her kitchen and kissed the back of her neck she practically went through the ceiling.

He laughed and put his arms around her, then pulled her hard against him. They kissed, deeply and fiercely, and fire leaped into her blood. The next instant she pushed him away and turned as if to hide, though there was no hiding from herself.

"Oren . . . the boys! They're just upstairs."

"Let me remind you that they aren't boys," he said, a good-natured grin on his lips and sex in his eyes as he tried to pull her to him.

She resisted and said smartly, "They are men grown, but I'm still their mother, and they aren't gonna see me any other way. Would you?"

That set him straight. "I guess I wouldn't," he admitted, dropping his hand.

"I thought you had to go out to Wings?" Suddenly she was hopeful that his plans had changed. "Can you stay after all?"

But he shook his head. "I just brought your basket and balloon. You left them in the car last night." He inclined his head, and Lorena saw the basket, with the balloon attached, sitting on the washer. He obviously saw her fallen expression, because he added, "Besides, absence makes the heart anticipate."

"Pretty certain of yourself, aren't you?" Lorena quipped, trying to appear cool, while inside her pulse hammered with longing.

His gaze was level. "Yes, ma'am, I am."

She smacked the dishrag at him, and he grabbed at her. His intention to push her up on the counter was clear in his eyes. Laughing, she eluded him. He was grabbing for her and she was smacking at his hands when Nicky walked in.

Lorena felt like a naughty little girl. Oren slowly straightened, and his face turned pink. Nicky stared, that horribly blank expression on his face.

"Hi, Nick," Oren said.

"Sorry to interrupt," Nick said tersely, and, his eyes carefully averted, he went to the sink. "I spilled a can of soda upstairs."

He got a cloth, and Lorena handed him a spray bottle of cleaner. He left without making eye contact, and pain sliced through Lorena.

Oren raised an eyebrow to her. "Is he angry—about us?"

"Well...I don't think he's happy about it. Jaime doesn't seem to care, but Nicky... You know, I would have thought it would be the other way around. Jaime was my firstborn. We were always so close. But these last years it's just been Nicky and me. He never seemed to pay me much attention, but he did know I was always here—just Mom."

Understanding glimmered in Oren's eyes. He reached for her, and she went into his embrace. He smoothed her hair, and she held on to him.

He said, "I'll talk to him."

But she shook her head. "Leave him be for now. It's best to wait for him to bring it up if he wants to talk. If he decides to let it pass, he won't appreciate having had it pressed upon him."

"But it hurts you."

Those words brought tears to her eyes, yet she chuckled. "It goes with the territory of being a mother."

He squeezed her to him and kissed the top of her head. It occurred to her that it had been many a year since anyone had held and comforted her, had tried to support her. She looked up at him, searching his face. There was a clear and uncommon strength in this man that she had overlooked all this time because she'd been seeing the years of difference between them, not the years of possibilities. She smiled at him, and he smiled at her.

The next instant her father appeared in the doorway. Oren dropped his tight embrace, but Lorena didn't move away from him. She had nothing to be ashamed of.

Her father's scowl deepened thunderously. "You here again?" he said to Oren.

Oren answered, "I don't know if it qualifies as again, but yes, sir, I'm here." There was respect in his tone, but not deference, no backing down in front of her father's powerful personality.

Her mother's heels pattered on the floor, and she pushed around her husband, still standing in the middle of the opening. "Well, hello, Oren. Nice to see you." Her mother's voice and eyes were alight with speculation. "Here's the fruit plate, Lorena. The melons are just wonderful this year." She began uncovering the dish she'd brought. "Are you joining us, Oren?"

"No, ma'am. I have to be goin'. I'll call you later," he said to Lorena. "Nice to have seen you," he added politely to her parents.

He left by the back way, and no sooner had the door closed than her father said, "You can't be serious about this. Oren Breen? Good Lord, he's a cloud-head, without an ounce of ambition. And what is he—five, six years younger than you are?"

"Ten, Daddy."

His eyebrows shot upward, and her mother said, "If you're worried about that, Max, what did you say to Jesse when he brought home Marnie, a woman almost young enough to be his daughter?"

"That's different."

"Why is that different?" her mother asked with a careful calm. "Just because Jesse is a man?"

"Absolutely," her father said. "And don't start on me, Petra, about equality of the sexes. While the sexes are as equal as two plus two, they are as different as one from a hundred and one. And, besides, Oren Breen *is* a cloud-head." He left the room on that note and, not to be outdone, Lorena's mother called after him.

"He may be a cloud-head, but at least he's a living, breathing male who likes to dance!"

Watching them both, Lorena had a suspicion that her parents' remarks to each other were only partially related to herself and Oren.

Her suspicions were proven correct when, as she and her mother were alone in the kitchen, cleaning up, her mother said out of the blue, "It's no different for us, you know."

SUMMERTIME

Lorena waited for more to come. Nothing did. Her mother was at the sink, scrubbing a pan with vigor.

So Lorena said, "What isn't different, Mama?"

Her mother said, "People think when you get older you don't fight... that you don't fight and you don't have passion. People don't realize that while the body ages, the mind has absolutely no age. A person can be just as immature at seventy as they were at fifteen. Your father is that way."

Oh, boy, Lorena thought. She really didn't want to hear this. She didn't want to be privy to her parents' struggle, but she was obliged to listen because she was her mother's only child, and a child should be a comfort to her parent, and besides, she was standing right there and there was no escape.

"I like to dance," her mother said next. "I've always liked to dance, and your father used to. I like flowers, too. I'd like him to bring me flowers... and to watch the late show in his arms... and to hold his hand. I always liked when he would kiss the back of my neck. Your father was a wonderful lover because he knew all the little things that went into it. He was never one to rush."

Lorena *really* didn't want to hear this. She broke in. "If you're sayin' Daddy's takin' you for granted, Mama, then I certainly understand. I think you and Daddy should go away for a long weekend, so you can discuss it. This is really something private between you two... something you two need to talk about." Realizing she was about to polish a hole in the glass she was drying, she put it down.

"I *have* discussed it with your father. He says he's old and that's that. The rub is that *I'm* not old. Oh, I'm his age, but I'm not old. It's all a state of mind. You know, the mind is the most important sexual organ for a human."

Lorena didn't say anything. She felt as uncomfortable and warm as if wearing an itchy sweater. She dried a glass, put it in the cabinet and took up another. She was unnerved and at first didn't know why. Then she realized that she was glimpsing yet another phase in her mother's life, a life that might resemble her own someday.

She didn't know anything else to do but put her arm around her mother's shoulders. "I love you, Mama." She couldn't recall saying that more than half a dozen times in all her years.

Her mother was surprised, and then a tender light lit her eyes. "I love you, too, darling." Her mother had never said the words much, either, and Lorena was surprised at the effect they had on her.

Then her mother, almost as if making a great discovery, said, "And, darlin', that is most precious—we should take what love we can while we may."

Her words seemed to hang in the air and echo inside Lorena.

Then her mother said, "Lorena, if you could find it in your heart to spare one, I'd like one of your kittens."

"Yes...I think you should have one—and Daddy should have one, too."

Chapter Eleven

Oren whistled as he walked along the hot concrete walk. He held a bouquet of bright flowers, and his heart floated in his chest. He was going to see his *lady*. He wasn't hiding it anymore.

He'd told Lorena he would come for her tonight at seven, but he couldn't wait that long, so he thought he'd drop in and see if she'd go to lunch with him. Oh, he knew she would get on him about how some people had to work—and he'd just tell her how great it was that he didn't have to be bound by such conventions.

"Mind your *p*'s and *q*'s, Harvey. This is a stuffy bank, and like as not they don't appreciate havin' a dog come to visit."

His boots echoed loudly on the parquet flooring; Harvey's toenails made a faint tapping sound. Prima looked up from behind the teller counter. She smiled, then looked pointedly at the flowers and raised her eyebrows. Oren grinned.

Lorena's door was open. She sat behind her desk, her attention focused on her computer, as usual. Oren stood for a minute just looking at her, at her shiny brown hair, the curve of her cheek, her small, firm shoulders. As if sensing his presence, she turned and looked at him. A bright, welcoming smile swept her face.

Oren stepped forward. "Hello, darlin'." He gave her the flowers with a flourish.

"Oh...Oren. They're beautiful." Breathless wonder echoed in her voice, and he felt mountain tall.

"So are you." He kissed her, right there, across the desk, quickly, but pulling away slowly.

Her face turned red, and her eyes shifted self-consciously past him. "People can see...."

"Do you care?"

Her eyes danced. "No."

"Can you go to lunch with me?"

"Don't you ever work?"

"Not if I can help it."

"I..." She glanced at her computer, then grinned at him. "Oh, this can wait another hour. Where shall we go?" She grabbed her purse.

"How about Amarillo?" he said, taking her hand and spiriting her out of the office and across the lobby, casting a wave at the smiling faces all staring their way. Even while she protested that she couldn't possibly go all the way down to Amarillo, he held on to her, and once outside the doors he broke into a jog, feeling the need to get her away from the bank before she could have second thoughts or something important could grab her away from him. Laughing, she came along. Catching their high emotions, Harvey padded off ahead of them with a rare spurt of energy.

They went to Amarillo for the entire afternoon, where they lunched on hamburgers at an old drive-in, took in the Quarter Horse Museum, perused a giant pet supply store where Harvey could join them, went to an elaborate photography store, where Harvey came, too, and where Oren bought film so he could take more pictures—he'd been taking them all day.

Harvey waited in the car while they capped their day with supper at the fanciest place in town, never mind that Oren wore jeans and a sport shirt and Lorena a simple blouse and trousers. Oren felt like a king with his queen. He wined her and dined her and danced her and drove her home in the intimate privacy of his grand pink chariot, with his arm draped around her shoulders and the sensual strains of Johnny Lee filling the air. It was a perfect time to ask her to marry him.

He'd thought about it off and on, he guessed, since he'd begun seeing her. And seriously since he'd slept with her. There was something about their sleeping together that made him feel he was already committed to her, certain there would never be another woman for him. He was ready for the public words and legal piece of paper that had seemed so unimportant before.

He thought he might be rushing things for Lorena, though. She had to think about everything six ways from Sunday, so he figured he'd better get started at persuading.

So he said, "You know, we could get married tonight."

She cut her eyes to him. The greenish glow of the dash lights shone on her face and her creamy neck. "You've been crazy all day. What happened—did you hit your head this mornin'?"

"I got up in love this mornin'."

She looked at him then and smiled slowly. "Me, too."

"Then what do you say, little darlin'? Huh? Wanna get hitched?" He made light of it, knowing she was going to refuse, back up, as she had when he'd first sought to get her to simply go out with him.

She chuckled. "Well, not tonight. I'm not dressed for it."

"We don't want to put this off very long, you know. Our lives are tickin' away, and I don't want to waste a minute of them."

She didn't answer. He glanced down at her. Their eyes met. She said, "I don't think we are." And he knew what she meant. And he noted, too, that she hadn't said an outright no.

All his instincts told him not to press. Lorena was like a donkey, and that was okay to say, because Oren had a high respect for donkeys. They were as reliable as the sunrise and as loyal as a hound dog, but they could also be very stubborn. All properties he could ascribe to Lorena. If you tried to push Lorena into anything, she naturally wanted to resist. She might out-and-out refuse, and he didn't want that. So he said no more. He'd planted the seed. Now he would wait to see what came about in her mind.

She invited him to stay the night, and he did. It was only their second time together, and they were as eager and excited as on their first. He made love to her in her bed, her scent and body all around him. Her passion took his breath. It was the stuff a man's dreams were made of.

The following morning he awoke, very tired, to find her already up and dressing.

"I have to catch up on all the work I let go yesterday," she said. "And I have a young couple coming in to see about a mortgage first thing at nine."

"How can you be so chipper at this time of the mornin'?" he grumbled.

Perky as a puppy, she came over and kissed him. "Because you have filled me with energy!"

He grabbed her and told her the young couple could wait, and she said she didn't want to do that to them. However, with him making breakfast, he had her to himself for another forty-five minutes.

That night he brought in fajitas, but just as soon as they'd eaten she led him to the door.

"I have to work tonight," she said. "Positively."

"I could watch television until you finish," he said.

"You wouldn't. You'd tempt me at every turn."

He grinned. "Maybe...maybe not. I can promise not."

"And I wouldn't trust you...or me." She chuckled. "You are simply too irresistible, Mr. Breen. And I need to work. I've been spending too much time thinkin' about you when I should have been workin'." Her smile was spicy sweet.

"And maybe you need your space," he said, reading between the lines.

She looked deep into his eyes. "Maybe I do." Her eyes searched his. "You understand?"

He nodded. "I guess I need a little of it myself," he admitted, suddenly realizing he did need time for himself.

She smiled with warm relief, then pushed him out the door. With her face poked around it, she said, "I do love you, Oren Breen."

"Bet you say that to all the fellas." He peered at her, his face near hers in the crack of the door.

"Oh...you!"

"I love you, Lorena. Let me back in to show you. Then I'll go home," he teased.

But she firmly pushed him away. He saw the flicker of fear in her eyes, heard a hint of panic in her voice when she said, "Go. We need some time apart. It's too fast."

So he went, knowing she was right, feeling a bit of fear at the power of his own emotions, yet also some relief at being on his own for an evening, even though he was longing for her. He must be in love, because he certainly did feel inside out.

After Oren left, Lorena wondered if she was losing her mind. She was at once glad to be alone and wishing she hadn't told him to go. With every moment she was falling deeper and deeper in love with him. What was going to happen? Where could they go? Marriage?

That scared her to death. So much separated them—yet her heart would not discount the idea.

The following evening Lorena had supper prepared when Oren arrived at her front door. She had romantic music playing softly and candles on the table. She took his hand and pulled him inside, leading him across the living room.

He stopped and jerked her back into his arms, then kissed her until her toes curled. "Food can wait," he told her. "I've missed you." And sweeping her into his arms, he headed for the bedroom.

She whispered into his neck, "So much for putting space between us."

As he laid her upon the bed she thought how she had to come to her senses...how this couldn't go on...how she would have to come down to earth...and she would...later.

For now she was a woman, with a woman's knowledge of exactly what she wanted and needed, and exactly what she was risking, for nothing in this world came without a price. And she knew, too, what she had to give, and how for her, at her time of life, all of this was a rare, fine thing and might never come again.

She kissed him, inhaled the man scent of him, took him into her and allowed rational thoughts to fade away. For now she chose this.

It came for them both as a mountain fire roaring to the peak, leaving them sweaty and pulsing and smiling foolishly at each other.

Later, while they were eating their supper in bed, both still nude, Oren asked her again to marry him. Her breath stopped in her throat as she saw the deep, sincere look in his beautiful blue eyes.

She adjusted the sheet covering her breasts and dodged the question. "Why not watch the late show instead?" she quipped, and twirled spaghetti noodles on her fork.

He didn't answer, only remained very still. She felt his intense gaze forcing her to look up at him.

"We can't go on..." He gestured and raked a hand through his hair. He broke the gaze and slid over to put his feet on the floor. "We can't keep doin' this and not talk about marriage, Lorena. It doesn't fit either of us. I may have slept with a woman once, even twice, and not felt any joinin' with her. Not felt anything more than a great physical release, to put it bluntly." His eyes came around to hers. "But I've made love to you more than three times, and that's something I've never done with a woman before. I love you, Lorena, and I want you all the time."

She reached out for him; she had to touch him, had to hold on to him. "It takes so much, though, to make a marriage. Love and desire are only a part of it."

"They're a hell of a beginnin', and I've always figured the rest came with time."

"Oren..." She breathed deeply. "I'm forty. Marrying me wouldn't be like you were marrying a woman who was lookin' ahead, thinkin' of children and later a career. I've raised my children and now I have my career."

"Does that mean you don't look ahead at life? That you're done with it?"

Startled, she said, "No, of course not. It's just that... I don't look at things the same as I did twenty years ago."

"Did it ever occur to you that that's what draws me to you? I want a woman who is full and ripe, not green and just a little tart."

She supposed she hadn't thought of that. Yet her mind demanded that she object. "I don't know if I could have another child, and the chances for something being wrong with a child I bear are so much greater."

"Have I said anything about wantin' children?"

That stopped her—and seemed to prove her point. "No. That's just it. We don't know enough about each other's plans to consider marriage."

"Then let's get to know everything."

"Oren . . ."

But he wouldn't let her beg off. He removed their dishes o a tray and propped himself carefully on a pillow. "Okay. don't really want a kid. I have a baby half sister and a nephew and nieces and another of those on the way. I'm the youngest of my brothers, and I guess maybe in some ways I never grew up. Whatever the reason, I just don't hanker after progeny. I'd rather get to be fun Brother and Uncle Oren and leave all the dirty parts of child-rearing to my dad and brothers."

"You say that now, but—"

"I say it now just like I said it ten years ago. I'm not sayin' I wouldn't love a child, but given a choice, I've just never felt the compulsion to have one." The truth was in his eyes.

But Lorena had to say, "What if I wanted a child?" Suddenly it seemed a possibility. Heavens . . . many women her age had children.

"If you want one, I'll do my best to give you one, darlin'," he said in a sexy tone.

She tried something else. "Where would we live?"

"Where do you want to live?"

"Here. I like my house." He wouldn't want that; he would want his own place, in the country.

But he said, "Okay," and gazed at her calmly, his eyes parkling.

"You're going to agree with everything I say, aren't you?"

"Yep."

"You're impossible!"

He took her wrist and pulled her down beside him. They kissed, and she held on to him.

He whispered into her ear, "Say maybe."

And she said, very softly, hopefully, fearfully, "Maybe."

"We'll work it out as we go along, darlin'. We don't have o have all the answers right at the start, you know."

She pulled back and gazed into his beautiful eyes. "I love you, Oren. And that's why I want to wait. I truly believe we should have more time."

She'd failed at marriage once, and she was frightened of trying it again. And she truly believed *he* should have more time, that he was going too fast for his own good. But she wouldn't tell him that, for he would say she was trying to think for him. Still, to her, this was the greatest gift she could offer him.

However, there was another gift that Lorena could give Oren—and herself—and that was to see about birth control. The following day she made an appointment with her doctor. She told the receptionist, and herself, it was just for a checkup, but deep inside she couldn't deny that she was doing this with the thought of marriage ahead.

During the rest of the week and into the next Oren and Lorena sneaked away for lunch, had supper out and brought supper in. They went all the way to Santa Fe for a large rodeo, where Oren took pictures. This time he'd been hired by the promoters to do professional shots for a publicity brochure. Lorena was quite impressed by him, but he shrugged it off nonchalantly, as was his way. His daring in getting some of them set Lorena's teeth on edge, but she had never felt so alive.

They watched movies at home on the sofa, sharing a bowl of popcorn, and played with the kittens and Harvey. Oren helped her with a new program on her computer, and she helped him with framing and hanging some of his photographs. It was then that she saw the photos that he'd taken of her the first night they met.

She chanced upon them when helping him get the framed prints that he'd stacked in his bedroom. There were three shots of her; one of them had parts of Prima and Mary Jean in it, too. Two hung near the head of his bed and one, the clearest close-up, sat on his nightstand. She stood there and stared.

"I've had them since that night," he said in a low voice. She turned to see him leaning against the doorframe. "I would look at them and dream of you, even before I knew who you were."

She could find nothing to say to that, but over the following days she would recall those pictures and the wonder would rise and tumble in her heart. She thought how she and Oren had been drawn together from the very first, for though she'd had no actual picture of him, his image from that first meeting had remained in her mind, too.

The days of summer were full and ripe for them. During those days they allowed themselves to be immersed in their own private world. They slept together twice more and that was all, as if each was holding back, waiting for their desire to reach the prime, dizzy peak before succumbing to its richness. For Lorena, it was a savoring of an experience she would hold to her heart and relive, treasure, thinking that perhaps each time would be the last.

Their private world was interrupted during the weekend—Friday night to Monday morning—when Nick came home. And for once, much to Oren's annoyance, Nick showed no interest in going off with his friends. No, sir, he made certain to be in whatever room Oren and Lorena were in and to make sure his mother knew he would be waiting for her return on Saturday, when she and Oren went off to the rodeo. He had designated himself the duenna, and a strict one, at that. His presence meant any physical contact between Oren and Lorena was kept to a bare minimum when they were at the house, and Lorena wouldn't stay long away from the house, either.

Oren was at first irritated with her for her coolness toward him in Nick's presence. However, he soon discovered it was a difficult thing to kiss a woman with her son looking on with a suspicious, disapproving eye. Each time Oren

spoke an endearment, reached for Lorena's hand or dared
to plant a quick peck on her cheek, he quite suddenly felt
like a thief and a perverted lecher.

He supposed he *was* a thief to Nick, who had for so long
had his mother to himself, had been the only man in her life.
Once, when their eyes met, Oren clearly saw the challenge
there. Nick was ready to fight for his mother. And Oren
wondered, if it did come down to a fight, whom Lorena
would choose.

He did not feel she would choose him over her son, so he
wanted to avoid a contest at all costs.

Early one morning Oren rode with Rory and the hands to
move cattle to fresh range. He'd gone along to take Matt's
place, because these days, with Annie's advancing pregnancy, schedules were arranged so that Matt could stay close
to home.

Oren had gone out eagerly. It had come upon him suddenly, this need to be out in the open, to feel a horse beneath him and the golden rays of the rising sun on his
shoulders, to rest his eyes on rolling hills of grass. It seemed
so long since he'd done so. He rode along, following the
slowly moving cattle, occasionally jogging off to nudge
strays back to the herd. He couldn't help thinking about
Lorena and speculating that she would enjoy this. He was
bringing a cow and her calf back when Nick rode up beside
him.

Nick didn't say anything at first. Oren offered how it was
a nice day. Still Nick didn't say anything. So Oren said how
the delicious chicken chili Lorena had fixed last night for
supper still had him filled this morning.

"Your mom is sure a good cook. No wonder you've
grown up so big." He figured this was about Lorena, so he
might as well open the conversation with her.

Nick cocked an eye at him. "You never did say anything
to Mom about me wreckin' your Cadillac."

Oren, feeling his way through this, said, "There wasn't any need. It was your business, and you paid to have it fixed."

Nick looked thoughtful, then squinted at Oren. "And just maybe you thought that would win you points with me. Give you a way to my mom." The challenge was clear in his eyes and in his voice.

Oren shrugged. "If you want to see it that way. But the truth is that I don't care one way or the other about winnin' points with you, *sonny*. I certainly don't need to use you to get to your mother."

Anger flashed in the younger man's dark eyes, and he bristled up like a porcupine. "You're sittin' in a sweet spot right now with my mom, but all it would take is a word from me and she'd shut her door right in your face."

Oren lifted his reins and halted his horse, focusing intently on Nick. "You think so, do you?"

Nick glowered and swiped his hand beneath his nose, then pointed at Oren. "I'm warnin' you. If you hurt her, I'll come after you. I don't care that you are a Breen and older. I'll come after you and mess up that pretty face of yours that the women are all so crazy for."

"I'm not aimin' to hurt your mom, Nick. I love her."

Nick cast him a skeptical look.

Oren said, "I intend to marry your mother. I intend to be there for her . . . when you and Jaime are off to school and jobs and your own families."

Nick glanced off in the distance.

"That she makes room for me doesn't shut you out, Nick. You're her son and always will be, but she has a right to her own life. She has a right to have someone share her life, especially when you're gone."

Nick shook his head and again focused his angry eyes on Oren. "You aren't good enough for my mom and never will be." With a kick to his horse, he loped away.

Oren pulled a handkerchief from his pocket and wiped a dribble of blood from his nose. Well, he thought, it could have gone worse. They could have gotten into a fistfight.

He worried that Nick might say that word to Lorena, that he might give her an ultimatum to be done with Oren. And, despite the confidence he showed Nick, Oren truly didn't know what Lorena would do. He feared she would please her son before she would follow her own heart.

Maybe it wasn't playing fair, but Oren made certain Nick had plenty to keep him busy at the ranch until dark. He didn't want to chance the younger man getting into town to speak to Lorena before he did.

He picked Lorena up from work and took her all the way to Raton for a romantic steak dinner. When they returned home he again asked her to marry him.

She pulled out of his embrace and raked a hand through her hair. "Oh, Oren . . . I don't want to rush into this."

"Lorena, I knew you were the woman for me the first time I met you—which was darn near four months ago, and I don't call that rushin'. And how long it's been doesn't make a difference. I'm not gonna change my mind about how I feel about you six months or six years from now, and I don't think you will, either."

"One thing I've learned is that none of us knows how we'll feel about anything tomorrow, much less six months from now. Marriage won't change that. Six months from now you could end up waking up and finding yourself married and wishing you weren't."

"I imagine that could happen sometime, but isn't that what marriage is about—dealin' with the changes together?"

Still she shook her head, then gazed at him with her warm brown eyes. "Waiting won't hurt anything. It can only be a good thing. Don't rush this, Oren. If it's real, it will be here tomorrow and the day after that and the day after that."

But Oren thought about Nick and old Max and how they could come between them.

She stepped forward, a sultry look in her eyes. He took a step backward and said, "If you don't want to marry me, we don't need to be sleepin' together." He waited.

Lorena stood there feeling slapped across the face. "If that's what you want." She spoke with careful quiet.

They dueled a moment with their eyes. Oren turned and walked out. The door shut behind him.

Lorena stood there in the middle of her living room, alone. Her chest felt so heavy that she could hardly get a breath. Anger swirled, but only for a moment, before sorrow drained all energy out her toes. She looked around, almost uncertain of where she was. It was as if a sudden whirlwind had come and swept her bare. She'd thought they would be together tonight...had thought of them making love...the clean, fresh sheets she'd put on the bed...the way she felt so full within his arms.

She walked to the stairs and rested a hand on the newel post. A great black hole of loneliness opened in her heart.

She hadn't meant to hurt him with her refusal—and it really wasn't a refusal. She'd only said to wait. What was so wrong with that? She'd meant to do the right thing for him. And maybe the right thing would be to break off. How could she marry him? Did they really have a chance?

The black hole of loneliness threatened to swallow her.

And then the front door opened with a soft creak. Lorena lifted her head to see Oren peeking around.

"Can I change my mind?" His grin was tender, electric.

Her heart soared. She rushed at him, and he grabbed her up into his arms. He kissed her, hard and deep and claiming. The next instant he slammed the door closed with his foot, swept her into his arms and carried her into the bedroom.

* * *

The room was bright with sunlight when Oren awoke.
Lorena's moving had awakened him. She was slipping gently
from bed. Peeking with one eye, he watched her graceful
movements and enjoyed a great view of all her creamy
curves.

She disappeared into the bathroom. He lay there waiting
to hear the shower running and recalling how it had been
with them in the night. He smiled. He heard the water start,
slipped quietly into the bathroom and opened the shower
door.

He scared her; she gave a small cry and almost smacked
him with the washcloth. He took her into his arms, and they
laughed together as the water pelted their heads, ran down
their bodies. His skin was slippery against hers. Hers felt like
warm velvet against his palm. He lathered his hands and
washed her. She did the same for him, until they were both
a lot hotter than the water coming from the shower head.

She said he'd planned this, and he said he hadn't, not really. She said they needed to get out, and he agreed. What
he needed was in the nightstand drawer. But, somehow,
neither of them made a move to part. The touching, kissing
and pelting hot water held them captive. And then neither
of them could say anything, and Oren could only think of
her body caressing him and the desire pounding through him
and how relief was a scant, warm, wet inch away.

Her breath came hard against his neck, and her small
whimper reverberated in his ear. As he took her to him, he
had the quick thought, a slice of fear, that this could be his
last time. He tossed the fear aside, but it caused him to hold
her tight, to drive into her, to savor the emotions and sensations that he'd never felt before, for this was the woman
he loved with all his heart.

"I'm sorry," he said, kissing the top of her wet head and
looking at her in the mirror. He thought how her pink terry

robe made her look beautiful. He really was sorry for taking the risk, he told her with his eyes.

She gave him a shaky smile. "I don't think you did it all by yourself." Then she turned and wrapped her arms around his waist. He had a towel around his hips, but his body hadn't forgotten how she felt against him. "I've made a doctor's appointment. I couldn't get in until Monday, but I'll see about getting a diaphragm." And the sparkle in her eyes told him that she was planning for the future.

"I'll get the coffee," he said and left, suddenly buoyant. Nothing like a little sex in the morning with the woman he loved to get a man going, he thought.

A few minutes later, when old Max walked into the kitchen, Oren thought that there was nothing like a little sex in the morning to get him into big trouble—in more ways than one.

He was pouring water into the coffeemaker when he heard the back door opening, then, "Damn, blasted cats." He recognized Max Sandoval's voice and saw a kitten come scurrying into the kitchen. The next instant, just as he was debating whether he should run or duck behind the island, old Max appeared in the laundry-room doorway.

The older man stopped dead-still and stared. His thick, iron-gray hair seemed to stand on end, his sharp features to turn to granite. His gaze moved from Oren's head to his feet—and Oren felt as if the towel he wore wasn't there at all—while fire seeped up into his eyes and flooded his face.

Oren said, "Good mornin'." Nothing else came to mind.

"What in the hell are you doing in my daughter's kitchen...like that?" Max's long arm came up, and his hand gestured violently.

"I'm makin' coffee." Oren lifted the now-empty pot as evidence, then jammed it in place in the coffeemaker. He wanted to run for the bedroom and his clothes—his single towel made him feel distinctly vulnerable—but he figured flight wouldn't help his case. He smiled. "Would you like some?"

Something like, "Arrggghhrraaa" came out of Max Sandoval's mouth.

Chapter Twelve

Oh, my Lord, it was her father! She recognized his bellow. With the curling iron wrapped in her hair, she turned for the door, then remembered the curling iron and struggled to get the thing untangled from her tresses.

As she emerged from the bathroom, Oren sauntered into the bedroom. "We have company."

Her father shouted, "What do you mean runnin' around my daughter's house without your clothes?"

Harvey gave a low growl, and Oren silenced him. Then he raised an eyebrow at her as he said to her father, who was now towering in the bedroom doorway, "I'll get dressed now, if you'll give me a minute." Calmly he moved to collect his clothes from the floor where they'd been tossed all helter-skelter, obviously in great haste, the previous night. Heat flooded Lorena's face when she saw her pink bra draped over the oak nightstand. Retrieving it now would only call attention to it. She whirled to confront her father, who stood there furious as boiling black clouds.

"Daddy, there's no need to yell. We can hear you perfectly well."

His eyes blazed at her. "I certainly thought I raised you better than this, Lorena Maria." He gestured at Oren. "Carrying on like a common...and with this...this...cloudhead." He'd obviously wanted to say something stronger than cloud-head, but Max Sandoval lived by a strict code.

"You certainly raised me better than to go into someone's house without knocking."

"Since when do I have to knock on your door? I do have my own key."

"A key you should use with discretion, Daddy."

Oren, clothes in hand, came to stand at her shoulder. She felt his calm strength and gazed up at her father. Would she ever fully get over feeling like a child with this man? she wondered fleetingly, and stood a little taller, tilting her chin up.

"If that's the way you feel about it," he said, his voice cold as winter glass, "here is your key." He held the key out to her.

"Oh, Daddy..."

"Take it." Pain flickered in his eyes. "I apologize for intruding. Go right on with what you were doing, by all means." He turned smartly and left.

Lorena and Oren looked at each other. Slowly, gently, the laughter came. Oren said, "Why do I suddenly feel I should be spanked?"

"Because that's my father's specialty—making people feel exactly like that." Then she went into his arms, pressed her nose into his sweet-smelling skin and held him to her almost with urgency.

He lifted her clear off the floor and twirled her around. His voice sounded raspy in her ear. "If you'll marry me, your father would feel much better."

"Or kill you." Strange tears welled into her eyes.

She pulled back and looked into his sparkling, beautiful, magnificent blue eyes. "I love you, Oren. I really, truly do."

He gave a whoop and twirled her again. Her heart rose like a balloon borne on a fresh spring breeze. She almost told him she'd marry him . . . but something held her back.

The realities of life had too strong a hold on her.

Lorena made time that morning to pay her parents a visit. Their house was a rambling brick ranch, heavy with the Spanish tones of their heritage. Large pots filled with colorful flowers dotted the walk and filled the entry courtyard. With some trepidation she opened the iron gate and entered the small courtyard. She dreaded an argument with her father.

She could see everything from his point of view—she simply didn't happen to agree with him. His ideology had always been very different from her own. Her father saw things as cut-and-dried, and he had a very rigid set of rules that he lived by. He'd never felt happiness was a requirement of living, and she had always believed—perhaps suspected was a better word—that, if not a requirement, happiness at least had an important place. She thought in that instant that what she'd been learning from Oren was that happiness was very much indeed a requirement for living, and it was in the degree to which one found true happiness that one was truly alive.

Her mother opened the heavy, dark door and cast her a mischievous smile. "Come to see your father, dear?" she said sweetly.

Lorena stepped inside, and immediately the familiar, dear scents enveloped her—her father's after-shave, her mother's flowers, the aging air conditioner. "You heard about it, I presume."

"That you and Oren are sleeping together? Oh, yes, though I didn't find it any surprise. Your father didn't, either, of course, no matter how much he's blustering. He knew it, or at least, that it was a distinct possibility. He simply didn't care to find out so clearly. It tells him that Oren, after all, isn't some passing fancy for you. Oh, the pain of it to him.'' Her eyes settled softly on Lorena. "But this is what he needs—a little shaking up. He's in his study, and I'm sure he's waiting, hoping you'll come.'' She inclined her head toward the door down the hall and quietly, gracefully walked away, her footsteps growing silent on the sitting-room carpet.

Lorena knocked on the door. "Daddy?'' She poked her head in.

Sitting behind his big desk, her father peered over his glasses. "Shouldn't you wait for an answer before you open the door?''

She withdrew and pulled the door shut, and he called for her to stop that nonsense and come on in. She did.

Her father sat behind his large desk, tall bookcases lining the walls behind him. She stopped beside him, but he didn't look at her and kept his gaze on the newspaper spread in front of him. She kissed his cheek.

"I'm not angry with you,'' she said, thinking the best tack was to go on the offensive.

"Humph,'' he grunted, glancing at her and then back to the newspaper in front of him. "He was here earlier,'' he said gruffly. "Your paramour.''

"Oren?''

"Do you have more than one?''

When he kept his eyes focused on the paper, she said, a little timidly, "What happened? I hope you two didn't fight.''

"Now what do you think we did? Sit and have cigars and drinks together?'' He snapped the paper. "I sent him away with a bloody nose.''

"You hit him?''

He shook his head, folding his paper and setting it aside. "Nope. Didn't have to. He gets a bloody nose when he gets mad, has since he was a boy—had some good ones in my courtroom—so I guess he hasn't grown up enough to rid himself of the habit. Didn't you know that? Seems like you should...since you know him so *intimately*." He folded his hands and leaned back in his chair, very much lord of his court.

"I do know that, Daddy." She moved things and rested her bottom on the edge of his desk, ignoring his frown at her actions. "And it has nothing to do with growing up—or maybe it does. Oren is the most mature person I know, because he's managed to grow up without losing the precious ability to feel his emotions and not be scared of them. Here...I brought your key." She laid it on the desk.

Her father blinked and silently told her that he wasn't relenting. That was to be expected; her father did not relent easily.

She said, "I know you disagree with my sleeping with Oren—" and that wasn't easy to admit to "—and I'm sorry for that. That aside, I'll say I'm sorry for our having words this morning, if you'll say you're sorry about bursting uninvited into my house and making a scene."

He stared hard at her. "I'm sorry for *bursting*, as you put it, into a house that I've been enterin' at will for the two years since you moved here. But I'm not at all sorry for anything I said. You've disappointed me, Lorena."

"Oh, Daddy, I've been disappointin' you most of my life." And that came out without thought.

Their eyes met.

"You think that?"

She nodded slowly. "We've never thought alike. My grades weren't as good as you'd like, and then I went and married Tony."

He stared at his desk. "All of that may be true—*is* true, I guess. But you've left out all the things I'm proud of about you. Like your abilities, ridin' horses like you did, goin' back to school like you did, raisin' those boys on your own."

He gazed at her intently. "And your grace. You're like your mother in that. You have great grace, and I've always admired that."

"You've never told me," she said softly.

He looked at her for a long moment. "You're a damn fine woman—a damn fine figure of a woman, too. That's why I'm so mad at you for this foolishness! Oren Breen—good grief, why does it have to be Oren Breen?"

"You wouldn't mind me sleeping with anyone else? Is that it?"

"No! That's not it. I'm not pleased about that, but I do know about life. I'm not dead, no matter how much your mother accuses me of being." He muttered the last. "But why did it have to be that cloud-head?" He raised his eyes to her. "And if you're going to carry on, you should be more discreet. What if I'd been Nicky—or does he already know? Have you been livin' openly with Oren in front of him and everyone else, and we're just the last to know?"

"No... of course not, Daddy. I've been very circumspect in front of my son. And as far as discreet goes, I don't know how to be more discreet than behind the walls of my own home."

"What about Nicky and Jaime? What kind of message do you think your behavior would give them? With their mother doing this, why shouldn't they think they can go out and do the same?"

"I certainly don't think it would be wrong for them to fall in love," Lorena countered. "And I hardly think anything I could say or do could prevent it."

Her father's gaze still demanded an answer.

"All right, Daddy. No, I wouldn't want either of them involved with a girl the way Oren and I are involved. But that's simply because they're so young yet, especially Nicky. His situation in life is far different from mine—you can't possibly compare the two of us. You simply can't. What I choose as a grown woman of forty can't be compared to Nicky's choices at eighteen, or Jaime's at twenty."

Her father nodded, his frown as deep as ever. "So, Oren Breen says he loves you. I'll give him that. He came here to tell me, quite quaintly, actually, that his intentions toward you are honorable. He wants to marry you."

"Yes," she said softly.

"Do you love him?"

"Yes, I do."

He passed a hand over his face and sighed. "Why should I expect you to see reason? You've always been an incurable romantic."

"Have I?" she asked, surprised. "I hadn't thought so—but I do now." She smiled at him and took his hand. "Why don't you give it a try, Daddy? There's nothing like a little romance to make you feel years younger."

"There's nothing like a little romance to make you foolish," he grumbled, but he squeezed her hand in return. Then he said, "I suppose you could do worse than Oren Breen."

Impulsively she put her arms around his neck, and in that instant she realized she hadn't done so in years.

"Thank you, Daddy," she said, meaning for everything over all the years, but mostly for his acceptance now. She knew it was hard for him.

That night Lorena and Oren had a picnic supper out at Lorena's grandparents' old house. He'd called from the ranch and arranged to meet her at the old place. He was there ahead of her, with Harvey at his heels, both waiting with the gate open. The delight she felt at seeing him there, blue shirtsleeves rolled, worn jeans hugging his hips, the golden western sun shining brightly on his straw hat, was so powerful as to be frightening. She recalled what she'd told her father: that Oren was a man who wasn't afraid of his emotions. He was teaching her to be like that, too, so she pushed aside the fear and let herself feel the intensity of joy.

She got out of the car, swinging the picnic basket with her. He gave her a quick but very warm kiss and took the basket. His eyes were as crystal-blue as the sky.

"You went to see my father this morning," she said first thing, as they headed up the sloping lane toward the house.

He nodded. "Didn't get me much, but I went."

"He said you asked for my hand."

He grinned and turned a little pink. "I figured he'd be impressed by something like that. Didn't seem to go like I wanted, though. He told me to drop dead."

"Oh, but he *was* impressed. He told me that I could do worse than Oren Breen."

"My, isn't that a compliment to me, though."

"It is from him." She laughed and kissed him.

They sat on the weathered boards of the porch, and she revealed what she'd brought, all his favorites: grilled hot dogs, hot pepper beans, vine-ripe tomatoes, Vidalia onion slices and chocolate chip cookies. The assortment appeared perfect for indigestion, but he seemed to have an iron stomach.

"Now, this looks like a meal after a man's heart," Oren said, and bit slowly into a hot pepper.

"It's what a woman does for the man she loves." Lorena spoke softly, feeling suddenly shy and focusing on feeding Harvey a piece of hot dog. She felt Oren's eyes on her.

"Is it what a woman does for the man she's going to marry?"

"Oh, I imagine." She didn't know why she couldn't say yes. She simply couldn't say the word yet. But when she finally looked up into Oren's eyes, she saw him smiling.

"You're right. It's real, and it will last. We don't need to rush." With his gaze locked onto hers, he bit very slowly into his hot dog.

A great joy came over her then, and she felt accepted, loved, just as she was with all her doubts and fears. She didn't need to have all the answers for them to be together.

After packing away the leftovers, Oren pulled her between his legs to lean against his chest, while he propped his back against a corner post. Not far away Molly grazed; she'd had her pan of grain and was hopeful for more. Harvey lay down in the cooler grass. Night birds called from the distant trees and taller grass, and the scent of coming evening filled the air.

As they watched the setting of the coral sun, Lorena felt Oren's heartbeat against her back and inhaled the musky scent of him. His arms were warm and sweat damp around her. She shifted and turned her head, reached up and pulled his lips to hers, kissing him deeply. She felt the acceleration of his pulse and knew she'd been the one to send it racing. With a woman's knowledge of what was to come, her pulse, too, began to rise.

She kissed him again and pressed her hip against him. Without a word she left his arms, retrieved the tablecloth they'd used earlier and spread it on the ground. She stretched out on it and looked up at the deepening sky.

"There's the first star tonight," she said.

He stretched out beside her, bringing the scent of a man with him. He propped himself up on his elbow and looked at her; she refused to look at him.

"What do you wish on it?" he asked, and began tugging her shirt from her jeans.

She smiled. "For our summertime never to end." His hand brushed her skin, and her heartbeat skittered over her ribs.

He caressed her belly, then bent to kiss her skin, murmuring, "Oh, darlin', summertime never does leave...it just changes a little."

Then they waited for the cover of darkness.

Lorena hurriedly dressed, wondering why doctors always kept their examining rooms so cold. Was it something to do with health? When she came for her physical she usually wore socks, and kept them on. Every stitch of clothing had to be removed, except socks. There was something about keeping her socks on that gave her the illusion of retaining a scrap of dignity. Socks and that stupid paper gown—what a fashion statement. Today, though, she'd come from work and forgotten her socks and had had to brave the experience with bare feet. She vowed never to do that again.

Dr. Yaeger was a hefty man, about fifty, very impassive. He would have been a great poker player. Absolutely nothing showed in his expression, so she couldn't explain the unease she'd felt as he'd examined her. She just thought he'd done a lot of unnecessary poking and frowning—no, of course not frowning. He had no expression at all. She was being imaginative.

However, five minutes later Dr. Yaeger came in, sat on the same short stool he'd used when examining her and told her that he believed she had something called a dermoid cyst. "In fact, there's a possibility that you have bilateral dermoids. I want you to have an abdominal X ray," he said, marking something on her record. "Can you go for one this afternoon?"

She heard his question, but her mind was still reeling with the word *cyst*. She'd always thought that another word for that was *tumor*. Her mother had had a tumor. A cold chill shot down Lorena's back. She said, "What is a dermoid cyst?"

He looked at her over his glasses and paused in his writing. "A type of ovarian cyst that forms from all types of human cells, very much like a fertilized egg, though it isn't, of course. We could wait to see if it disappears. If it's a dermoid, it won't. Also, tiny teeth form within a dermoid and can be seen on an X ray, if the cyst is far enough along. It's a dermoid for certain then, and it must come out. I'll have my nurse arrange your X ray, if you can go over and have it done now."

"Uh . . . yes."

He started to rise.

"But I haven't had any problems," she said quickly. "Not really. I've been late a couple of times, but that isn't unusual for me."

"It's not unusual not to have symptoms, though you probably would have sooner or later." He moved to the door.

"Can they be cancerous—these cysts?"

"Not likely, but it's always a possibility. There's no way to know that until the surgery, Mrs. Venable," he said with thinly disguised impatience. "I can tell you that less than one percent of these things become malignant, so you might as well not waste your time worrying about that. The worst that you are probably looking at is that we'll have to remove your ovaries altogether, but at your age you're almost done with them, anyway. Hopefully we'll know a bit more after your X ray. My nurse will arrange it." And then he was gone.

She stared at the open, empty doorway. "But I thought I might want another child," she whispered. "Another life."

After the X ray had proved him correct in his assessment—not only one dermoid cyst, but two and complete with teeth forms, no less—Dr. Yaeger seemed almost jubilant. He showed his nurse and receptionist the X ray, talking about this being a case for the textbooks. Lorena felt like some kind of prized item held up for show-and-tell, and she wouldn't have been surprised had he dragged in other patients to show them.

"I believe I will get a second opinion," she said when he began to schedule surgery.

He looked at her a long moment. "Of course, that's your prerogative," he said with a frown. "But I wouldn't wait too long. One or both could burst, and the consequences could be serious."

"Just what do you call your wanting to remove my ovaries and throw me into early menopause, if not serious?" She almost shouted it at him. He and his staff were shocked, and Lorena was more than a little surprised herself. She'd never shouted at a doctor before.

But she certainly wasn't sorry. She wasn't letting anyone cut away precious parts of her body if it could possibly be avoided.

The doctor's office was in Raton, and Lorena drove all the way back home to Clayton with his words echoing in her ears, almost in the rhythm of the spinning car tires or the passing fence posts. *We may have to remove your ovaries... have to remove your ovaries... have to remove...*

Odd that she was so aware of that part of her body, could almost feel the cysts poking her, when this morning she hadn't felt a thing. Now she felt almost as if she were carrying around two ticking time bombs.

Perhaps she and her mother had never had an especially close, confidential-type relationship, but this proved to be a time when Lorena went straight to her mother. Thank goodness her father was out playing golf. Lorena was trying to be rational and composed, as she'd been brought up to be. As she'd always been, before Oren had taught her that having emotions was equal to living. Now her emotions were bare. She entered the house with a lump in her throat, and by the time she finished telling her mother, tears were streaming down her face.

"Oh, Mama... he says he doubts it's cancer, but I could be that one percent. And even if it isn't, they still want to cut out my ovaries. I'll have no hormones. Oh, I know they can give me replacements, but it isn't like the real thing. You know that—look what you went through." The tears came harder as she recalled her mother's experience with total hysterectomy and hormone therapy.

"Stop crying, Lorena. Tears aren't going to help." Her mother handed her a tissue.

Properly scolded, Lorena tried to stop her tears.

Her mother said, "It isn't the end of the world, you now. I've managed, though I agree, it isn't the ideal thing." he frowned. "And you're too young. I was fifty-three, just out in my change, anyway."

Lorena clutched the tissue, trying to get hold of her emoions. "Mama, I have seen what early ovary removal does. he only woman I know who welcomed it was Marion Valler, and I think hers had stopped producing for years. he already was a recluse, so her life certainly didn't aange."

Her mother got up and went to gaze out the window.

"I'm sorry, Mama. But, not thinking about the cancer or ot having a choice, did you really welcome the ending of aat part of your life?"

Her mother breathed deeply. "No...no, I despised it."

Lorena said quietly, desperately, "Oren...I can't do this Oren."

"What do you mean 'do this to Oren'? What has it got to o with him?"

"Oh, *everything.*"

"Lorena, if he loves you, this won't make a scrap of difrerence. It isn't like you'll be deformed, for heaven sake."

"I'll be different." She pressed a hand to her chest. "My ntire nature could change...and my skin and hair...my ones. I won't be the same. I'm already ten years older than e is. Without hormones I'll be much more than that. Oh, ord, I don't want this! Not now. I'm not ready! And, ord, if it's cancer..."

Her mother's face cracked with true emotion for the first me, and her hand came tenderly over Lorena's. "Listen to ie. You're rushing ahead to the worst. You told me yourelf that the doctor said the chance of cancer was small. And ou don't know for certain that you'll lose your ovaries. You on't really know very much at all, and I'd like a word with aat doctor about his manner, let me tell you." She waved a dismissive hand. "The first thing you need to do is get a second opinion. No one should have surgery before getting a second opinion. You have to have more information, Lorena."

Lorena nodded. "I know." She rubbed her forehead. "I don't know who to call, though."

"We'll call Esmerelda. She said something about bowling with a head nurse from over at the hospital." She reached for the telephone.

"Mama...don't tell anyone else. Oh, you can tell Esmerelda—she can keep her mouth shut. And you'll have to tell Daddy, I guess. But please, I don't want to worry Nicky or Jaime. There's no need until we know something for certain. And I don't want Oren to know."

"Lorena, with the relationship you two have, hiding this is not a good idea. And considering how small this town is, it's probably impossible. He'll sense something is wrong anyway."

Lorena breathed deeply. "I don't want Oren to know. He has such a loyal heart. No matter how bad it could turn out to be, he'd want to stand by me, and I can't let him go through that. He's only thirty. He deserves to have a wife who's all woman."

"Lorena, ovaries aren't all that make you a woman," her mother said sternly.

"No, but they're at least half of it. Oh, I can't explain it, Mama. I just don't want him to know. Please. Not right now."

That evening Oren insisted she come to his house for supper and a movie afterward. She told herself that wanting to cling to her own home was not rational behavior and went. She kept imagining she could feel the cysts inside her bouncing with each step, taunting her with their threat.

Oren was joyous and playful, singing and dancing while they put their meal together. She tried to join him but felt as if a dark shadow weighed her down.

Once he asked, "What's wrong? You seem awfully quiet. Have a hard day at work?"

She nodded, claiming the perfect excuse. "Nothing seemed to go right."

He stepped close and began massaging her neck. "Maybe we should take our plates into the living room and relax on the sofa. Hey... wasn't today the day for your doctor's appointment?"

She didn't look at him. "Yes."

"So? Did you get what you went after?"

She glanced up and saw the funny, wicked gleam in his eyes.

"No. I didn't have time to get the prescription."

"Ah, well, it doesn't matter. Come on in here and sit, while I get the rest of supper."

"I'll help."

"No. Come on, darlin'. You need to rest and relax." He took her by the upper arms to steer her from the room.

"I do not." She pulled away from him. "I'm perfectly fine. What bowls do you want to use for the fruit salad?"

He cast her a curious glance, then got the bowls. She wished she hadn't spoken so sharply. Tears were close to the surface. Fine. Start crying. And then what would she say to him?

Later, they sat close on the sofa, watching the movie. Though neither of them truly watched it.

They made love, right there on the sofa. Lorena blocked out her worried thoughts and threw herself into making love with such wild abandonment that she amazed herself. She felt their special time slipping away from her, and she wanted to wring from it all that she could. And perhaps a part of her wanted to refute all the doctor had told her and

to believe it was all a nightmare. She could do that by losing herself totally, absolutely, wonderfully in Oren.

Completely satiated, Oren dozed. He awoke sometime
later to find his skin sweaty against Lorena's and the fabric
of the sofa rubbing uncomfortably against his back. The
movie had shut itself off, and a late-night talk show flickered on the television screen.

He gazed for a moment at Lorena, and images of what
had transpired between them a scant hour before flitted
through his mind. She'd set him on fire. Now the wisps of
hair at her temples were damp; her skin glowed all over with
dampness. He caressed her ivory breast with reverence for
a woman, *this* woman. And then he gazed again at her face.
It was pale in the silvery glow from the television, and she
looked exceedingly young. She frowned in her sleep.

A tiny shiver crossed his shoulders, and caution whispered at the back of his mind. She'd been different tonight,
he thought. But he was too sleepy to puzzle it out—and
damned uncomfortable, too.

Carefully he slipped from the sofa. By the glow of the
television he lifted her and carried her into the bed. She
roused, and he thought with disappointment that she would
insist on going home. She always did, saying that Nicky
might show up or call, and that it was easier getting ready
for work. Valid excuses, Oren could admit, but they were
also a means of keeping the distance she needed between
them, a distance that gave her a sense of protection.

But this time she lifted her arms and reached for him instead. This time she wrapped her legs around him, taking
him into her again.

Chapter Thirteen

Oren slipped into his jeans and rapped on the bathroom door as he zipped them. "I'll make coffee."

"I don't have time" came Lorena's muffled reply.

He went ahead and made coffee quickly, anyway, because he wanted to hold her to him a few minutes longer.

Something was wrong. The thought came unbidden, and he passed it off as he opened the door to let Harvey outside. The heat of a late summer morning hit him, and he thought of the way it had been between them last night, like wildfire. Lorena had been almost feverish in her passion. He could honestly say it had never been like that before, not with any woman in his life. He wanted to tell her, though not with words. It wasn't something he thought he could do with words. He wanted to tell her with touch.

Yet this morning, when she'd awakened, she'd been distant. He'd tried to kiss her, and she'd eluded him, gotten up and hurried into the bathroom. Embarrassed, he thought with a soft grin. She was embarrassed about letting herself go so completely last night. Letting herself go was a hard thing for Lorena.

And then he thought how last night had been another time when precautions had been forgotten. Maybe that was troubling her. Twice now it had happened. It wasn't a big thing for him, but it could be for her. If she got pregnant, things could be tough for her—unless she married him. Of course, things could be tough for her even then. Babies weren't easy.

He thought all this as he poured a cup of coffee for her and half of one for himself.

When he rounded the bedroom door he saw her there, staring at photographs on his wall. She wore only one of his shirts that covered her to her thighs. His eyes roved over her back and down over her bare legs, and he imagined what she looked like underneath. Then he softly came up behind her and enveloped her while balancing the hot coffee.

He guessed he startled her, because she jumped slightly. "Good mornin'," he murmured into her hair.

"Good mornin'," she said softly.

He felt her warmth against his bare chest, right through the cotton shirt. "Thanks for last night."

"Umm . . . you, too." She shifted out of his arms, gently, but pulling away just the same. "Is this your gallery of children?" she asked and nodded, indicating the pictures she'd been looking at.

He handed her the cup of coffee and gazed at the wall. "Yeah . . . guess so." These were all of his nieces and his nephew—his favorite animals, too. He pointed that out. Most of his private family photos he kept in this room.

"Are you sure you wouldn't like to have a child of your own, Oren?" She flicked him an intense gaze, then shifted her eyes again to the pictures.

"If you want one, I do."

"I didn't ask that. I asked what *you* wanted. You obviously like children. I've seen you with the three from next door. You enjoy them." She aimed her eyes at her cup.

"I do. Part-time. I'm not certain how I would feel about one twenty-four hours a day, through diaper changin', throwin' up and back-talkin'. Does this have anything to do with us slippin' up last night?"

She shook her head and walked toward the door. "No, I just saw the pictures. I have to get ready for work. It's late."

At the back door he grabbed her arm and pulled her to him, kissing her. She kissed him in return, but there was something wrong between them. He felt this with the part of him that didn't need to see to know something existed. It was as if she were retreating back to the shelter of the place where she'd been months ago when he'd first met her.

He thought then that she had come out of herself to him... but she had never taken him into her private place.

The earliest Lorena could get an appointment with the doctor that Esmerelda recommended was still a week away. Not ideal, but patience was a virtue, so the saying went. Lorena had a good talk with herself, going so far as to stare at herself in the mirror while she was at it. "There's no sense in thinkin' about it, Lorena Maria," she said, sounding very much like her father. "There's nothing you can do about those stinking little cysts, so there's no sense in thinkin' of them at all."

So she didn't, or at least she managed to push the thoughts aside into a deep inner pocket every time they came crowding in. She had to, for she didn't want Oren asking questions, and he was a most perceptive man.

Both Oren and Nicky were around her all weekend, which helped to keep her thoughts off herself. She went on a cleaning spree and pressed both of them into service. After an entire morning of that, Oren decided her Mustang needed a tune-up. Nicky chose to go help; he was barely on speaking terms these days with Oren, but he apparently felt Oren's company and tuning up the Mustang preferable to housecleaning, so Lorena was left on her own, and happily so, she had to admit.

It was comforting, though, to know the two of them were just out there in the garage. A number of times she went to the window and gazed out at them, just stood there recording in memory the color of their hair, the set of their shoulders. Once she came out with glasses of iced tea for them and chanced to catch what she knew she wasn't supposed to hear.

Oren was speaking. "I can back off, if you want, Nick. But the fact is, I'll still be here with your mom after you've gone off to college in a few weeks."

"Yeah ... well, maybe I won't go."

"I don't have any say over what you do. You can be stupid, if you want. Whether you're here or not—I will be."

"I guess that's up to my mom, isn't it?"

Lorena stepped in at that point. "Well...how's it comin', you two? Thought you might want somethin' cold to drink about now."

Oren smiled, and Nicky tried to; clearly neither wanted her to know what was going on with them, and perhaps that was best.

Saturday evening she and Oren went out to Joe Gonzales's ranch for a calf roping. Joe had asked Oren to take pictures of the ropers. Nicky decided to go, too, which was something of a surprise, until Lorena realized he'd done it in order to irritate Oren, and in order to make time with Corinne Hunsicker, who turned up there, too. Lorena bit her tongue against criticizing Corinne, who, at around twenty-one, was too old for Nicky. And it was not the years that troubled her, but the experience. Corinne far outdistanced Nicky in experience.

Sunday morning her mother and father showed up, bringing an entire noon meal; apparently her mother had the idea Lorena shouldn't be cooking. When they were cleaning up, the dishwasher coughed and fainted, and her father, Nicky and Oren spent two hours together, trying to fix it.

"You're doing well," her mother commented, while they sat together listening to the men arguing in the kitchen. There was a question in her eyes.

"There's nothing else for me to do," Lorena said.

"There's such a thing as holding in too much," her mother cautioned.

"Not right now. Now's the time for holdin'."

At that particular moment her father's voice rang out. "Get out of my way, the both of you! I know how to hook up a hose!"

Her mother smiled. "I think those three are learning to get along well, don't you?"

"Yes . . ." They were, she thought. At least none of them came storming out. They were finding a way. Surely she couldn't have anything dreadfully wrong with her now. Surely not now, with life going along so wonderfully and normally, with the sun shining and her loved ones shouting and arguing around her.

That evening, as he said good-night—at her door because Nicky was there—Oren asked, "Is anything wrong? You've been awfully quiet this weekend." His gaze was intense.

"Have I?" She focused on the placket of his shirt, knowing he might read her eyes.

"Yes...I'm sorry about gettin' in that argument with your dad."

She smiled and smoothed his collar. "Daddy loves it. He loves to see your nose bleed."

"I'll try to refrain, then. Is there anything wrong? Are you worryin' about Nick goin' off to college in a few weeks?"

"A little. It's not easy to let him go." She looked at his lips, because she couldn't meet his eyes, when she wanted to tell him all. "I'm just tired. You know, women get times when everything gets a little off the level," she said, chuckling dryly.

He propped his forehead against hers. "I don't know about women, Lorena. I really don't." His voice was a husky, plaintive whisper. She pulled back and looked at him. His eyes regarded her tenderly, even apologetically. "There was just me and Dad and Matt and Rory for so long that I guess I really don't know very much about women at all."

"Oh, Oren." She hugged him, listening for long seconds to his heart beating in her ear.

Monday came, and Nicky went back to the ranch, but for the next two days and nights Oren was kept at the ranch, too, taking over range work with the cattle for Matt. As much as she missed him, Lorena did find it easier to be alone. While alone she didn't have to pretend to be normal. She quilted until all hours of the night and ate half a bag of Oreo cookies. She realized she had the annoying trait of thinking the worst, when it was just as possible the best could happen and all her worry would turn out to be for nothing. Why not think the best? At least then, while she waited to find out, she would have some peace.

At last came her appointment with Dr. Anthony Torres. By the time she entered his office she had almost convinced herself that he would refute all of Dr. Yaeger's findings and that she'd been foolish to get herself into such a state.

But that wasn't to be. After examining her and studying her X rays, he agreed with the diagnosis of dermoid cysts and went into greater detail in describing them and said they were large enough to be of concern and would have to be removed. He believed the chance of them being malignant was slim to none, but he did admit to the possibility.

"I have discovered that anything is possible with the human body," he said, gazing at her with a warm smile across his large desk. He was a short, balding but very attractive man whose eyes smiled even when his lips didn't. He ran a hand over his shiny head. "The medical texts tell us that most dermoids occur in women in their twenties, but obviously the operative word here is *most*. Since medical school,

e youngest patient I've personally seen was sixteen years
d and the oldest, thirty-two." He grinned. "In that light,
rhaps it could be of some comfort to you to believe your-
lf remarkably young for your years."

She smiled in return, to be polite. "I don't want to lose my
aries," she said, quite firmly. For her part, she didn't care
ere the cysts came from or where they were going. She
s interested in preserving her body.

The doctor sobered and nodded. "That is the ideal. You
e a fairly young and very healthy woman, with twelve or
ore years yet before menopause, and it is preferable to let
e body alone as much as possible. The human body is set
work a certain way and reacts badly if tampered with."
gain came the smile.

Then his gaze became intense. "However, you must un-
rstand that I cannot promise that both ovaries won't have
be partially or even totally removed. This type of cyst can
twisted, causing a number of difficulties in extricating it
om the ovary. And cysts must be removed entirely, or they
ll recur. If the ovaries are only partially removed, your
dy will go along producing hormones as usual, and you
uld even become pregnant. But, again, there may be a
cessity to remove one or both in their entirety. Also..."
e paused. "As I said, I cannot sit here and rule out can-
r. What it comes down to is that total or partial removal
something the surgeon won't know until she goes in. What
an assure you is that the surgeon I recommend is one of
e best in the field and won't cut out what she doesn't need
. I assure you that every effort will be made to do the least
nount of tampering possible, but I must tell you that you
ll be asked to sign a paper authorizing total removal if
cessary."

"I see," she said tightly.

There it was before her. No need to cry over it. Crying
sn't going to help now. With perfect outer calm, she took
t a notebook to write down the particulars the doctor told

her. His office staff would make the arrangements with tl
specialist in Amarillo and notify her as soon as possible.

She was shaking when she came out into the receptic
area, and her thoughts were tumbling over themselves. Sl
would have to tell Paul that she needed time away... ar
there would be the daily paper to take care of for
week... and her mail... and Nicky—oh, my, he was to leav
for college soon... and Jaime... *and Oren... my heave*
what will I say to Oren?

"Lorena?"

It was Annie, sitting there smiling. Jada Cobb sat besic
her, and her eyes were highly curious.

"Hello, Annie. Miss Cobb." The address felt formal, bi
that was where Lorena wanted to keep it. She nodded ar
smiled at each woman, then focused on Annie. "How a
you, Annie? Oren has said everything is goin' fine." H
mind had trouble focusing, but once ordered, manners bo
of years came to the fore.

Annie said she was doing wonderfully, that her fir
pregnancy hadn't been easy but that this one was a breez
and, yes, it was to be a girl, as Oren had already told Lor
na. Modern medicine could tell these things early now. A
cording to the doctor, the new little Breen, who didn't y
have a name, was due to put in her appearance in five sho
weeks. However, Jada had figured at least six using da
from *The Farmer's Almanac.*

Lorena noticed that Jada wore a white duster with a nan
badge, and Jada explained that she volunteered at the ho
pital several times a month. She made the comment that D
Torres was beloved by all, and then she said, "I hope yo
visit wasn't for anything serious." She very obviously wasn
one to bother to hide her curiosity.

Lorena shook her head. "Nothing as exciting as bein
pregnant," she said outright, because she knew that was tl
real question. "I was just getting a checkup."

"We've been hopin' to have you out for supper, Lor
na," Annie interjected quickly. "Matter of fact, I've su

ested it several times to Oren, but I think he wants to keep
ou all to himself as much as he can." She smiled with warm
merriment.

Lorena felt her face flush and managed to say she would
e happy to come anytime. Then she looked at her watch.
I really need to be getting back to work. It was nice seein'
ou both."

She walked away, thinking that they probably wouldn't
ay anything to Oren about seeing her here. There wasn't
ny need for them to. And if they did, she would simply ex-
lain that she'd been getting a checkup from a new doctor.
Oren might ask why, but she would just explain it away.

But she couldn't explain away the surgery, now could she?
That sat there, big and deep and wide.

She wanted to put her head down on the steering wheel of
he Mustang and sob. But the car was a blast furnace at that
moment, not to mention being in full view of the world. She
started the car and meant to head for the bank; they would
e expecting her to return, after all. But then she drove right
n by and kept on driving out of town, without a true des-
nation, simply driving. She liked to drive and thought how
driving was something having ovaries or not wouldn't af-
ect.

She drove north toward Rabbit Ears Mountain, which
tuck up like some man-made edifice from the flat, sum-
mer-browned land. The sun was bright, the air condition-
ng blowing full blast. She thought maybe it wasn't so much
he car being hot, as herself. Her mind was going ninety
miles an hour.

It could be cancer...chances were slim, but the doctor had
aid he couldn't discount it...she should be worried about
hat...but funny, all she could think of was that she could
ose her ovaries and overnight become a menopausal
woman. Might as well take everything from inside her and
e done with it, she thought coldly.

The other side of a normal menopause was the best time
f life, Aunt Esmerelda had said. But brought on by sur-

gery was another matter entirely. Lorena had seen that wit
her own mother.

She'd known a number of women who'd lost their ova
ries to surgery, and according to most, life was never th
same—no matter what doctors said and no matter that the
took replacement hormones. Their hair wasn't the same
their skin wasn't the same, their moods weren't the same an
sex certainly wasn't at all the same.

She'd been so happy. It wasn't fair.

And wasn't that a stupid statement? Life was never gua
anteed to be fair, and she'd never before expected it to be.

Oh, Oren. Her dear Oren. She smiled softly. He'd taugh
her so much ... funny, that, for she was the older one. Th
one who'd lived more life, so to speak. But he was the on
who wasn't afraid of himself, of being exactly who he wa
and the world be damned.

If anyone had asked her a month ago if she could lov
him as she did now, she would have laughed. She hadn
known she was capable of loving someone the way she love
Oren. No, she hadn't known that love like this could exist

It was this deep, abiding love that made her want the be
for him.

Oren would say that none of this mattered to him. Tha
was what he would say, because he was a romantic soul an
loyal as a knight in shining armor. And because he had n
idea what it would mean in terms of the changes that woul
come upon her. The losses. And when she had those losses
he would, too.

She didn't want that for him. He deserved better tha
that.

Clayton dozed in the hot afternoon sun. Oren wished he'
put the top up on the Cadillac; Harvey's tongue was hang
ing out, and he was slobbering on the seat. Nights wer
cooler now, though, and this one would be nice.

He saw Lorena's Mustang still parked in the bank's lo
when he drove past. It was going on five; the bank closed i

nother half hour. He started to stop, then decided to go on
o the grocery store and pick up things for tonight's supper.
He hadn't seen her in nearly three days. Tonight was a cause
or celebration.

At Aragon's Grocery he picked up his favorite hot dogs
and Mexican hot beans for him, and brown sugar baked for
Lorena. She didn't like buns; she liked to grill her hot dog
until it was almost burnt and then cut it up into her beans.
He zipped down the aisles, snatching anything from the
shelves that looked good or that he thought Lorena might
like: green olives, pickled beets, homegrown tomatoes, a six-
pack of Coca-Cola, chips and salsa, an apple pie and a
bouquet of bright flowers from the bin at the checkout. On
his way to the house he stopped and bought a bottle of
chardonnay, Lorena's favorite.

Knowing Lorena would prefer to eat at her own table, he
carried his two sacks of groceries over and went in by her
back door, trying not to step on the kittens in the process,
as they raced in with him. Perfectly at home in her kitchen,
he poured a bowl of milk for the kittens and one for Harvey,
too, put the wine on ice, popped the lid off a cold beer for
himself and set about making a tossed salad. Lorena was a
nut about salads for vitamins, to which he gave thanks because it obviously worked for her. Oren figured he would
take his vitamins in a pill. Lorena always told him that was
the ten year difference between them. He was thinking about
that, and about how Lorena had been acting lately, when the
telephone rang. He decided to let the answering machine get
it; his hands were covered with the juice of the tomato he
was cutting. But when the telephone reached the third ring
he realized the machine hadn't picked up, and thought it
could be Lorena herself.

Frantically he reached for a towel, then stretched for the
phone, knocking over the bottle of olive oil in the process.

"Hello?" He tucked the phone on his shoulder and
righted the bottle. Oil spread slowly across the countertop.

"May I speak to Mrs. Venable, please? This is Dr Torres's office calling."

He took hold of the receiver. "She hasn't come in yet May I take a message?" Dr. Torres—that was Annie's doctor.

"Would you please tell her to call our office first thing in the morning," the efficient voice said. "Oh, and we found a gold pen in the examining room after her visit today, and we thought she might have dropped it."

It was a second before Oren got his thoughts in line to answer. "Okay... yes. I'll tell her. And if the pen has a flower engraved on it, it's hers."

"Oh, it does. I'll have it here for her."

He replaced the receiver, thinking, *she saw this doctor today.* His gut tightened. What was this all about? She'd had a doctor's appointment last week. That was what she'd told him ... and thinking back, he thought she'd said something about her doctor being over in Raton. Today she'd seen Dr Torres, and she hadn't said anything about it.

Something was going on here—*and she hadn't told him.*

A cold chill of alarm spread across his shoulders. What if something was wrong with her? Anger came next. He told himself not to imagine things. There could be a perfectly reasonable explanation.

But she hadn't made any explanation at all, and the anger grew with that thought.

Lorena sat behind her desk, working to catch up on things she'd let go the past weeks. Things that would need to be done before she had to take off for her operation. She immersed herself in the work, seeking a center of calm. She hardly realized when the lobby clock chimed out five-thirty.

At the final chime, Paul entered her office.

"Working late?" He looked surprised. She hadn't worked late in a month.

"Yes... I need to catch up on some things. The Gonzales's loan, for one. The appraiser is dragging his feet.

And, Paul, I'll be needing to take time off, I'm afraid." By the look in his eyes she knew he expected her to say she needed a week for a wedding and a honeymoon. When she said maybe as much as six weeks, his eyes went wide with concern.

She didn't go into great detail, other than to explain that he needed an operation. "It's one of those woman things...." She asked him to keep it confidential for now.

At six Delores closed the drive-up window and bade Lorena goodbye. Lorena was glad to be alone. She needed this time. She kept trying to work. To hide there in her work and not think.

But then she realized she was staring at the papers on her desk but not seeing them. And that there was no place to hide, anyway. Slowly removing her glasses, she sat back. The setting summer sun slanted golden through the window blinds, falling on one of those silly little bank cars that Oren liked so much.

At that moment the telephone rang. She knew it was Oren checking on her, since she hadn't come home yet. She let it ring three times before finally answering. She told him she would be a bit longer, and she halfway hoped he would say he'd see her tomorrow, then. Instead, he said he would have hot dogs and beans ready. "I'll be waiting," he said firmly.

She hung up and continued to sit there. The sun sank lower, and the light turned coral as it slipped away.

She had to let him go, she thought. She had to tell him they were through. If she didn't, he would stand by her no matter what. If she came through without her ovaries, or having to deal with cancer, he would still be with her. He would feel obligated to, of course, no matter that, as time went by and she wasn't the same, he would grow to resent being attached to her. His time with her would have been wasted, when he could have been in love with a full woman and had a family. Or at least a chance for a family. By then there would be things in life he could never recover.

There was the chance that she could come through the operation perfectly intact, or at least nearly so. Nothing would change for them, then. Yet somehow she couldn't shake the worry, the fear that this was just the beginning of so many problems.

And if the worst happened, she could end up ruining Oren's life. She couldn't chance that. She loved him too much.

She loved him. She didn't want to be the cause of changing him as she would be changed.

Slowly she gathered her things, rose and turned out the light. Twilight was coming outside, and she thought how she'd kept Oren waiting for a while. Town was quiet, though the kids were beginning to cruise for the evening. Lorena recalled doing the exact same thing up and down the exact same streets. And she thought it a fine night for being young and cruising and necking.

Five minutes and she was driving down her street. The Feldmans had company parked out front. Aggie Pacheco and Joe Sanchez were sitting in lawn chairs. The living-room and porch lights shone from Lorena's house. Oren's house was dark, but his Cadillac was in the driveway.

She pulled the Mustang to the back, stopping in front of the garage. Her foot was on the step when she looked up and saw Oren sitting there in the dimness on the deck. The porch and garage lights cut across him. Long and lean, with a beer in hand, he had the patio chair cocked back, his boots propped on the rail, and he gazed at her intensely.

"Hello, darlin'. Have a rough day?" he asked and rose. There was something deliberate, powerful, in his movements.

Her heartbeat quickened, and Lorena averted her eyes. "Yes…a long day." It wasn't going to be easy, she thought, her gaze coming around involuntarily to linger on his lean, hard frame. Her body betrayed her by responding.

Chapter Fourteen

Oren moved quickly to hold the door open for Lorena, then followed her into the house. She didn't pause to give him a kiss, though she did say hello to Harvey, who had elected to lie in the middle of the cool, tiled kitchen floor. Oren told Lorena to go ahead and change into something more comfortable.

"Everything is warmin' in the oven," he said. "I'll put it on the table while you're gone."

She nodded and without a word went on into her bedroom. He watched her. Few women could walk as gracefully as Lorena, whose movements drew a man's eye, no matter if he was mad, or afraid, or confused as hell.

He was sitting at the table, waiting for her, when she returned. She wore what she would normally clean house in—faded baggy overalls and a short-sleeved T-shirt. On her the attire looked damn sexy. She stood in the archway and stared at the table. "You set the good china?"

"Yep...thought it was appropriate." He leaned over, took up the bottle of chardonnay and filled her glass. "Thought we should celebrate, since I've been gone several days and you need cheerin' up." Out of the corner of his eyes he saw the strange look she gave him and her hesitancy in coming to sit. She was hammering a wall in place between them, as surely as if she'd gone out and bought lumber to do it. And he damn well wanted to know why.

He sat back, lifted his glass and started to offer a toast. But something in the way she looked stopped him. He took a deep drink of his wine, then picked up the bottle and poured more into his glass.

"The flowers are lovely," she said.

"I thought so," he said and plopped a fat hot dog on a bun. "So, you've been havin' a rough time at the bank the last couple of days. What's been goin' on?"

He expected her to evade him, and she did. "Oh..." She poked her fork around her plate. "The usual, just more of it."

"Makin' lots of loans, are you?"

She nodded and reached for her wine.

They ate in uncustomary silence. Oren asked if the Mustang was running all right since they'd tuned it, and she said it was. She said the meal was good and commented again on the flowers. Other than that, neither said anything and both knew something was wrong. An alien dropping in from Mars and seeing humans for the first time would be able to tell right off that something was wrong, Oren thought hotly.

About every other second he wanted to ask her what it was, why she wouldn't tell him. But he wanted her to tell him on her own. He didn't want to have to ask. He *shouldn't* have to ask!

Then he thought that women were funny and that maybe she wanted him to ask. Which he shouldn't have to do. But he couldn't take it any longer, so he said pride be damned and asked.

She looked at him and put down her fork. "We need to talk."

"I guess we do," he agreed. "Something's been up with you for days." It was odd, but just in that moment he realized something had been bothering her since last week, since the day she supposedly went to see a doctor. Alarm came back, cold and hard. He waited and watched her searching for words. When they finally came, they weren't at all what he'd thought they would be.

"Oren, we have to break off." She looked at him and then back at her wineglass.

He sat there. "Break off? As in stop seein' each other and call it quits?" The anger returned, overriding the alarm. *She was driving him crazy!*

She nodded. "There's just no way I can marry you. It simply wouldn't work. There's just too much difference—"

"Are you sayin' you don't love me enough to marry me?" he broke in.

She took a deep breath, then nodded slowly. "Yes . . . it just wouldn't work."

He stared at her. "You're lyin', and I want to know why."

She stood. "I've told you. It just wouldn't work." Her brown eyes, like the eyes of a trapped doe, met his and skittered away. "Our . . . affair has been wonderful. It's still wonderful. But there's no sense in lettin' you think we can get married, because we can't. It's just nonsense, and you'd be wastin' your time, when you need to find a woman who would be right for you."

"And you don't love me?"

"I . . ." Her eyes came to his. "Not enough for marriage."

He rose and reached for her arm. "Kiss me and tell me that."

"Oren . . ."

She tried to elude him, but he held her, found her lips with his own and kissed her deeply. He felt her react. He knew he did.

She pushed him away. "I told you, it won't work." There was a sob in her voice. She whirled and ran for the kitchen.

He followed, grabbed her again and enveloped her in his arms. "You told me you didn't love me." He kissed her until he lost his breath, and then he kissed her again. She stiffened at first. He plunged his tongue into her mouth and ran his hands down the curves of her body. He moved until he had her trapped between the counter and his body, then rubbed against her. "Tell me again that you don't love me," he whispered hoarsely and kissed her, not giving her a chance to say or do anything.

She was stiff against him, fighting him. He persisted. Kissed her lips, her cheeks and on down her silky throat, shoved his hands beneath her overalls to caress her curves, making her his, trying to tell her that he loved her.

And slowly she began to soften. To meld and pulse against him. He felt it, the way he could feel his own blood through his veins. "Tell me again that you don't love me," he whispered, angry and frustrated and afraid of losing her.

"Oh, Oren…" She laid her forehead on his chest and held on to him.

She quivered. His hand was on her bare flesh beneath her shirt. She was hot. He was hot. He felt her quiver again and knew she was crying.

"What is this all about, Lorena?" Taking a step back, he wiped his nose with the back of his hand and saw a streak of blood. "Why did you go to see Dr. Torres today? Are you pregnant? If you are, I'm sorry if you're upset about it, but it's okay with me. I've told you that."

Her head came up then, her eyes wide and perplexed. "How do you know that—about Dr. Torres?"

"The doctor's office called. They want you to call them back in the morning."

She turned from him and said in a small voice, "I gave them my work number."

"It was nearin' six. Guess they thought you'd be home." He stared at her shoulders and thought how small they seemed, wiped again at his nose and felt the frustration building. "What in the hell is it?"

At last she faced him. "I have two ovarian cysts that have to be removed. Dr. Torres was to make arrangements with a specialist in Amarillo. That was probably what the call was about. His office was to call to let me know the date and time."

He gazed at her and swallowed. Not pregnant. He thought about what an ovarian cyst probably was. He couldn't say he knew all there was to know, or probably even the half of it. Beyond what could be seen on a woman, and what couldn't be seen but felt awfully good, he didn't know much. "What exactly is an ovarian cyst?"

"A growth on each of my ovaries. Do you know what those are?"

He nodded. He could see from the look on her face that this was serious business, and the fear came creeping back over him again. Fear and frustration because he was having to pry all this out of her. "Are you talkin' cancer?" His throat was dry as toast.

She breathed deeply. "Maybe, but it isn't likely to be. Still, the cysts have to come out, and since they're attached to my ovaries, there's a chance I may lose them, too. The doctor said nothing could be certain until they go in."

"Okay." He sought equilibrium. "But what has that got to do with you tellin' me that we're through? And why in the hell didn't you tell me any of this? You knew it last week didn't you? Why not tell me, Lorena?"

She gestured with her arms, as if at a loss. "Oren...if I lose my ovaries, I lose my hormones. Most of them, anyway. Just the same as if I went through menopause."

He watched her face and saw the pain and fear there. He halfway understood it all—except why she'd wanted to keep it from him. "I still don't know why you didn't want to tell me. There's nothin' to be embarrassed about. Women have problems...so do men, all the time. That's why there're urologists, you know." He stumbled over the unfamiliar word. "Do you think I'd want out? That I won't love you if you have this operation?"

"No. I thought—I think—that you'll still believe we can go on, but that's because you don't realize that it won't be the same. Without my ovaries *I* won't be the same." She jabbed a finger to her chest, and her voice rose. "Hormones govern everything—skin, hair, disposition...and sex, Oren. It will affect sex."

"Do you think that's all I'm concerned with? After all these weeks, all that we've been—is that what you think of me?" He darn near yelled that.

She waved a dismissive hand. "No, of course not." Her eyes came up, pleading. "You are...I want you to..." She took a breath. "Oren, I want you to be able to have it all—a woman of vitality and passion and life. I don't know if I'll be able to give you that after this operation."

He gazed at her, astonished, scared, frustrated. "So you just thought you'd go and break it off and never tell me any of this?"

"There wasn't any need to tell you." She jutted her chin. "There isn't anything you can do about it. I've got to have the operation."

"What operation?"

They both turned their heads to see Nick standing in the kitchen doorway. His gaze moved back and forth between Oren and Lorena.

"Your mother and I are havin' a private conversation," Oren said. "When we're done, it'll be your turn. Right now, you can get out."

"This is my house, too, you know," Nick said. "Mom?"

"I'll talk to you later, Nicky. Please, give us a few minutes."

He looked at Oren as if Oren were an escaped criminal, then back to his mother. "You sure you're okay?"

"Yes...give us a few minutes alone."

With his chin jutted as stubbornly as Lorena's, he nodded and stepped back out the door.

"At least I'm not the last to know," Oren said. "How in the world did you possibly think you could keep me from finding somethin' like this out?"

She rubbed her forehead. "I didn't think I would. I just thought...oh, I don't know what I thought! Okay? I was just doin' what seemed best."

"For me. You were doin' the best thing for me. Thanks a lot, Lorena. Everyone knows I'm not smart enough to think for myself. I don't know at all what I want—I need you to do the deciding for me. Damn it, Lorena!"

"Well, *forgive* me for thinking of your welfare." Her voice dripped with sarcasm.

His frustration boiled. "Thinking of me? Huh! What's really going on is that you took me into your bed, into your body, but you never let me get in here." He jabbed two fingers to his breastbone. "You never took me into your heart."

"I've loved you, Oren," she said in a low voice.

He shook his head. "You've loved me, but you won't let me love you. You won't *let* me, Lorena. You want to give, but you won't take. It's a two-way street, you know. I want to love you, Lorena. I want to be as much a part of you as I feel you are of me. That's what it's all about—givin' and takin'. Bein' there for each other for things like this. You should have come to me, let me share the fear with you, but you had to carry it all alone. And then you had to make my decision as to whether or not I wanted to stay with you. That's a hell of a decision to make for a man."

"You can't know what it will mean for me to have my ovaries removed."

"I don't have to know. All I have to do is share it with you. You've said over and over that the age difference between us is a problem. Well, ten years isn't a blink of an eye, and it sure as hell has little to do with what separates us. What separates us is you—that you can't trust me enough to let me into your heart. The years have nothin' to do with it, and I don't think it's just me, either. I think it would be this way with *any* man. If you let someone into your heart, you lose control of yourself, and you're damn scared of that!"

Tears coursed down her cheeks. She said, "Damn right I'm scared. And it's my right to protect myself from any more heartbreak than I have to endure. I've learned from my mistakes.... I have ten years' worth of those on you."

"Yes, you do. I guess you're right about that." He couldn't deal with this anymore. He was at the point of saying things he could regret. "You'd better talk to Nick." Turning on his heel, he strode away to the front door.

Lorena watched him go, stared at the archway to the dining room and listened to the front door slam hard enough to rattle the windows. Would he return? Or had she succeeded after all in ending it between them?

Oh, Lord, what have I done?

The tears came full and hard, and she thought she was going to come apart.

Nicky came in the back door. "Mom?"

She quickly turned toward the counter, hiding, just as Oren had accused her of doing. But she had to protect Nicky; it wasn't the natural order of things for a son to see his mother coming to pieces.

"Mom...are you bad sick?" Raw fear traced his voice.

"No, darlin'." She turned then, trying to swallow her emotions. He looked so young in that moment. She touched his arm. "Please don't be scared about that. It's an operation, but I'll be fine. But...right now I have to be alone. Just give me a few minutes, and then I'll tell you all about it." And she raced away to her bedroom.

Two minutes and Oren was out of town, driving off into the night, with the top down and cool wind blowing all around him. His nose had bled off and on for a whole minute after he'd left Lorena's, but it had stopped now. He was still furious, though—with himself as much as with Lorena. You handled it all real smooth, he told himself caustically as he switched on the radio. Nice and understanding you were, buddy. He switched off the radio.

She'd hidden this from him and then tried to order his life around as if he didn't know enough to order it for himself.

She should have come to him, told him and let him share this with her. Let him carry the fear with her, because she was obviously scared to death. But she'd shut him out. She hadn't had enough confidence in him to believe he was strong enough to carry the load with her. To believe she could lean on him. Lord, that hurt.

He drove and drove, trying to come to terms with his feelings. He, too, was scared. She'd said that cancer wasn't likely, but it was a possibility. He knew enough to know that cancer could always be a possibility when dealing with growths. At least, he thought he knew that; he really didn't know much at all about the human body—little about a man's and almost nothing about a woman's.

He found himself driving toward Wings, and when he got there he pulled into the lot of Cobb's Drugstore. Jada's apartment was right above it; lights were on up there. He stopped near the wooden back stairs that led up to the door and stared up for several minutes before getting out and going up.

The door opened, and Jada stood there in the yellow dimness of the porch light. Her red hair was in perfect order, and she wore a shimmering, bright red robe, looking for all the world as if she were expecting a lover. Oren had never seen Jada disheveled. Her eyebrows rose with surprise.

"Are you alone?" he asked.

"Yes." She smiled that sexy smile she always liked to assume and backed out of the way to let him come in. "What's doin', darlin'?"

Oren stepped into her entry and raked a hand through his hair. "Lorena has cysts on her ovaries that are gonna have to be removed."

Her smile fell. "Oh, my Lord."

"I really don't know what goes on with a woman so I was hopin' you could explain all of this to me. Lorena and I...we've just had a fight."

She blinked, and a tender smile curved her lips. "Suppose we have some coffee?"

Sitting there with him at her small, round oak table, drinking coffee out of sky-blue mugs, Jada explained the workings of a woman's body. Oh, he'd had all this in school, but at that age his mind had been on girls and what they looked like on the outside and how they responded to him. He hadn't cared about these details. Jada also covered a lot that wasn't ever spoken of in school, like what happened to a woman as she got older and exactly what happened when certain things were removed. Sexuality was a part of Jada as much as her skin, and she told him everything without embarrassment, even to using illustrations from her encyclopedia. The most important thing she explained to him, however, was what Lorena was feeling. "This kind of thing will throw the most sensible woman into a tizzy, believe you me," she said. Jada even seemed to take it all as hard as Lorena.

He was quiet for a long minute after she'd finished, drinking his coffee. At last he said, "The sex is good between Lorena and me, and I...and I won't say it doesn't matter. But it isn't the only thing, not even the most important thing."

Jada gave a small smile. "Honey, sex, in all its varied forms, is with us from the time we're born until we die. It's at the core of our being, and there's no escapin' that. And sex, one way or another, has made or broken more than one relationship. It can make your life heaven or hell.

"You can't completely understand what Lorena's feeling, Oren, simply because you're a man. But not many men would go to this much trouble to try. You must love her very much. Go and tell her that. She needs to hear that now. And no matter how much she tries to push you away—and she will, simply because it's the way of a strong woman—don't et her. She needs you. You're the only one who can give her what she needs right now."

Oren drove around for a while after he left Jada's. It was a time of searching his soul. He had to admit that he had expected his and Lorena's sex life to just get better, and he wouldn't care for them to have problems in that way. And he wondered how he would feel if he knew for certain he would never have any children of his own. When he thought of it, he had to question if he would be disappointed.

It was nearing two o'clock when he arrived home. Lorena's house was dark. Nick's truck was gone from the driveway; he'd probably gone back to the ranch, since it was a weeknight. Oren pulled the Caddie into his own driveway and then walked along the sidewalk over to Lorena's. He thought how the night was what his father always called soft.

He went around to the back and still saw no lights. Using his key, he let himself inside. He wondered what Lorena had done with Harvey. All was quiet. There was enough light shining in from outside that he could walk through the house without turning on lights. He headed for Lorena's bedroom, walking softly.

The glow of the streetlight fell through the window and across the floor to the bed. Harvey, who lay beside the bed, raised his head when Oren entered.

Lorena was curled on her side, with her head upon two pillows. One of the kittens was curled beside her. Somewhat uncertain, Oren tossed aside his hat and sat on the bed. He wondered if she was going to send him away. His heart pounded as he thought how she'd told him at supper that they were through. He switched on the bedside lamp and sat there for several seconds just looking at her. Her brows were furrowed, her nose pink, and there were dark shadows beneath her lashes, signs she'd been crying.

"Lorena..." he said softly and touched her. He bent and kissed her. He saw her eyes flutter open.

She looked at him and her eyes melted. "Oh, Oren."

He opened his arms, and she came to him.

Lorena pressed her face into his cotton shirt, inhaled his scent and held on to him for a long time. They both whispered, "I'm sorry," at the same time.

"I didn't mean to hurt you, Oren."

"I know.... I didn't mean to hurt you, either."

"I don't know what I was thinking. It all just piled up." And then she said, "It's so silly, Oren, but I'm so scared." It was an immense relief to admit it aloud.

"It isn't at all silly—and I'm pretty scared, too."

She cried then, into his shirt. And this time she just let go of sensible and cried her heart out. Dimly she thought she was being awfully silly, but something inside her just had to cry.

Oren stroked her hair and murmured something about how she should cry it all out, and she thought she couldn't do anything else, and she thought also how she was so glad he'd come back, and how she hadn't known she could be so silly. She mumbled that, and he told her he was glad to see it, and how it made him feel better about being silly himself.

Gradually she became aware of his hands firmly stroking down her back. Her blood began to warm. She slipped her hand up his smooth, hot neck and found his lips with hers. He shuddered. Sensations washed over her, and she gave herself to them, letting her sorrow be forgotten in the precious magic of making love with Oren. And she pressed it all into memory, the way his hands played over her body, the way his satiny skin felt to her palm, the way his hard muscles rippled and the way his scent enticed and raised her high. She allowed herself to live totally, completely, in that moment.

Dawn was lifting the deep darkness. The birds' songs outside were growing louder, and inside the flower sprigs on the sheets were appearing. Lorena reclined with Oren upon the pile of pillows, safe and secure in the crook of his arm.

They talked about it all, deeply and freely, about exactly what Dr. Torres had told her, about the risks and fears and hopes. Lorena felt her strength returning as she shared this with Oren, and she had to admit her thinking had been all confused by her fear. But she couldn't agree with Oren that her reasoning in not telling him had been taking over his life for him.

"I was tryin' to protect you because I love you. That's a normal thing for a person—trying to protect those they love."

"It was denying me my right to choose," Oren insisted. "And treating me like a child."

"Do you mean like you always check to make certain I wear my seat belt?"

He looked at her a moment. "That's way different."

"How? Isn't that something you do with a child?"

At last he nodded. "Okay. I can accept you were tryin' to protect me. You try to do that with everyone. But another reason you didn't tell me was because you couldn't lean on me," he said quietly. "You didn't trust me enough to lean on me."

And she knew she'd hurt him with that. She said, "I've always had a hard time leaning on anyone. I don't know why. I just do. It has never been easy for me to...reveal myself."

"I know."

They were quiet then for several minutes. Lorena took his hand and cradled it in both of hers. He rubbed her thumb with his. She stroked the hair on his knuckles. The clear song of a meadowlark filtered through the partially opened window. Lorena saw Oren smile. His eyes came to hers. She sank into them, and she smiled, too. She didn't think she had ever known such a feeling of being alive.

Then Oren took her hand, playing with her fingers as he spoke. "I did a lot of thinkin' after I left here. I understand better now what is goin' on with you and what you were tryin' to tell me. I've thought about everything six ways from Sunday, so I'm not speakin' lightly. I want you to marry me, now, as soon as possible.''

"Oh, Oren—"

His expression stopped her. "Lorena, just hear me out." She gazed at him, into his beautiful blue eyes that entreated her.

"I want you to marry me *before* you have the operation. I want you to give me that trust."

"It has nothing to do with trust."

"Then what does it have to do with?" His gaze was calm and steady, unrelenting. "It has to do not only with trusting me, but with trusting yourself and the goodness of life, no matter how much facts tell you not to. It has to do with havin' hope, darlin'. I can give you that, if you'll let me."

She didn't know what to say. She looked down at his hands, ran her fingers over their backs. He had wide, strong hands, and the image of him holding the camera, his careful manipulations of it, came full into her mind.

It was a difficult thing for her to break past the bond of her reserve, of her self-protection.

Slowly his head came forward, and he kissed her gently, tenderly. Then he lifted his head and stared into her eyes.

"Yes," she said simply, gloriously.

The wedding was held the following morning, at dawn, at the Breen ranch, down by the pond beneath the willow and cottonwood trees.

Dawn was Jesse's idea. Like the director of a Broadway play, he assembled everyone in their places upon the close-cut, damp grass. There were chairs for Aunt Josephine and Oren's aunt Ina and Annie. The rest of them stood.

All was still, as if the whole earth was waiting for the sun to rise. The leaves above didn't so much as rustle, and the pond was like glass.

"Are you cold?" Oren whispered when Lorena shivered.

She shook her head. "I'm excited."

She was holding on to Oren's hand tightly. He bent and
kissed her cheek. Jesse tutted and told them none of that.
Lorena looked at the sky to the east. It was turning a paler
coral.

She turned and looked at everyone.

Aunt Esmerelda smiled and waved and whispered loudly,
"You look beautiful!''

Lorena's mother beamed, though her eyes were teary.

Lorena caught Marnie's eye and sent her a private smile
of thanks for the loan of the wedding dress. The only dress
Lorena had was the black-and-white suit that she'd gone to
Ricky's graduation in, and she certainly wasn't going to be
married in black. She felt the most beautiful she'd ever felt
in her life in this dress. And using the dress was somehow a
symbol of her joining the family.

Her gaze skimmed over faces—Jada Cobb's, smiling at
her, Annie, Zoe, Jesse, who winked.

She looked at Nicky and Jaime. They stood right behind
her and were to give her away. Jaime grinned, and Nicky
looked as solemn as his grandfather, the judge. He reached
up and tugged at his tight collar. Lorena let go of Oren's
hand and stepped over to adjust the tie for him.

"You look so handsome,'' she said.

He said, "I feel like a stuffed turkey.''

"You look like one, too,'' Jaime said, even though he was
twenty.

Nicky smiled then, and the expression he cast on Lorena
turned tender.

"Damn fool idea, Jesse,'' Lorena's father grumbled. He
stood with his book open in his hand, facing Oren and Lorena. Oren had the feeling from Max's looks that the old
man would rather have a shotgun in his hand than the
book—and not to marry Lorena, but to send Oren packing. "It's supposed to rain,'' the old man groused. "Those
are clouds over there.''

"It won't rain,'' Jesse said calmly. "It's gonna be a clear
blue dawning.''

Oren thought how even Mother Nature wouldn't g[o]
against his father. When Jesse Breen wanted something, h[e]
usually got it.

He took Lorena's hand again. He looked down into he[r]
face; it was light enough now for him to see the shades o[f]
brown in her eyes. She appeared perfectly calm.

"Once I've made up my mind, Oren, I've made it," sh[e]
seemed to say.

Little Mary Regina cried for her daddy to hold her, an[d]
Little Jesse said he had to go to the bathroom. Matt too[k]
him off behind a tree, because Jesse said there wasn't tim[e]
to be going up to the house. Rory caught Oren's eye an[d]
laughed.

"How long are we gonna stand here, Jesse?" old Ma[x]
demanded.

"Hold your horses, Max. It isn't like you have som[e]
where to go."

Old Max glared at Jesse, and when Oren chuckled, Ma[x]
glared at him and murmured, "I could make your life hell,["]
and his voice held high satisfaction.

Matt returned with Little Jesse and took up his place a[s]
best man. He seemed to have a faraway look in his eye, the[n]
he looked at Oren and grinned with the knowing look of [a]
man who had stood in the same place.

A hush seemed to fall over everyone as the sky grew sud[-]
denly lighter, pale pink fading into pale blue.

As Jesse watched the golden ball that was the sun pee[l]
over the horizon, Marnie tucked her hand into his. H[e]
squeezed her hand, then ran his gaze over all those assem[-]
bled there, touching briefly, like a blessing, on each mem[-]
ber of his family and resting lastly on his youngest son.

Max Sandoval cleared his throat and began to speak th[e]
words that would join Lorena and Oren as man and wife.

Once again, it was another great day in the Breen famil[y.]

Epilogue

One year later...

Lorena was gasping for breath and whispering, "I think I can, I think I can...."

Oren said, "What?"

"It's...from *The Little Engine That Could*," Lorena said breathlessly. "Didn't you...have...that when you...were young? Ohooo."

"Guess so." Oren squeezed her hand. "Pant, darlin'." And he did so.

She snapped, "Oh, you...pant for both of us." As far as she was concerned, she was ready to leave this mess right now.

"Push, Lorena." That was Dr. Torres.

Lorena tried, but didn't know if she did very well. Her head was spinning, and she just wanted to go home. "How did I get myself into this?"

"If you don't know, it's a little late to tell you," Dr. Torres said brightly.

Lorena opened her eyes to see Oren's worried face. "I'm all right...." She tried for a smile, but it turned into a grimace as her body contracted. She refused to scream, not so much for pride as because she worried that Oren would go to pieces.

"Here he comes," Dr. Torres called.

"Is he...Oren, I love you."

"I love you, darlin'."

"I'll love you as much as the baby."

"I know."

"Push, you two, and save the mushy stuff for later!"

Lorena grasped Oren's hand and gave a mighty push, feeling her baby come into the world.

Dr. Torres said with triumph, "I told you that you could have a baby with only part of one ovary!"

The baby, a perfect red raisin of a baby, let out a scream. Dr. Torres laid him carefully on Lorena's abdomen, and Lorena held him to her with one hand and held Oren with the other.

It was over. He was here. She had it all, and life was good.

"Here is Maxwell Oren Breen, darlin'," she said at last.

Oren's eyes, filled with wonder, were fastened on his son, and he began to cry through his smile.

Fifteen minutes later, in the arms of his proud father, the new little Breen greeted his family through the nursery-room window. Petra was smiling and crying and said he looked like Oren. Max said heaven forbid—the babe was much more handsome and definitely more Sandoval, with that head of black hair.

Jesse ordered Oren to hold his son's head better, and Max told them both to be careful with his grandson. Marnie took the first picture of the new Breen.

Annie held almost-one-year-old Jemma up to see her cousin, and Matt held Little Jesse, who knocked on the glass to say hello. Rory held up both Glory and Mercy, and they were properly impressed when Zoe told them that they would have a little brother or sister just like this one come Christmas.

Jaime and Nicky rushed up, with a policeman following right behind them. They pressed their noses against the glass and stared with amazement.

And little Maxwell Oren Breen simply slept, dreaming of rolling grassland, fast horses and flashy cars, boots and jeans, and pulling little girls' heartstrings.

*   *   *   *   *

SALLY JANE GOT MARRIED
Celeste Hamilton

Everyone believed Sally Jane Haskins was the town bad girl—except widowed father Cotter Graham. When a night of passion suddenly meant they were expecting, a trip down the aisle was the only choice. Sally Jane hoped that this, at last, was her chance at happily ever after....

Celebrate Sally Jane's nuptials in Celeste Hamilton's SALLY JANE GOT MARRIED, available in February.

She's friend, wife, mother—she's you! And beside each Special Woman stands a wonderfully *special* man. It's a celebration of our heroines—and the men who become part of their lives.

Don't miss **THAT SPECIAL WOMAN!** each month—from some of your special authors! Only from Silhouette Special Edition!

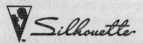

Silhouette
SPECIAL EDITION™

WHAT EVER HAPPENED TO...?

Have you been wondering when much-loved characters will finally get their own stories? Well, have we got a lineup for you! Silhouette Special Edition is proud to present a **Spin-off Spectacular!** Be sure to catch these exciting titles from some of your favorite authors.

HARDHEARTED (SE #859 January) That Special Woman!
Chantal Robichaux's baby is in jeopardy, and only tough cop Dylan Garvey—the baby's father—can help them in *Bay Matthews's* tie-in to WORTH WAITING FOR (SE #825, July 1993).

SUMMERTIME (SE #860 January) *Curtiss Ann Matlock* introduces another of THE BREEN MEN when Oren Breen must convince the reluctant Lorena Venable that he's her man!

FAR TO GO (SE #862 January) One of the twins, Joe Walker, has his hands full when he's hired to protect the willful Lauren Caldwell in the latest from *Gina Ferris* and her FAMILY FOUND series.

SALLY JANE GOT MARRIED (SE #865 February) That Special Woman!
Sally Jane Haskins meets Cotter Graham, the man who will change her life, in *Celeste Hamilton's* follow-up to her CHILD OF DREAMS (SE #827, July 1993).

HE'S MY SOLDIER BOY (SE #866 February) *Lisa Jackson's* popular MAVERICKS series continues as returning soldier Ben Powell is determined to win back Carlie Surrett, the woman he never forgot....

Don't miss these wonderful titles, only for our readers—only from Silhouette Special Edition!

SPIN3

CONVINCING ALEX

Those Wild Ukrainians

Look who Detective Alex Stanislaski has picked up....

When soap opera writer Bess McNee hit the streets in spandex pants and a clinging tube-top in order to research the role of a prostitute, she was looking for trouble—but not too much trouble.

Then she got busted by straight-laced Detective Alex Stanislaski and found a lot more than she'd bargained for. This man wasn't buying anything she said, and Bess realized she was going to have to be a *lot* more convincing....

If you enjoyed TAMING NATASHA (SE #583), LURING A LADY (SE #709) and FALLING FOR RACHEL (SE #810), then be sure to read CONVINCING ALEX, the delightful tale of another one of THOSE WILD UKRAINIANS finding love where it's least expected.

SSENR

If you are looking for more titles by

CURTISS ANN MATLOCK

Don't miss this chance to order additional stories by
one of Silhouette's most popular authors:

Silhouette Special Edition®

#09589	INTIMATE CIRCLE	$2.95	☐
#09601	LOVE FINDS YANCEY CORDELL	$2.95	☐
#09668	HEAVEN IN TEXAS	$3.25	☐
#09695	*ANNIE IN THE MORNING	$3.29	☐
#09757	*LAST OF THE GOOD GUYS	$3.39	☐
#09805	*TRUE BLUE HEARTS	$3.39	☐
	*The Breen Men miniseries		

(limited quantities available on certain titles)

TOTAL AMOUNT	$
POSTAGE & HANDLING	$
($1.00 for one book, 50¢ for each additional)	
APPLICABLE TAXES**	$ _____
TOTAL PAYABLE	$ _____
(Send check or money order—please do not send cash)	

To order, complete this form and send it, along with a check or money order
for the total above, payable to Silhouette Books, to: **In the U.S.:** 3010 Walden
Avenue, P.O. Box 9077, Buffalo, NY 14269-9077; **In Canada:** P.O. Box 636,
Fort Erie, Ontario, L2A 5X3.

Name: _____

Address: _____ City: _____

State/Prov.: _____ Zip/Postal Code: _____

**New York residents remit applicable sales taxes.
 Canadian residents remit applicable GST and provincial taxes.

CAMBACK1

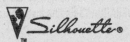